To: Sandra

From: [illegible] Daly

It was so nice meeting you and Austin I will definitely keep in touch

GOD Bless

xoxo

B.V.

LSDV PRODUCTIONS PRESENTS

IF ALL MEN CHEAT, ALL WOMEN SHOULD TOO!

By: LaShonda DeVaughn

Printed in the United States of America 1 2 3 4 5 6 7 8 9 1 0

PUBLISHER'S NOTE:
This book is a work of fiction. Names, characters, businesses, organizations, places, events and incidents are the product of the author's imagination or are used fictionally. Any resemblance of actual persons, living or dead, events, or locales is entirely coincidental.

Editor: Tina Nance, Perfect Prose Editing

In Loving Memory of Andre Stone…In my heart forever

Other Titles by LaShonda DeVaughn

A Hood Chick's Story 1

A Hood Chick's Story 2

A Hood Chick's Story 3

I'd Rather Be Single

Chapter 1

Loving him hard was all that I could do, no matter how hard I tried, I couldn't leave my boo. This is my story…

"You gonna wear what I bought you when I come through?"

I could hear the bass in Tae's deep voice coming from behind the closed door to the bathroom. He was trying to whisper to whoever he was on the phone with. I carefully pressed my ear against the door, trying to make out what he was saying.

He was talking low and sexy. "Make sure you put on them red heels I bought you too."

I placed my hand over my mouth as butterflies fluttered in my stomach, my feelings were beyond hurt and I couldn't take listening to any more of his conversation. I burst through the bathroom door like I was the damn police and shocked the fuck out of his ass.

"Who is that!?" I demanded, charging toward him while he was nestled on the toilet.

He quickly hung up and tried to disregard my question. "Don't you see me in here taking a shit? Why the fuck you busting in the bathroom Janae?"

I frantically took in deep breaths. I couldn't believe he had the nerve to try to act like he didn't know what I was talking about.

"Tae, who were you just on the phone with? I heard you telling her to wear some heels that you bought for her. Are you out here spending money on other women? Was that Sharece? Are you still cheating on me with her?" I questioned.

Tae continued to downplay the situation, pissing me off even more. He shook his head.

"Yo, this shit is crazy! You didn't even cook shit for a nigga today and you in here questioning me about some bullshit?"

"Tae, I know what I heard. I'm tired of going through this with you!"

I covered my mouth with both hands. I felt myself about to cry. I tried to stifle it, but I couldn't. On top of already being a sensitive woman, I was two months pregnant so hormones were raging and the tears slid from my eyes effortlessly.

"Man shut the fuck up and get out. Shut the door! I was on the phone with Eric. I'm meeting him tonight to work on some plot plans!" He smirked at my tears and grew even more irritated. "What the fuck are you crying for?" He shook his head again and threw up his hands, highly annoyed. "Man, I gotta get out of here yo, like I said, I'm getting up with Eric, we have to handle some business for work. I can't take this shit right now Janae, all you do is cry!"

I wiped my tears with the back of my hand before responding to his bullshit.

"Whatever Tae," I sniffed. "You're just making up lies so that you can get out the house again."

He frowned up his face and pointed to the door. "Bitch get the fuck out and let me finish shitting!"

I turned and foolishly dashed out of the bathroom in tears. His disrespect didn't shock me; he was becoming an all around cold hearted man. And it didn't make sense for me to continue with the confrontation. It was obvious he wasn't going to tell me the truth. Tae and lying ran hand and hand. He was just a lying ass nigga! It was like he had no respect for me anymore at all and I guess I brought it on myself. No matter how bad he treated me, I would always take him back and he knew it.

Tae and I had been together for four years and he'd cheated on me the whole time. Not to mention, this wasn't the first time I had caught him sneaking around on the phone talking to other women in our own home. And he was so slick about it too, trying to be sneaky whispering and shit. Each time I caught him; he would stand in my face and lie with a straight face.

I did everything for Tae, so I never understood why he carried on these affairs when I was giving him a hundred and ten percent.

It was around the second year of our relationship, and about five side bitches later, that I had lost confidence in myself and forgotten the person that I was. I had exhausted my body trying to make him happy and each day I lost sight of myself while trying to please him. Every time I took him back, I would hope that it would be the time he'd change and then I would go the extra mile to make things work. And each time I got shitted on.

Don't get me wrong, it wasn't like I caught him with the bitches in bed or anything. Most of the time, I would just hear rumors or he would slip up and leave his phone laying around and I would read text messages from hoes thanking him for busting them open the night before. He always had a lie ready after each incident and would never admit to anything.

After the first time he cheated, I did what every other woman would do and tried to figure out why. It wasn't long before I realized that the obvious answer to why men cheat, is that they are selfish!

Still, I didn't want to give up on Tae. I decided that maybe if I corrected the flaws within me, he might change and realize what he had at home. But that shit didn't work. Tae's selfish ass wasn't changing for anyone. Looking back, I wish I would have left after the first time I caught him cheating. I would have probably been married to Mr. Right by now, but my dumb ass settled for less and I truly hated Tae for it.

After a while, he stopped answering me or grew extremely defensive when I questioned him about other women. He probably figured that I wasn't going anywhere and that I needed to just go with the flow. He had basically turned into his father, the same cheating, womanizing man he hated for hurting his mom. I turned into what my mom became to my father; the wife amongst many other women. The only difference was that Tae and I aren't married.

Lately, I'd been under the impression that Tae was growing bored with me and that I wasn't as exciting to him as I used to be. I couldn't remember the last time he'd taken me out. There was no affection between us at all and he never complimented me anymore. All he did was take from me; both emotionally and physically. The closest I got to feeling wanted was when we were fucking. That seemed to be the only thing that we had that hadn't stopped. Tae had the stamina of a damn horse and it was hard for me to get wet because I just wasn't into it anymore.

I was the type of chick that believed in love making, so sex without feeling loved wasn't appealing to me. I would cringe as I fantasized about him sexing other women when we fucked, and sometimes I would cry with him right there on top of me. He had scarred me so much, that mentally I had a hard time getting into our lovemaking sessions. Hell, the only reason I was doing it was out of hope that he wouldn't go out and get coochie somewhere else.

The women Tae cheated with couldn't hold a candle to my looks and it honestly lowered my self-esteem. I mean, most of these women looked liked they had just stepped off the stage of a broke down strip joint. I, on the other hand, had the body of a goddess. My hazel eyes complimented my butter brown skin and I had curves systematically 36-24-40 which was almost perfect in a man's eyes. My body was one of the things that attracted Tae to me in the first place, besides my innocent persona.

Unfortunately, my good looks and my fat ass weren't enough to keep him faithful. And although the other women were busted, there had to be something within them that piqued his interest; something that I must not have had. It made me feel imperfect.

Finally, I heard the toilet flushing and I could hear Tae's footsteps creaking on the wood floors headed toward our bedroom. I was sitting on the edge of the bed feeling sorry for myself. I just couldn't contain my emotions, no matter how hard I struggled to do so.

Tears were strolling down my cheeks left and right. I just wanted to be happy and feel loved and Tae wasn't delivering. I waited for our bedroom's clear door knob to turn and for him to enter. I could predict his next move. He usually headed for the closet to grab a fresh set of clothes and head out to meet whatever woman he was seeing behind my back. I waited and watched.

He strolled through the door, and as expected, aimed straight for our large open closet. He sifted through his clothes, searching each hanger and appearing frustrated when he couldn't find what he was looking for.

"Boo have you seen my black True Religion shirt?" he asked, shouting each word as if I wasn't in the bedroom just steps away from him.

I glared at him pitifully without answering and I put my head back down. There was no way that I would help him find clothes to look good for another woman.

He shot me a look when I didn't respond quickly enough, and commenced to talk to me like I was his child instead of his woman.

"Janae, you hear me talking to you? You just gon' sit there looking stupid and not answer me or are you going to help me find my shirt?"

I combed my long bang out of my face with my fingers and picked up my head.

At that point, my mind was gone. I was too busy focusing on the fact that he probably wasn't going to come home that night.

I faced him again; he stood tall staring at me with impatient eyes.

"No Tae, I haven't seen your shirt," I said as I wiped the tears off my cheeks. I shut my eyes. We were together but why did I feel so alone?

Tae was tired of seeing me cry and he had always showed

disgust toward my sensitivity. All he had to do was stop dogging me out and he wouldn't have to see my tears so often. I can't front though; crying was all that I had found myself doing almost everyday for the past few years. I was starting to be overly miserable. I felt like I was stuck and the biggest reason was that I didn't like the thought of moving on. I guess you could say I was a little too comfortable, fuck it… a LOT too comfortable.

I watched as he slipped on a brand new pair of jeans. At that point, working on plot plans with Eric had become a highly imaginative lie which I was already aware of.

Shameful to admit, but sometimes I would try to trick myself into giving him the benefit of the doubt, trying to believe him when he told me some bullshit. In reality, I was only playing myself. My intuition never steered me wrong when it came to his cheating.

While looking for his shirt, he occasionally glanced in my direction.

"Wipe your damn face Janae! I'm tired of you looking pitiful all the time. And you wonder why I'm never home. Shit, that's why we ain't having no kid right now, cause you ain't ready! Matter fact, did you make your appointment?"

I wanted to cry even harder, but I didn't want to fully bawl out in front of Tae. I didn't understand how he so-called loved me, but wanted our child aborted? This was the second time that he was forcing me to do this.

I had never believed in abortion and my mom was probably rolling over in her grave after seeing that I had already gone through with the first one. I had waited until the last minute to abort my first baby, thinking, hoping and praying that Tae would change his mind, but he never did. I was actually showing when I got my first abortion and I had acquired a few stretch marks on the sides of my hips which helped to knock down my self-esteem even more.

"No, I didn't make the appointment." I whined.

My light tears turned to heavy drops as I stood to approach him. "I don't want to do it Tae; I want to keep the baby." I cried as I clutched my belly with both hands.

Tae huffed and brushed his hand over his freshly groomed goatee. "Yeah aiight. Yo make that appointment first thing in the morning." He pushed his way through me as I stood speechless.

Damn, I thought to myself. *As if it was that easy.* This nigga acted as if I was getting rid of a pet fish instead of our own flesh and blood that we had created together.

He spotted his True Religion shirt hanging deep in the closet. "Here's my shit," he said grabbing it and then stretching it on. He slipped into his Prada sneakers, snapped on his diamond encrusted bracelet, kissed me on the cheek and headed down our long hallway toward the front door.

Just that fast, my emotions sank deeper turning into an uncontrolled anger. I felt like I needed to do something quick. I stormed behind him at full speed, he was going out to do me dirty and it was painful to just sit and let it happen. I grabbed hold of him.

"You're not leaving Tae!" I shouted tugging on his shirt.

"Janae, don't start with this bullshit!" He squeezed my wrists trying to release the grasp I had on his shirt.

In lightening speed, tears sped down my face as I started beating on his back with my fists, "You're not leaving to go cheat on me! You're not going to do work with jewelry and new clothes on Tae, that's bullshit! I'm in here pregnant with your baby and you're going out tonight to be with another woman and I'm tired of it! Why do you keep hurting me Tae! Why huh, whyyyy?" I screamed at the top of my lungs.

He looked at me like I was stupid. He had no regard for my feelings. All he screamed before breaking away from me was, "Yo get off me, I'm out."

I stood screaming through the door as if it would do any

good. "I hate you! I'm tired of going through this with you Tae, I can't take it anymore!" I cried each word as if I sang them.

I put my hands on the top of my head and gripped two fists full of my hair until I heard his car leaving the driveway.

I stood there feeling helpless and foolish before crying my way back into my large bedroom. I crawled into bed and stretched my delicate body out on my soft brown cashmere quilt and held my belly.

"I love you." I said crying aloud as if the baby could hear me. I wanted my baby so bad; I was already attached to it.

I shifted and squirmed around in bed for about twenty minutes. I was nauseous, a headache ignited and my body was a mess. I was worn down from dealing with another night of drama. *Why was I so stupid? Why couldn't I just leave this man?* I questioned myself. I knew good and well that he wasn't meeting Eric, but there I was letting him walk all over me.

Eric was his boss at the construction company he worked for. Eric was married and very dedicated to his family. When it was quitting time at work, that's exactly what it was for Eric. He would go straight home to his family and do what he was supposed to do as a man. Take care of home first.

Tae constantly used him as his scapegoat to get out of the house, using the fact that he is his boss as an excuse.

Tae's job at the construction company was steady and I worked in the admissions office at Clark Atlanta University, so we were doing pretty well with our combined income.

That's why I didn't understand Tae's reluctance toward us having a child. The only reason I could think of was that he didn't want his mistress or mistresses to find out about it.

Mainly, this bitch Sharece. He cheated on me with her so many times over the years that I was almost confused with thinking that she was wifey and *I* was the mistress. That's how bad it was. She was the one chick on the side that seemed to not be only a hit it and quit it type thing; there were feelings involved.

I mean, the entire neighborhood knew about their relationship before I did. It was the most degrading feeling in the world. Even some of the students who attended the college where I worked knew about Tae's side dealings with Sharece. The students would point and snicker at me, and I prayed that the nasty rumors would fade. They supposedly ended their affair last year when Sharece found herself her *own* man and finally left mine alone.

When Tae and I first met, he was what you would call a bad boy. He was a small time hustler; he stayed flossing all of the latest brands and always dressed to the nines. He was extremely popular and all the neighborhood girls drooled over his existence. He stood about six feet tall, milky brown skin, pecan shaped eyes with deep outlining eyebrows that made him look mischievous.

I was the shy good girl with curves in all the right places. They were kept neatly covered up because I didn't like the attention. I was known to be shy, but very intelligent. A lot of guys liked me, but none had the luxury of getting up with me because my mom was too strict. That was until Tae put that charm on me.

I remember the day we met like it was yesterday. It was as dramatic as how the rapper DMX and his wife met; it was rumored that they met while DMX was robbing someone. I guess it's true what they say about good girls attracting bad boys.

The day we met, Tae was outside of the corner store by his mother's house beating the shit out of some dude. I had never seen anything like it in my life. I mean, Tae was stomping the guy in the head with his Timberland boot and all I heard was the dude crying out like a chick, pleading for Tae to stop.

"Nigga you're gonna kill me! Stop dawg!" The dude kept crying out each time Tae stomped. He was on the ground in a fetal position covering his head with both hands but the stomps were too vicious to escape.

"Stop, dawg stop!" he cried.

His head thumped back and forth on the sidewalk as Tae stomped repeatedly. I pushed my way to the front of the crowd.

"Could you please stop?!" I shouted as I joined the onlookers watching Tae torturing the dude on the cement sidewalk.

"Mind your fucking business!" Tae shouted still stomping. He didn't even look to see who I was; he was too much into conducting his ass whipping.

"That's enough!" I shouted out again.

He gave his last forceful thump and blood splattered out of the dude's mouth, sprinkling onto the sidewalk and landing on some of the crowd's shoes.

Tae angrily faced the crowd to see who was doing the shouting. Everyone turned their heads in different directions so that he wouldn't focus on them. When he realized that it was me that had been crying out in the dude's defense, we instantly locked eyes. And he stopped.

Something about him turned me on. I immediately recognized him for being one of the bad boys that my mom warned me to stay away from, but something about him made me want to know what was behind his mischievous spirit. We stared at each other for a good five seconds until he ran away, due to the loud police sirens that were getting closer.

I, as well as the other onlookers stood in shock at the results of Tae's bashing. Dude just lay there and didn't even move. I was dead scared! Judging from his swollen face and all the blood around him, I thought that Tae had killed him until he finally started moving one of his legs and struggling to get up.

"Are you okay?" I bent to ask him. But there was no response.

"Uh uh, come here Janae, don't get into that, mind your business!" My best friend Sarah shouted behind me. Sarah didn't want anything to do with the beef. She was always very street smart and was always getting on me about being naïve.

I was the type of girl who wanted to lend a helping hand to people in need. And I'll admit, sometimes I could be a little too nice. Sarah's famous words were always "fuck them." No matter who it was.

I glanced up at Sarah with sincerity imprinted in my expression and I nodded. "No! We have to see if he's okay, we can't just leave him here."

She placed her hands on her petite hips. "Bitch, this is the hood. You see everyone else leaving?" She pointed to the scattered crowd. "Well that's what we need to be doing, that dude will be a'ight. Come on, let's go."

I glanced back down at the dude and I hesitated for a few seconds before deciding to take Sarah's advice and mind my business.

All Sarah cared about was taking care of herself. She was raised by her mom who everyone called Ms. Michelle. Ms. Michelle never acted like a mom; she acted more like she was Sarah's sister. She was wild and it just wasn't normal.

We were only nineteen years old at that time, and her mom used to tell us the craziest shit. She would sit and tell us how we should suck our man's dick on a daily basis to please him, morning, noon and night. She would actually demonstrate on bananas and I could never understand what her point was. She was single herself, and every man that she had ever been with had left her, but she was always telling Sarah and me different ways to keep a man.

I will never forget the day she said, "If you want to keep your man from cheating, you have to keep him pleased in all forms, toss his salad and all."

Even Sarah didn't know what Ms. Michelle meant, so we looked at her curiously until I popped the question.

"What is tossing a man's salad?"

Her mom, with her deep Southern accent proclaimed, "Licking his ass!"

"Ughhhhh!!!!" Sarah and I screamed out in unison.

Her mom was still poised with a serious look on her face as if she had just taught us something valuable.

"I ain't playing! And I'm not ashamed to tell my daughter how to please her man. Sometimes you have to do nasty shit that you don't think you'll ever do. All men like their ass licked, trust me."

Ms. Michelle never held back, she had acted as if she was Sarah's sister ever since I could remember. She did appear young in the face and she and Sarah had the same brown tone to their complexion. I always told Sarah that she looked like Gabrielle Union and her mom looked like a thick Angela Bassett. But as ghetto as her mom was, it rubbed off on Sarah.

After leaving the scene that Tae put on, Sarah and I had to walk down the same street that he disappeared on when he heard the sirens. There was this particular gray house that Sarah and I would pass on our way home from the store where a lot of guys hung out, smoking, drinking and rolling dice. They often had a radio on the porch playing loud rap music and they'd be play fighting and clowning around with each other.

Sarah and I would purposely walk on the other side of the street to avoid them. Little did I know, I would come to know that house very well. It was Tae's mom's house.

For some reason we didn't cross the street that day. I remember seeing Tae on the porch with a few of his boys boasting about what he had done to the dude down the street. His friends were praising him and carrying on about the next guy they wanted to beat down.

Tae loved the attention and was on the porch gloating like he was the toughest nigga alive for putting in work.

He cut his conversation short once he saw Sarah and me passing. He ran off his porch calling himself trying to holler.

"How you doing shawty?" he asked walking up on me.

"I'm good." I said rolling my eyes and trying to keep up with Sarah who appeared nervous as if Tae wanted to rob us.

"Girl come on!" Sarah said nervously before walking up and eventually leaving me walking solo. I tried to catch up to her, but Tae followed and stalled me.

"Damn, can I talk to you for a minute?" He asked.

I stopped and sassed him, "Why do you want to talk to me? So you can stomp me like you did that dude down the street?"

Tae smiled, "I knew that was you yelling out from the crowd. You was the little pretty girl sticking up for that nigga. I don't want to harm you boo. Shit, I want to get to know you. I'm glad I found you shawty." He stared at me for a moment, locking his eyes around my shape first and stopping at my face. "You have some beautiful eyes," he said.

I blushed and turned to look away from him.

"So what's your name?" He asked.

I was torn. The bad boy in him was so attractive to me and I was digging his baggy jeans and sweatshirt too. But I was still clueless of his intentions, so I brushed him off.

"Why do you want to know my name?"

"Why wouldn't I?" He asked.

Okay, this dude got game, I thought to myself.

"My name is Janae." I said finally.

"I'm Dontae, but everyone calls me Tae."

I peeked up at his eyebrows again, they were so dark and deeply defined; they truly made his face.

"So can I get your number?" He asked.

"Well I'm not allowed to give my number out."

"Whoa! Are you serious, ain't you like 18 or 19?" He asked surprised.

"Yeah I just turned 19, but my mom don't play that. I come from a very strict household."

"You're right about that, after eighteen anything goes."

"Well not in my household." I added.

"Well that's cool because I've been looking for a good girl like you."

"How do you know I'm a good girl?" I asked batting my eyes.

He pursed his lips to the side and stepped back.

"Look at you, I could just tell. You got innocence about you and it's sexy. Plus as you said, you come from a strict household so I'm sure you haven't had too many relationships."

Tae was right, he read me like an open book. I was truly a good girl and had never had a relationship with a boy; my mom wasn't having that. Especially with a bad boy like him. He reached for my hand and did some real old school flirting. He pulled out a blue ink pen from his pocket and wrote his number down in the inside of my palm. When I went home, I copied it into one of my notebooks and drew a heart around the number. I placed it on my heart, cheesing from ear to ear.

From that day forward, I was sneaking to call Tae from my mom's phone as well as secretly going out on dates with him. Because my mom kept me so clustered in the house, the edge that Tae showed me had me feeling like I was finally living life. He made me feel beautiful, wanted, attractive and special. He showed me a side of myself that I never knew existed; a wilder side. It didn't take long for me to fall in love with Mr. Dontae "Tae" Harris.

Four years later, the same man that made me whole; had made me miserable, and I didn't know how much more I could take.

Chapter 2

If loving him was wrong, I didn't want to be right. His love had blinded me. Dontae was my life…

Riiiing!!!

"Admissions office, Janae speaking."

I tried to sound as cheery as I could while answering the phone at work the next day, but the morning sickness had my stomach in twirls. I was nauseous and had already thrown up three times on the way in to work.

"Hey Boo, it's Tae." I shut my eyes. This voice, those words used to light up my day. But, seeing as though he didn't come home the night before, that voice, those words, disgusted me.

"Why didn't you come home last night Tae?" I whispered while eyeing the busy office and hoping that no one was listening.

"Oh um, me and Eric was up all night working on those plot plans for this new job that came up and I ended up falling asleep at his crib. I didn't even notice that I fell asleep till this morning, but I said fuck it and went straight to work from there."

I pursed my lips to the side. "Oh, so you're at work with your True Religion shirt, jewelry, new jeans and Prada sneakers on?"

"Yo Janae, I didn't call for this shit. I called to say good morning."

I always called Tae out when I knew that he was full of it. He was too much of a pretty boy thug to work at his dusty construction job in his stylish wear. I hated when he called acting as if everything was fine after not coming home.

On top of that, he could never get his lies straight so, as usual, his next words were "Yo, call me later." Followed by a click.

I slammed my phone down on the receiver and then brushed

my hand over my bone straight hair, pondering my life. I was so damn unhappy. I put out more than what I received and Tae was taking complete advantage of my kindness.

This was as good as it was going to get with him. He wasn't going to change no matter how hard I loved him. I knew that I couldn't take another four years of the same shit.

The first two years were our best years; he was perfect. Taking me out, making me laugh and adoring me in every way. The third and forth year has been the most miserable years of my life.

Suddenly, my work phone rang again and it was a call that I looked forward to even less than Tae's.

"Admissions, this is Janae." I answered.

"Hi Janae, this is Monica Rice calling from Planned Parenthood. I got your message regarding setting up an appointment to terminate a pregnancy."

Tears filled my eyes immediately and I stared out into the air, clutching my belly with my free hand.

"Yes, I called."

"Okay Janae, when would you like to come in?"

What kind of question was that? What did she mean, when would I *like* to come in? I wouldn't *like* to come in at all. I didn't want to kill my baby; I was being forced to.

"Hello? Janae are you there?"

I tuned back in. "I'm here," I said regretfully. "What days are available?" I asked.

"Well, let me see here." She paused, then her voice came back across the line. "How about next Monday, the fifteenth? We have a twelve o'clock and a two o'clock."

I hesitated before answering. Maybe that would buy me five more days to convince Tae that we should keep our baby.

"Alright, you can put me down for the twelve o'clock appointment."

I heard rapid typing.

"Okay, I just put your appointment in the system. Have you

done this before? Would you like me to go over anything with you?"

"Yes I have, I know the procedure. I'll be there at twelve next Monday."

"Okay, just make sure that you bring someone to take you home after the procedure is completed."

"Okay." I said before hanging up.

I decided that after work, I would have a serious talk with Tae. After all, we were in our mid-twenties, had a luxurious, not to mention spacious two bedroom apartment and a pretty good amount of savings stored away. Maybe if I came at him correct enough to convince him that our baby would actually bring some stability into our relationship and possibly slow him down, he'd listen.

I wasn't trying to trap Tae, but I was convinced that having our child would turn him into the family man that I longed for and get our relationship back on track.

I suddenly got an idea. The best way to get Tae's attention or any man's for that matter was through his belly. Tae loved to eat and was always expecting a meal when he came home from work. I quickly devised a plan to have a sit down with Tae and put our important issues on front-street.

I would make a special candlelit dinner, and serve him wearing little to nothing. It would be something out of the ordinary for me *and* for him. And while he stuffed his face, I could sneak in the serious discussion regarding our child. I would let him know how miserable I had been lately, with hopes that he would come to terms with wanting to start our new family together and change for the better.

When quitting time arrived, I headed straight to the supermarket. I picked up some blade steak, a pack of frozen diced onions and peppers, corn-on-the-cob, potatoes, and flour for gravy. I rushed home because Tae usually got home two hours after me, which afforded me plenty of time.

I set everything up perfectly. I lit two tall ivory candles in the middle of our glass kitchen table and I set the kitchen studio style lights to dim. All the food was done except for the steak and the smell of the seasoning smothered the entire house. Tae liked his steak to be a touch before burnt, so I kept it covered up to cook to his liking.

I soon heard his car pulling into the lot and I pushed my D-cups together and ran to the full-length mirror to see how my bra and thong looked with my lilac stiletto pumps. I smacked on some lip gloss and scurried to the door.

When he came in, I walked up on him and softly pecked him on the lips to greet him. He stood frozen with a shocked look on his face and didn't kiss me back. He watched as I turned, his eyes beaming on my ass as it hugged my thong with each cheek smacking each other forcefully as I walked up to the stove to check on the steak.

I could tell that he was wondering why I was being so nice to him. Usually he received the silent treatment from me for weeks at a time when he pulled his occasional "not coming home" stunts. I was giving hope one more try, because I was tired of being his doormat.

I hoped that this talk would even make him ease up on keeping me sheltered in the house away from my friends and controlling me. I let the controlling go on for so long, because my mother had treated me the same way all my life, so I was used to being confined.

I was my mom and dad's only child and felt like a prisoner at home. They wouldn't let me go anywhere and Tae kept me just as sheltered as they did. I had lost all of my friends because no one wanted to adapt to the 'only seeing me when Tae permitted me to hang with them' rule. Thank God Sarah stayed in my corner.

After Tae got over the shock factor, he didn't say a word about the setting at home. He headed straight for the shower and freshened up. Thankfully, his stint in the shower gave me enough time to make our plates and prepare myself to confront him. My morning sickness had eased a bit; I was still queasy, but remained focused on this moment.

He returned from the shower and we were both seated at the table. The air in the room seemed to be just as heavy as my nervousness. A few minutes of silence later, I finally broke the ice.

"So, how was your day?" I started out while sifting salt into my mashed potatoes.

"It was cool. Busy. What about you?" He said picking up his fork and diving into his meal.

"The same. I wasn't feeling well all day, but I managed." I replied.

"Mmm," he said focusing more on his food.

"I wanted to talk to you Tae." I said peering over at him across the table.

He waved his free hand signaling for me to continue.

"Well as it stands, my life is already pretty routine. I go to work, come home, cook, clean and cater to you when you *do* come home."

He choked on his steak, "Cook? You don't cook everyday, don't even give me that shit Janae."

I sucked my teeth and picked up my fork, scooping up some mashed potatoes as a diversion. I was hoping that his out of the way comment wouldn't ruin our dinner or my speech that I had prepared. I did feel the need to defend myself because I broke my neck to make sure Tae was fed; he just had a complaint for everything I did.

I let out a small sigh. "Tae, I do cook for you basically everyday. The only time that I don't cook for you is when the fridge is on E like it was last night. It's usually only on E because I'm always cooking you big meals. You don't have a normal appetite Tae. You don't just want chicken, rice and corn; you want chicken, rice, corn AND pork chops."

"Yeah whatever, get to what you want to talk to me about. I

knew you didn't make me this food dressed half ass naked with candles lit and shit just to be doing it." He panted rudely.

I wiped my mouth with my napkin and conjured up some courage to continue.

"Well honestly Tae, right now I'm not happy."

He took his face out of his plate and looked up at me as if he was shocked.

"But, I think our relationship still has potential. I'm willing to forgive you for everything that you have done. I won't even bring up Sharece anymore when we argue. I'm even willing to forgive you for cheating on me with whoever the woman was you were talking to on the phone last night about the red heels when you were in the bathroom, because I'm sure that's where you slept last night. I will put all of that in the past if you just agree to start fresh. Cut off all of your extra-curricular activities, stop the sneaking around on me and trying to control me and let's start all over as a family. You, me *and* the baby."

I finally sat my feelings on Tae's lap. I tried to read him, but I couldn't. Tae was just like his father, he never wore his feelings aloud so it was always hard to discover his thoughts. He sat stiff looking at me with a straight face. I would think that any man would take this agreement. A man's wifey dismissing all of his past conduct, even as early as the day after, to start off fresh? What man would resist having a clean slate with his woman after being grimy to her for so long?

Seconds after I laid everything out, we continued to sit in an unpleasant silence until I took matters into my own hands. I got up and walked over to him. I pulled his chair to face me and I sprawled down on my knees. I unbuttoned his jeans and put his dick in between my breasts allowing myself to be tittie fucked before taking his penis into my mouth. I was like his personal superhead; I was a boss in this field. I continued to suck, lick and stuff my jaws with Tae's meat for a good while. His shoes were off so when I saw his toes curl I knew he was about to bust. He pulled out his dick and jerked his sticky white nut all over my face. I shut my eyes, revealing my sex face and acting as if I enjoyed it.

Tae was still groaning and stroking himself to release all of his cum. I slowly opened my eyes smiling at him with my face full of his nut.

"So Tae, are you willing to start over as a family?"

He let go of the grip on his dick and exhaustedly gazed down at me; his eyes looked pleased and I was anticipating his agreement.

"We ain't having no baby Janae."

"What?" I asked with a lump caught tight in my throat.

Tears were forming at my eyes and I felt foolish.

"We are not having no baby, I don't know why the fuck you keep bringing it up. I already told you this."

"So are we going to continue our relationship like this Tae, with you sneaking around with other women while I'm stuck at home alone wishing you were here? I feel like I'm being tortured Tae, why can't we have this baby?" I stood off my knees and held my belly with both hands.

Tae shook his head and slid his sticky penis back into his boxers.

"Janae, we will have kids, but not right now and that's that. Don't ask me about this shit again."

I snatched a napkin off of the table to wipe the nut off my face that was now mixed with salty tears. "So you just want me to kill another child? Because that's what I'll be doing Tae, killing the baby. The baby is innocent, it didn't ask for you to nut inside me, create it and then want to kill it. I don't want to do it! Please don't make me kill the baby Tae!"

"Well you have no choice." He said nonchalantly.

He beamed hard at my body as if it disgusted him.

"Look at you, you got new stretch marks on your sides, your stomach is already mad big and you're only like two months. You need to hurry up and make that appointment before your body get's fucked up even more."

I paused and took a deep breath as I took in all of his slander.

"So that's all that you have to say to me Tae? After everything I sat here and said to you tonight?"

"Yeah." He said with the highest arrogance.

I tucked in both of my lips, shaking my head. My feelings were hurt beyond belief. He had ripped my heart right out with his sharp words.

I had the option of having the baby and raising it on my own, but I didn't want to struggle alone and cheat the child out of having two parents. More importantly, I didn't want to have to struggle on my own with only my income. Maybe I was making excuses for the fact that I felt like shit because the father didn't want it, but I hated the thought of raising a baby alone.

The conversation with Tae didn't cater to my objective and I was forced into an unwanted predicament, I had to abort my baby.

A cloudy Monday came sooner than I wanted it to, and noon rolled around just as fast. I dreaded driving up to the hospital. I cried the entire way because I knew that I was actually going through with the procedure.

Heavy raindrops began to fill the Atlanta streets. To the average Joe, it was just a rainy day. For me, it felt like a sign from God telling me not to go through with the procedure, but I forced myself to keep driving.

I arrived at the hospital and sat numb and alone in the waiting room full of deep emotion. I didn't have anyone to call to express how much I didn't want to do this. Sarah knew that I was getting an abortion, but I didn't want her to know that Tae was the one forcing me to do it. She already preached to me about being stupid for taking him back all the time and if she knew that the decision for the abortion was Tae's and that I didn't agree, I wouldn't hear the last of it. Needless to say, I was a wreck.

It didn't take long before the doctor called my name. I struggled to get out of my chair. I felt like I just wanted to crawl somewhere and die. I resisted and hesitated to get up as the doctor continued to call out, "Janae Rogers?" while scanning the waiting room.

I knew I had to get it over with, but I was glued to my seat.

It took every piece of strength for me to allow myself to stand up and get out of the hard waiting room chair. But I had to get up because the doctor almost gave up on calling my name.

On shaky limbs, I followed behind the doctor while rubbing my belly whispering sweet 'sorrys' to the baby under my breath. Something told me that the baby would have been a girl. I was so attached in wanting to keep her that it killed me to take each step toward the hospital room. I was only hastening my innocent baby's horrible death.

I was convinced that she would have been me and Tae's princess. All he had to do was give fatherhood a try. I'm sure he would have quickly grown attached to our little girl and loved her whole-heartedly. I shook off those thoughts and quickly dismissed that fantasy to bring my attention to what was about to happen.

I stepped into the small gray hospital room with my face saturated with tears. I traded my clothes for a thin blue and white hospital robe and lay on the stiff hospital bed staring at the bright lights on the ceiling while tears streamed down the sides of my face.

And that day, at that moment, in plain words, I killed my baby.

God please forgive me, and mom, I'm sorry.

Chapter 3

No Change, Plenty Pain. If I stay, things will remain the same.

Sarah called my phone a little after my procedure was over.

"Are you okay Janae?" she asked sympathetically.

I sniffed and wiped my nose with my crumpled tissue.

"No Sarah, I'm not. He didn't even come up here with me, could you believe that? He could've at least done that much. He went to work this morning and I was expecting for him to take off early because he knew that my appointment was today. But no, he didn't call me or anything. So I'm up here by myself and I'm not supposed to leave without a ride. I'm still a bit out of it, but I'm fine."

"No you're not fine! I'm on my way to get you. I can't believe that asshole didn't come up there to pick you up. Fuck him! I swear I hate him. But girl, I'm on my way."

"Thank you so much Sarah."

"You don't have to thank me, I'll be there shortly."

I ended the call with Sarah and sat there waiting and feeling horrible. Not only was I sore, but my conscience was scarred for the second time. I held my belly and cringed at the fact that my baby wasn't in there anymore. I whispered a silent prayer asking for forgiveness because I felt like killing another baby had definitely secured a place for me in hell.

I clutched my cell phone, hoping that I would at least get a phone call from Tae, but he never called.

Sarah picked me up shortly after our phone call and took me home. She left me with her usual advice before I got out of the car. "Janae, you have to stop being so nice. It's time for you to put your foot down and stop letting him walk all over you."

She was right, but I slammed the door after thanking her for the ride and painfully walked into my apartment.

It just wasn't that easy for me. I didn't have the willpower to leave him, as much as I wanted to. I prayed for strength all the time; strength to leave Tae and the power not to love him so much.

I went straight to bed without even taking my clothes off. I wanted to sleep this bad dream away. Words couldn't express how I was feeling at that moment. I was empty and I felt abandoned. Before long, I was knocked out in bed.

Hours later, I heard noises. I peered at the neon red highlighted digits on our alarm clock, which was the only light in my pitch black bedroom and noticed that it was one thirty in the morning. I quickly made out the squeaking footsteps of Tae sneaking into the house. He tried to peel off his clothes silently and slip into bed.

One thirty in the morning was actually earlier than usual. Four in the morning was the norm for him. I guess whoever he was out with that night didn't give up the panties, because he expected me to roll over and assume the position. Ass out.

My ass was already facing him and he poked at it through my clothes with his dick.

"Stop Tae," I whispered.

"I can't get no pussy?" he asked.

I rolled my swollen eyes. "Are you serious? We can't have sex right after an abortion."

He moved back and asked, "Oh yeah, how that go? You a'ight?"

"No I'm not," I said, as if it wasn't obvious.

"A'ight I'll buy you some flowers or something tomorrow a'ight?" He rolled over and paused for a second.

"Janae?" he asked. "How long did they say we had to wait to have sex?"

I couldn't believe this bastard. He was more concerned about sexing me rather than my health. And flowers? Was he serious?

"I don't know Tae." I lied, pissed at myself for even answering such a thoughtless question.

Sarah was right. I let him walk all over me. I was supposed to be cussing him the fuck out for not calling me all day and not accompanying me to my appointment. But I felt the need to steer away from confrontation with him as much as possible, I didn't like drama.

The overbearing stench of his Obsession cologne invaded my nose which confirmed that he had been out with another woman while I was disposing my body of our precious fetus. And like always, I just let it go.

I shut my eyes and tried to sleep off the pain. At the same time, I was beating myself up for allowing him to get away with murder… literally.

The next morning, I woke up feeling the same way; like shit.

I had taken the rest of the week off work in advance so that I could heal, which meant that I had nothing but time on my hands, because I literally had no life.

Tae had already showered, got dressed and left for work when I was just starting to gather some strength to get up and start my day. I carried my weak body into the living room glancing at our suede couch, matching suede curtains and squeaky clean glass end tables. I then peered into our granite kitchen and everything was spotless so there was nothing for me to clean. That's when I knew that boredom would consume my day.

Tae constantly stayed on me about keeping the house clean and I was always one step ahead of him to avoid any arguments. I did everything for him. It was like Destiny's Child wrote that song *Cater to You* from viewing all of the work that I put in for Tae. On top of keeping an organized house, I ran his bathwater, ironed his clothes, kept him fed, never held back on all sexual activities, and I would spend my last dime to buy him the latest brands.

"Uhhhh." I let out an exhausted sigh before I plopped my sore body down on the couch and gazed out of our oversized bay window. I realized that I wasn't getting anything good from Tae in return, after everything I was putting out. Yeah, he bought me things in the past, but it was usually out of guilt and not because he wanted to.

I was even stupid enough to give him the majority of my tax refund every year and the earnings that I did keep were still eventually spent on buying something for him. Honestly, I had always thought that what I was doing for him was out of love, but when you're not getting anything sincere in return and there is no change, how is it love?

Having this second abortion had opened my eyes to a lot of things and I was trying to think of anything that I had in my life that was good. My dad died of cancer when I was fourteen and my mom died of the same disease just before I turned twenty. I had no other family left in Atlanta.

Deep in thought, I smiled at the fact that I had Sarah in my corner; I truly needed her crazy ass. She was the strength that I wished that I had.

Due to Sarah's upbringing, she was truly a "wild child." That was up until I got a phone call from her hours later that day. I have to admit, I have never been jealous of another female in my life, but when Sarah called me with her news… I was officially HATING.

"Girl, guess what?" She asked with intense excitement.

"What? You got the promotion?" I smiled and paced the kitchen gaining excitement for her.

She had been waiting to hear the status on a new position as a supervisor at the telecommunications company where she had worked forever. She had just bought a condo with her new boyfriend, so getting the promotion would be a helpful addition to her new lifestyle.

"No, I still haven't heard anything; they are taking their time with promoting me so fuck them. This is even better than that."

"Really? Then what is it?" I asked curiously.

"Okay girl, get ready for this." She paused and then screamed out, "Girl, Curtis asked me to marry him!"

Jealousy danced on my emotions as I quit pacing the floor and paused in mid-step with my mouth opened, largely not knowing how to respond. I was happy for her and all, but she had only been with Curtis for one year. I had been with Tae for four years and the closest that I got to a ring on my finger was a Tiffany ring that he got me to go with my charm bracelet, out of guilt for calling Sharece from our house phone.

How was Sarah getting married before me? It just didn't seem fair. To top it off, Sarah had cheated on every man that she'd ever been with, including Curtis. She didn't care about how much advice her mom gave us about "how to keep and please a man," Sarah was all about herself.

No matter if we went out to get drinks or out to catch a movie together. If she spotted a potential prospect that she wanted to creep with, she would leave me by myself and fulfill her fantasy or whatever you want to call what she was doing with these strange men. And now Mr. Curtis was locking her down.

"Congratulations." I let out reluctantly.

"Why you sound so sad, ain't you happy for me?" She took her excitement down a notch.

"Of course I'm happy for you girl. I'm very happy for you." I lied, *or did I?*

"Did ya'll set a date yet?" I asked.

"Yeah, we were looking at the calendar and I'm stuck on June 13th as the date. You know I don't play. And Curtis agreed, shit he had no choice."

"Wow, June? Sarah that's only three months away!"

I was super hating at that point. Setting a date always made the engagement more official, it meant that they would actually be getting married and that he wouldn't just have Sarah toting a ring to hold her.

"Yeah I know it's only three months away, but that's plenty of time."

I heard the exhilaration in her voice and she started to speak really fast and all over the place. "I want to have my bachelorette party as soon as possible. Oh and I want to have my wedding outside in the back of our condo, it's big enough. We have to go pick out my dress because I want a pink and white wedding and I want an ill ass white three-tier Gucci cake with pink trim. Girl this is going to be fun! I'll have my mom call you so y'all can start pitching ideas for the bachelorette party. I want strippers and all types of crazy shit. I can't believe I'm getting married girl!"

"Well congratulations again Sarah, whatever you need for me to do, I'm here."

"You damn right, you're my maid of honor." She said.

My jealousy instantly dissolved and turned into excitement. "Wow Sarah, I'll be honored to be your maid of honor." I smiled.

She cut in.

"Oh and tell Tae's ass that he's going to have to let you out the damn house for my bachelorette party. All that damn cheating he do and he be trying to keep you confined in the house, I just don't understand that shit."

I rolled my eyes and pulled the phone away from my ear while Sarah continued her rant. Comments like these made me regret telling her any of my business. I usually tried to just ignore her or change the subject.

I pressed the phone back to my ear. "Alright Sarah, congratulations again, I got to go," I said rushing her along.

"Okay, I have to get back in the restaurant anyway. Curtis is in there waiting for me; I just came out here to tell you my news. I'll speak to you later girl."

"Okay Bye." I hung up the phone, green with envy once again.

This time I was jealous of the fact that Sarah and her man were out at a restaurant.

Curtis catered to Sarah like she was Princess Diana. He made sure that she knew her worth as a woman and I had longed for that type of relationship my whole life. I can't even remember the last time that I had been wined and dined. Hooters downtown Atlanta isn't exactly being wined and dined, but that was Tae's idea of a fancy restaurant.

As soon as I put my phone down on the receiver, it rung again.

"Hello?"

"Hey Girl."

It was Sarah's mom Ms. Michelle.

"Hey Ms. Michelle how are you?"

"I'm good. I know Sarah told you her good news," she said singing her last two words.

"Yeah she told me," I said forcing a smile.

"See, she listened to her mom, she got that man to marry her! My baby must be putting in some work in the bedroom."

I blurted a slight giggle. It still felt funny even as an adult, hearing Sarah's mom talking about sex, but she was so entertaining.

"Yeah, well I'm happy for her Ms. Michelle."

"Okay, well listen. Sarah told me that you have the rest of the week off of work so get dressed. I'm coming to pick you up; we need to go to the mall to start picking things up for the bachelorette party."

"Ms. Michelle, she hasn't even been engaged for twenty minutes and you want to go buy bachelorette items now?"

"Hell yeah! She's getting married in three months so we have to start now. This party should be thrown within the next three weeks."

"But Ms. Michelle, I don't feel good; I'm still recovering from my procedure," I explained, assuming Sarah had already told her mom my business.

"Girl please, you been through that before, you gon' be alright.

Throw some clothes on, I'm on my way." She hung up as I was still holding the phone to my ear.

She and Sarah were so much alike, it wasn't even funny. They wanted what they wanted, when they wanted it, with no exceptions. I hadn't seen or spoken to Ms. Michelle in a while, but when we hung, it was more like chilling with a close friend rather than a friend's parent.

I took one last look around at my tidy apartment and decided that I wouldn't let boredom consume the rest of my day. I was taking Ms. Michelle up on her offer, besides, shopping for a bachelorette party should be fun.

I pulled open the freezer side of our stainless steel double door fridge and took out some chicken so that it would be thawed by the time I got home.

I took a brief shower and threw on some jeans and a white wife beater and slipped on my white *bebe* flip-flops. I grabbed my cell phone feeling like I was a child calling to ask a parent for permission, but I had to let Tae know that I was stepping out. He answered the phone as if he was busy and bothered.

"Hello what is it?" he asked.

"I was just calling to let you know that I was going out to the mall with Ms. Michelle."

"You ain't going to no damn mall. And why you trying to go out with that crazy lady?"

"She ain't crazy Tae, don't be disrespectful. I'm just stepping out for a minute."

"Well how the hell are you going to the mall, when I couldn't get no pussy last night? I thought you couldn't do nothing after an abortion."

"I can walk Tae. Walking and having sex are two different things."

"Well you need to stay your ass in the house."

I huffed and glanced over at the pack of frozen chicken sitting in the sink, "I'll be back in time to make you dinner okay?"

He hesitated for a second, "A'ight, well grab me some Jordans and a few Polo shirts. I gotta go. I have to get back to work."

"Alright, see you later." I ended.

"Wait Janae, what mall y'all going to?" He asked.

"I don't know yet, why?"

"Forget it, see you when I get home."

"Alright bye."

Not long after I hung up, I heard Ms. Michelle pulling into the driveway bumping her old Snoop Dog CD. She'd had a thang for Snoop since Dr. Dre days. The things she said she would do if she ever had the chance to meet him shouldn't be repeated, that lady was one big freak.

I ran to my room to grab my purse and then sprinted outside to the car.

Ms. Michelle was on fire that day. She had on small jean shorts with a fitted baby blue ruffle top and matching blue kitten heel shoes. Her ponytail was pushed back neatly and she looked like she had lost about twenty pounds. I actually saw her figure for the first time even while she was seated in the driver's seat. "Wow Ms. Michelle, you look good." I said.

"Thanks girl, I always look good," she said bobbing her head to Snoop Dog's old ass song, *Sexual Seduction.*

"Yes you do." I agreed playfully.

She turned down the music and pointed her extra long blue colored fingernail to the glove compartment as she drove away.

"Reach in there for me baby and pull out the list that I made. We should be able to find everything on that list in the mall today. I told Sarah that we didn't need to rent out a hall, because most venues would probably be booked since we are pressed for time. I told her that we can have the party at my house."

I unfolded the list and couldn't help but laugh at some of things that were listed. "Excuse my language Ms. Michelle, but chocolate dicks as party favors, a penis shaped cake and penis party hats. Ms. Michelle what is going on here?" I giggled.

She looked at me as if everything she listed were normal items. "What? If I left it up to you we would be having a party at church. You have to stop being so neat and prissy. Get loose. Once you loosen up, maybe Tae will marry you. You have to show him your freaky side sometimes. Show him you can be his girl and his mistress all at once.

"I try Ms. Michelle."

"Well try harder. Make your man happy, you can't expect for him to please *you* all the time. That's the problem with y'all young girls, you wait for the man to cater to you, meanwhile he's out getting what he don't get at home from someone else. You have to give a man your all, loosen up Janae."

She was serious as a heart attack but once she saw that I was ignoring her instead of agreeing, she apologized, apparently realizing that her words stung.

"I'm sorry baby, you know how I am. I can't help myself. Stop being so sensitive girl, life is too short, loosen up sometimes baby," Ms. Michelle preached in her parental voice.

She stopped at a red light and shook my shoulder to loosen me up and tears instantly fell from my eyes.

"I'm sorry Ms. Michelle, I don't mean to be so sensitive but you don't understand. I feel like I have given him more than all of me. I have nothing left in me to give and he still isn't appreciating me. I feel like I wasted four years of my life with him." I sniffed and reached in the glove compartment for a Kleenex. "This is all that I find myself doing; crying everyday," I said pointing at my saturated face.

"Well stop crying and apply the energy you use for crying to making that man happy."

"That's all I do Ms. Michelle. My whole life is Tae and his whole life is Tae too. He's so selfish, I'm invisible to him."

We pulled up to the mall and veered into a narrow parking spot. She took the keys out of the ignition and looked over at me. Tears blurred my vision as I tried to hold eye contact.

"Baby, if you have given a man everything that you have and more and he still can't seem to see who he has in front of him, then that muthafucka ain't worth it. You have a good heart Janae, you have always been beautiful, sensitive and loving. Any man in this world would die to be in Tae's shoes. Don't waste your tools on a broken product. You hear me?"

Her words were stern and forthcoming. I smiled while I swallowed her advice whole. I needed an authority figure to talk to sometimes. It was easier to accept her advice than Sarah's because she was my elder, so I respected what she said.

"Thanks Ms. Michelle."

She nodded while reaching for her purse in the back seat. "You don't have to thank me child. A woman crying in the middle of the day is usually due to men problems. Put a smile on your face, you'll be alright. If Tae ain't the one, then Mr. Right will soon come. Now wipe them damn tears and come on in this mall."

I almost forgot how outspoken she was and I laughed off her demand. I grabbed my purse and we headed into the mall.

I made Tae's purchases first, a pair of Jordans and two Polo shirts. After that, Ms. Michelle dragged me in just about every store for what seemed like hours at a time. We did however, manage to find a party store that was able to order the seductive items that she wanted to accessorize the bachelorette party. The sales clerk informed us that our items would arrive in just two weeks.

We also wrote down gift ideas for the guests to bring Sarah's freaky ass. Ms. Michelle wrote down the majority of the gift ideas. They were mainly explicit lingerie and freaky oils for Curtis to lick off Sarah's private parts as well as eatable panties and bras. We found these items inside the store's catalogue.

Ms. Michelle fell in love with that book and she even ordered a few items for herself. She was speaking so loud and being extremely obnoxious in the store. It was nothing out of the ordinary for Ms. Michelle, that's just how she was.

"Girl they got some cream you can put on your clit, it supposed to make it tingle and give you an orgasm!"

Embarrassed, I looked around at the surrounding customers. A white couple scrambled to cover their young daughter's ears, but the little puppy eyed girl had already heard Ms. Michelle's rant. The couple had blue balloons and teddy bear party favors in their hands for what looked like a child's birthday party, but Ms. Michelle clearly let what our visit was for be known.

"Ms. Michelle there are people around us." I whispered through my teeth. She shot a look at the white couple.

"Please girl, they the biggest freaks in here." The flamboyant sales clerk that was helping us almost choked on his spit.

"Okay ma'am, would you like me to place a jar of that on your tab too?" he asked.

"I sure the hell do!" Ms. Michelle replied.

"Okaaay." The gay clerk replied adding to Ms. Michelle's final order. Him and I shared a glance and then we giggled together. Ms. Michelle was truly a trip, but her humor was what I needed to keep my mind occupied.

I pulled my cell out of my purse to check the time. The screen revealed 6:55PM and the mall was about a half an hour away from my house. I hadn't even started on dinner yet.

"Ms. Michelle after we leave this store, I gotta get back home." I said.

"Alright, I just have to run in Victoria's Secret real quick so I can pick up some shower gel and lotion. I ain't gonna be long."

"That's what you said in every store we been in. Seriously, I have to go." I said adamantly.

"Oh girl please, I'll have you home shortly."

We exited the store into the crowded mall amid rushing shoppers and loud teenagers. I was over the whole shopping experience for the day. I decided to sit on a nearby bench to call Tae and explain why dinner would be late while Ms. Michelle continued with the rest of her shopping.

As I dialed Tae's number, I was continuously sent to his voicemail each time. I tapped my flip-flop on the mall's floor growing increasingly impatient while repeatedly trying Tae's phone. I peeked at the line in Victoria's Secret and found that Ms. Michelle didn't even find a place in the staggered long line yet.

Trying to take my mind off of hearing Tae's mouth, I sat back with my arms folded across my chest waiting impatiently as I watched the shoppers pass me by.

Suddenly in the midst of the passersby, I saw a familiar face. I stood and squinted to be sure I recognized him. In plain sight, it was Tae.

It was out of the ordinary to see Tae hit a public place with his work clothes; he was normally all decked out when he stepped out so I figured he must've come with some of the men from work. He was standing by the restroom area as if he was waiting for a companion and I started toward him smiling. Shit, I was hoping we could grab some take-out from the food court and I wouldn't have to cook.

Another familiar face walked out of the ladies bathroom and immediately clutched Tae's hand. My heart stopped and every dark disturbing emotion hit me all at once when I realized that the girl was none other than Sharece. When the smiling duo looked up and saw me, I could tell that their hearts stopped along with mine. Tae was clearly taken aback and we locked eyes before I dashed forward to confront him. He stood frozen and looked like he was scared out of his fucking mind.

"So is this why you wanted to know what mall I was going to? So that you wouldn't get caught in the mall with her?" I asked while pointing my finger toward Sharece's face.

Tae didn't utter a word, he let go of Sharece's hand and stood speechless.

"Oh no, grab her hand Tae. Why are you letting go now?" I mocked.

I paused and looked him up and down pitifully.

"You don't bring me to the mall, let alone take me places hand in hand. I just killed our baby yesterday and you repay me by still messing with Sharece!" I threw his shopping bags at his feet. "Here's your Jordans and shit you asshole!"

I turned to walk away but Ms. Michelle sped toward me and grabbed my arm, dragging me back over to Tae. "Oh hell no, pick up those bags, we are taking that shit back! You don't give him some shit you bought him when he's here with another bitch." Ms. Michelle took her blue coated fingernail and tapped Sharece's forehead, "Let *this* bitch buy him some Jordans."

I tearfully picked up the bags and got in Sharece's face. "I thought you had a man you liar, you just couldn't stay away from mine huh? You are a sorry excuse for a woman."

Sharece was short and petite with frizzy, but fine hair. She looked like a broke down Tyra Banks. She nodded and backed up, "You need to take this up with him." She said pointing to Tae.

"Bitch you're in this too!" Ms. Michelle barked. "Janae smack her!" Ms. Michelle demanded. "Smack the fuck out of this hoe and if you don't, then I will do it for you."

Sharece fearfully began backing up even more.

Ms. Michelle walked up on Tae and smacked him upside his head. "What the hell is wrong with you, doing this to Janae? You got a good woman right here and you are in the mall with this crack head looking bitch. You got to be the dumbest muthafucka alive."

"Yo, man Janae, I didn't come here with her." Tae explained, blatantly lying as usual while ducking to avoid another hit in the head from Ms. Michelle.

Sharece folded her arms and crunched her forehead.

"Don't lie Tae, how else did I get here? I ain't gonna sit here and be made a fool of. Now stop lying and tell her."

"Tell me what?" I asked curiously.

"Tell her what?" Ms. Michelle shouted with both hands planted on her hips.

"Excuse me! You are going to have to take this outside of the mall." A stocky security guard said, escorting us toward the door. Sharece escaped with another guard who was forwarding her to another exit while Tae, Ms. Michelle and I were pushed toward the front entrance.

As security whisked us away, I looked back at Sharece, my eyes barreled down stopping at her red pumps and that's when the fuckin' plot thickened. I realized immediately that Sharece was once again the woman that Tae had been lying to get out of the house to meet. That must've been what she was trying to tell me. It all made sense. She was the same chick he was whispering sweet nothings to on the phone in the bathroom a few nights ago when I in anguish confronted him while pregnant and emotional. The red pumps gave it all away.

"Man, I didn't do shit," Tae proclaimed as we exited through the double door front entrance.

"You're an arrogant little bastard aren't you?" Ms. Michelle alluded.

"Man whatever," he said waving her off."

She continued to cuss him out while I turned away, sinking in my thoughts.

How dare he do this to me! I can't believe this shit. How could Sharece be an issue again?

The daggers that Tae had constantly thrown at my heart had nothing on that very moment. This killed me. She was supposed to have moved on, how did she find Tae again? Or how did he find her? I just killed our baby and he was bold enough to be with another woman the very next day?

Maybe Tae was really in love with her.

Did he really think that I wouldn't go anywhere? Did I really appear that weak to him? Sharece was such a sensitive subject because she wasn't just a one night stand; they had an affair. Cheating should never be justified, but having an affair meant more than a one night stand, it meant feelings were involved, which made it hurt that much more. Tae *has* to love or have strong feelings for her to uncover an open door that I thought was shut and dead bolted a year ago. And of all days, the day after my abortion!

I closed my eyes tight. I was lost. All of my distorted thoughts made me lose my mind and caused me to think vividly into my profound imagination. Maybe Sharece didn't have stretch marks or maybe she could cook better than me. Or maybe he thought she was prettier than me. I tried to stop comparing myself but I couldn't help it. I just wished that I knew why.

The stupid single word question that all women who have been cheated on wanted to know was, *why?* I was losing my damn mind. I took too much shit from Tae and I couldn't stand around and watch him manipulate me again and tear my world apart, only to patch it up with lies. Fuck irrefutable evidence, the proof was clearly in front of me and there was nothing for me to question. It was time that I made a tough decision and finally put Janae first.

I snapped out of my zone once I didn't hear Ms. Michelle screaming anymore and I turned toward her.

"Where did Tae go?" I asked frantically looking around.

"That bastard went back through the mall probably to find that bitch and take her home. I used to like Tae, but that muthafucka don't deserve you. He didn't have shit to say. A man don't bring his mistress in public, that's rule number one. Fuck that shit."

Looking through the clear double doors I didn't see Tae anywhere.

"Come on let's go." Ms. Michelle suggested.

We walked to the car and all I could do was think of Tae leaving with Sharece and it hurt like fuck.

"Janae, sometimes I forget that you are from the same rough neighborhood in BankHead that I raised Sarah in. I'm not the one to condone violence but you should have smacked that bitch." Ms. Michelle pronounced before we got into the car.

I stretched my seatbelt across my chest. "Ms. Michelle smacking her wouldn't have changed the fact that my man brought her to the mall, so it wouldn't have made me feel any better."

"Well, it would have made me feel better, shit."

I shook my head and allowed Ms. Michelle to continue to ramble. Needless to say, she rambled the entire ride back. I drifted my focus out into the busy street, thinking hard. My thoughts were muffled and I felt dizzy, but my mind was in the right place.

First things first, I needed to figure out where I would go. The only thing that kept my mom and dad in Atlanta was the fact that they were both professors at Clark Atlanta University; we had no other family in ATL. My two aunts and grandparents resided in North Carolina, which was out of the question for me. My grandparents were still alive but even to this day, they lived by strict military rules. I wouldn't leave Tae for another shallow life; it would be like going from one prison to the next.

Sarah was my next option, but I wouldn't dare burden her and her new fiancé. They would soon be newlyweds and they would need their own space.

"You need to come stay with me for a while to get your head together." Ms. Michelle offered as if she were reading my thoughts. There was no question that her place was an option, but Ms. Michelle was a bit too wild for me. If she was still anything like she was when I was growing up, I wouldn't be able to deal with the whole men coming in and out of the house at all hours lifestyle.

"Thanks for offering, Ms. Michelle, but I'll figure something out."

"Well you fucked up by letting Tae's boss get y'all the hook up on that apartment, because he put it in Tae's name. Other than that it would be his ass that needed to get the fuck out."

As we approached my apartment, Tae's car was conveniently parked in the driveway, but I was even more pissed to see that parked alongside it was his boss Eric's green Range Rover. *No this nigga didn't*, I thought to myself.

Tae was good for putting Eric into our problems because he was the perfect mediator. But I could always tell that Eric didn't want to get in the middle of me and Tae's drama from his body language. He would roll his eyes and shake his head with frustration over Tae's countless mistakes, but still wouldn't take sides. He spit thc usual, 'Janae, just be patient with Tae, he means well' bullshit. I usually respected Eric enough to let him counsel us because he was such a great, respected individual. He was an ex OG who still held his street credibility, but now had a great career, great family, picture perfect life and plenty of great advice to share.

In this particular case, I didn't think there is anything that he or anyone could say to save Tae's ass.

Chapter 4

Should I stay or should I leave? What's standing in the way of my needs? I think about his feelings but what about me?

"Make sure you call and let me know if you need me Janae. My doors are always open if you change your mind. You're like another daughter to me and I just want you to be alright. I ain't gonna sit here talking your head off, giving you all types of advice and shit. I'm gonna let you figure this one out on your own. Now go inside and handle your business." Ms. Michelle encouraged.

"Alright, thanks for everything, Ms. Michelle." I replied calmly. The truth was, I didn't hear any of her words, I was too hurt to listen to what she was talking about; other shit clouded my mind.

I stepped up to my apartment door and entered slowly, unsure of what to expect. Eric's wife Deborah was seated on the couch in the living room. She stood when she saw me and extended her arms out.

"Aww, come here sweetheart." She said as I accepted her embrace. Judging from her embrace, she knew that my feelings were shattered and that Tae had once again fucked up. I cried on her shoulder while she stroked the back of my hair. "Cry it out honey. I know it's hard." She sighed. "You just never know what you get when you're dealing with a man. You just have to pray for strength and follow your heart." I smelled the scent of her Doublemint gum as she spoke. It was Deborah's signature gum. Deborah had a calming appearance which gave off the impression that she conquered life with ease. Her form fitting dresses always hugged her solid frame and she kept decorative shoes and handbags for added glam.

Like Eric, Deborah often lent out words of encouragement

and her warm hearted personality was addictive. She was a God-fearing woman and maintained a positive spirit. She was the type of woman that said all the right words and made them feel meaningful as if she were talking from her own life experiences. You would never think that there were any imperfections in her relationship with Eric, from the outside looking in. They seemed like they were so meant for each other; like they were soulmates.

"Trust me baby, I have been there before." Deborah admitted.

I suddenly broke loose from her embrace, wiping my tears to look in her eyes. "Huh? Are you saying that Eric cheated on you before?" I asked smudging my tears into my foundation.

Deborah twisted her lips giving me an obvious look as she took a seat on the couch.

"Honey, I have never met a faithful man in all of my thirty-nine years."

I bent to sit next to her, curious for her to continue.

She looked to the floor and shook her head as if she were revisiting painful memories.

"Janae, trust me honey, I have been in your shoes more times than plenty. Trust and believe that. But Eric has done a complete 180 since back then. I blame the majority of his cheating on immaturity because we were both young. We met when we were in our early twenties. He had his flings here and there with different women and I would always find out. He broke my heart so much to the point where I just…" She paused while being swallowed in painful memories. It appeared that she was tunneling into thoughts that she hadn't unraveled in years.

She then looked up and peeked down my long hall to see if Eric or Tae, who were apparently in my bedroom were anywhere around before she continued.

"Janae honey, he hurt me so many times that I even cheated on him once." I sat all the way back on the couch with my eyes bucked; shocked at Deborah's revelation.

I couldn't believe what I was hearing. She was hurt from Eric's cheating, but turned around and did the same thing that he had done to her. I couldn't understand it.

"Don't give me that look sweetheart, love will make you do some crazy things. I never thought that I could ever let another man touch me, let alone sleep with one. But honey, Eric had pushed me to my limit. He was out at all times of the night, he wasn't paying me any attention, and after rejecting men who approached me throughout our relationship, I decided that I would actually let one take me out. And that's all it took. My new friend catered to me and filled the void that Eric had left unfulfilled. He paid attention to me, made me feel beautiful and it was everything that I had wanted from Eric. However, it was short lived because my heart was with Eric. And to be honest, as guilty as I felt, I feel some sort of validation for what I had done. I felt like I had paid him back from the years of him stressing me and hurting me and ripping my heart out. Eric had even given me a disease, twice at that, and I *still* took him back."

"Well did he ever find out about the guy?" I asked curiously.

"No, not officially. But one day while riding with Eric to get our car fixed… I'll never forget the day. We had an old Chevy back then. Little did I know that he was going to the same shop where my special friend worked. When I realized where we were heading, I tried to talk him into going to another mechanic, but he insisted that this particular shop had the best prices. It was *very* awkward when we got there. My special friend knew about Eric, but of course Eric didn't know about him. We kept stealing glances at each other as he spoke with Eric about what needed to be done to our car and Eric kept looking at the both of us strangely wondering where the weird tension was coming from. What made matters worse, was that one of the workers that hung with my new friend spoke to me as if he knew me casually. He was like, 'Hey Deb what's going on with you today?' When he realized that I was at the shop with Eric and not for his friend, he tried to play it off cool and walk away. And that was it for me, after that day, I ended it. Slowly, but surely, Eric changed his ways. To be honest, I think that Eric knew what the weird tension between me and my friend was about, but he never said anything."

Deborah began whispering the story just in case her husband was listening from my bedroom where Tae was receiving his pep talk.

"Girl, my friend was very handsome and he owned and operated that mechanic shop back then, which was way before Eric had his own construction company. I knew that he was a threat to Eric and it probably messed with his pride. I think Eric secretly compared himself to my friend and realized that he could possibly lose me to someone else, and worse, someone who was more established than he was. To this day Janae, I don't think that I regret what I did, because in one way or another it changed Eric and in some form it changed me."

"How did it change you?" I asked.

"Well, it just put things into perspective for me. I've learned that I'm the ruler of my destiny. Back when Eric was cheating on me, I left my feelings in his hands and each time he hurt me, I had blamed myself. However, when I met my friend, it felt like I took my life back; like I was back in the driver's seat again. I now know what I'm capable of and if Eric hadn't changed, then I knew that if I had enough courage to cheat on him, then I was strong enough to leave him."

"But me and Eric had to be meant to be, because he had changed." Deborah then pointed toward my bedroom, "And that man back there that you and everyone else loves and respects is now my husband." She concluded with a smile.

After listening to Deborah's story, I wasn't sure if I should think of it as a beautiful love story or two people who had betrayed each other.

Suddenly, my bedroom opened and Eric came walking out toward me. "Hey Janae, I want to speak to both you and Tae in here, alright?" He asked pointing to my bedroom.

Ms. Deborah smiled and nodded her head. "Go on sweetheart, I'll pray for you. Just follow your heart."

I stood and followed Eric to my bedroom, regretting the fact that I had to see Tae's face. When inside, I noticed that Tae was sitting on the opposite side of our king size bed facing the wall. All I saw were the waves in the back of his pitiful head. His ass was too much of a coward to face me.

Eric didn't waste any time getting to the point. As soon as the door shut behind me, he spoke.

"Now Janae, I was just talking to Tae about this bullshit. He told me everything that happened. Y'all are two grown adults and you both know what's right from wrong. Now either y'all work this shit out or go your separate ways." He then gestured toward me. "Now Janae, I know that Tae can be an asshole, but I do believe he loves you. I was just in here talking to him about fucking up. All that cheating and bullshit and treating you bad get's old. A woman ain't gonna take that bullshit for too long. Sometimes a man can get so caught up in his shit that he doesn't see what's important. There comes a time when a man has to be a man before allowing pride to force him to lose everything."

Tae sucked his teeth from the other side of the bed and it agitated Eric.

"Tae this shit ain't a game young brother, this is life. You have a good woman here."

He motioned toward me, "Excuse my language for this Janae, no disrespect to you at all." Then he referenced back to Tae. "Tae, half these no good bitches out here won't put up with half the bullshit that you put Janae through and if they did, they wouldn't still have your back a hundred percent like she has yours. So take heed to what I'm telling you before what you have is gone. Now I hope this is the last time that I'm put in the middle of your mess, Tae. Man up!"

"Now I'm gonna go out here and take my lovely wife home so that we can enjoy our dinner and I can watch what's left of the game. Y'all have a peaceful night. See you at work in the morning in one piece Tae. Try to relax tonight Janae."

"Alright, thanks Eric."

He bent to hug me goodbye and the way he rubbed my back almost felt like he was caressing it. I actually felt a little uncomfortable.

"Okay, good night Eric." I said breaking our embrace. The last time Eric put Tae in our bullshit, Eric hugged me the same way when he left our house. I just brushed it off as his way of feeling sorry for me for being so stupid in love.

I led Eric and Deborah out and returned to the bedroom to finish up with Tae.

I had hoped that Eric's words had stuck with Tae, but then I had to remind myself that Eric had given us good talks in the past when bullshit like this occurred, and it never seemed to change Tae. I was still set on finally doing what was best for me and that was moving on. I was still in disbelief that my mind was actually really made up and that I was finally giving up my four years of getting nowhere with Tae to have the freedom of getting to know myself again.

Tae finally decided to talk to me as I kicked my shoes off by the bureau. However, he was still facing the opposite wall with his head down.

"I'm sorry Janae, for real. I don't love Sharece, I'm not fucking her and I don't want to be with her. I want to be with you and I hope you will forgive me."

His apology was flat, fake and shallow as fuck. He wasn't even looking at me so I couldn't even respect him or his lame words. Not only that, no man would be holding hands in a mall with a woman he had no feelings for. Especially, the day after his woman had an abortion. The whole shit was a bit too extreme for me to handle.

"Tae you're right, you are sorry. A sorry ass man." I picked up two pillows and threw them at the back of his head. "Here, take these pillows and get a blanket out of the linen closet. You can sleep on the couch. I'll talk to you about my plans tomorrow." I said in a calmer manner than I set out for.

Tae got up and took the pillows and walked out of the room, avoiding eye contact. I shut the door tight behind him and locked it. I peeled off my clothes and laid in bed with only my panties and bra on to marinate on the day's events. I was so hurt and I felt so weak and worn down for always giving him my all, for nothing in return. I turned off the lights and drifted off to sleep.

The next day I slept in. I woke up extremely late, near noon, but my body needed the rest. I was half asleep, but realized that Tae had somehow opened my locked bedroom door and left a peck on my cheek before heading out to work. I didn't have the strength to wipe it off when he did it, but when I got up, my face was the first thing to scrub. Who knows where his mouth had been? I was seeing him in an even dimmer light; he disgusted me.

I lazily moped around the house for a few hours before I retired to the shower. I was drying myself off after just stepping out of the shower when I heard the door bell. I ran to the window and saw Eric's Range Rover parked in my driveway.

I figured that he was picking up something that Tae needed for work because there was no other reason that I could think of for Eric to stop by unannounced. I tightened the belt to my bathrobe and slipped on my black fluffy slippers and scurried to the front door.

"Hey Eric, come on in." I widened the door.

"Thanks Janae," He stepped in and looked around hesitantly. He had on his dusty jeans, white t-shirt splattered in dirt and his aged beat up construction boots. He was built just like my father. You could tell that he was a muscular fella in his day, but was now built like a healthy, in-shape forty something year old. Even the gray hairs hinting from his chin reminded me of my father's because there weren't many.

"I came by to talk to you for a minute." He said.

I was curious to know what Eric wanted to talk about, so I led him to the living room. I was hoping that he wouldn't tell me that Tae had gotten hurt on the job. I sat impatiently waiting for him to speak.

"Can I get you anything, coffee, tea or something else to drink?" I asked hoping he didn't want anything; I wanted him to get to the point.

"Nah, that's a'ight I'm straight." He responded, helping himself to a seat next to mine on the couch.

"Tae is really taking this hard; he's not focusing at work." He started.

I sighed. "Well he should be taking it hard Eric; he really messed up with me this time. I'm finally washing my hands of this relationship. But other than that, is he okay?" I asked.

"Yeah he's okay, I mean I would like for him to be more focused on his work, but he's okay. He kinda reminds me of me when I was his age." He scooted closer to me. "When a man like me and Dontae feels like we don't have control over a situation, we fold. He doesn't know what do with himself because he thinks he's finally going to lose you this time."

I rolled my eyes, it sounded as if Tae was really being pathetic at work.

"Tae is a grown man. He will have to eat his mistakes one day. He has pushed me to my limit. I hope he is eating each one of his fuck-ups until he is full."

"Haha, I hear that, young sister. You have the right to be mad."

"I sure do." I said confidently.

Eric then paused and gazed directly in my eyes. It was a bit awkward, so I pulled my bathrobe a bit closer together, wishing that I had thrown on more clothing. After about two minutes of uncomfortable silence, I started to feel a lot uncomfortable. I've never seen Eric's eyes whispering flirty advances to anyone other than his wife Deborah.

He then scooted even closer to me and that's when I had to

draw the line. I stood with intentions of showing him his way the fuck out of my house, but he stood at the same time. He put his hands around my waist and pulled me close. Close enough to feel his dick rock hard against my pelvis.

"Eric get off me!" I shouted pushing him away. I looked at him as if he was a total stranger. I couldn't believe what he was trying to do.

"You know you want this Janae. Dontae has been doing it to you for years. Why not get yours with someone you trust? He would never have to know."

"Eric, you're not serious right now? What are you doing? I can't believe you! Stop!" I said struggling to push him away from me.

"He won't have to know Janae; you can maintain your household while we do our thing on the side."

I was completely caught off guard! I couldn't believe what was going on. He puckered his lips and leaned toward me while trying to pin my arms to my sides.

I lifted my knee and jabbed it into his dick. I kneed him hard enough to crush both his balls.

"Aaaaah!" He screamed out in pain, kneeling with his balls clutched in his palms. I ran for my cordless phone and then dashed toward my front door and opened it wide.

He glared over at me, his eyes soaring in pain.

"Get the fuck out of my house before I call the police." I demanded.

He wasn't moving fast enough, I pressed the talk button on the cordless phone to let him know that I was serious. He finally got up and limped past me. I quickly slammed the door behind him, locking all three of the dead bolts that Tae had recently installed because of all the break-ins in College Park.

What just happened? I thought to myself while my back was against the closed door. I and everyone who knew Eric had respected him as a role model and father figure, why did he just try that stupid shit? And with me of all people! He knew that I didn't get down like that; did he think that I was that vulnerable? I immediately thought deeper into the situation and I took it personal. I felt bamboozled.

Eric and Deborah had come to our house plenty of times for dinner and vice versa. Eric was on our Christmas list, we even threw him his surprise fortieth birthday party at our house last year. I paid the majority of the tab because I felt that Eric worked hard and deserved to play hard.

Deborah was another major concern. She thought that she was dealing with a changed man, but she was actually dealing with a fucking pervert. Should I tell her? Should I tell Tae? I had no idea what to do and the only thing that came out of me were tears. I thought about telling Sarah, but I didn't think that I even wanted her to know because Sarah never kept anything from Ms. Michelle. Ms. Michelle would sure enough spread the news around town and I didn't want to risk people not believing me. Eric was respected around most neighborhoods in Atlanta and if I outted him, it would surely shatter his image.

I avoided the living room because it reminded me of what just took place with Eric and I ran into my bedroom, slamming the door behind me. I balled up on my bed wondering what I should do. I contemplated calling Tae, but he was sure to lose his job or possibly go to jail because he would try to bring it to Eric right there on the job for violating me. Still holding the cordless phone, I decided that I would tell Sarah. She began blabbing as soon as she picked up.

"Hey Janae girl, I've been meaning to call your ass. You know my mom told me what happened at the mall. I hope you bleached that niggas clothes, nah matter fact, I hope you burnt his shit."

I shut my eyes, forgetting that Ms. Michelle probably called Sarah as soon as she pulled away from the curb after dropping me off and ran my business about Tae.

"I'll talk to you about that later Sarah, something deeper than that just happened."

"What the hell can be deeper than your man holding hands in the mall with that bitch? Did you catch them in bed together? Hurry up, fill me in!"

"Can you just shut up and listen for a second?" My tone involuntarily became thick because a lump crept up in my throat as I began crying thinking about Eric's actions.

"Eric just left my house."

Sarah cut me off. "Why did he come over in the middle of the day? Did Tae's ass put him in the middle of your business again? See, he needs to stop doing that to Eric. Eric has his own problems; he's running his company and catering to his own damn wife."

"Yeah he caters to his wife alright. He just tried to force himself on me."

I heard a weird blowing noise on Sarah's end. "Hold the fuck up Janae. I was sipping orange juice and just spit that shit all over my computer screen. Did I hear you right? You said Eric tried to force himself on you?" She asked in a shocked tone. "I don't even know if I could believe it, not Eric. Eric's a good dude; he's like a pops to us."

"That's why I'm still in shock Sarah. He pulled me close to him, his dick was all on my stomach, talking about Tae don't have to know. Then he tried to kiss me. It was so degrading."

"Well you know what Janae? I know that Tae is in the dog house right now, but you need to have him whip Eric's old ass. Fuck that. He violated and I lost all respect for him. What else did he do, did he try to rape you?"

"If he would have stayed any longer he would have. But after he pulled me close and tried to kiss me, I kneed him in the balls and made him get the fuck outta my house. I don't know what to do right now Sarah. I'm lost, that's why I called you. I don't know if I should call Tae, tell Deborah about it, or what."

"Damn J, that's a hard situation. But I do want Tae to beat his ass. Then again, he would lose his job. And Deborah idolizes the ground Eric walks on, so I don't even know if she would believe you. Shit, I don't know if anyone would believe you, niggas act like Eric is Tupac reincarnated. Everyone respects that man."

"So you're saying I should just keep it to myself? I can't just let this shit go, Sarah."

"I know Janae, we'll figure something out. I have to get back to work, I'll try to come by later on to scoop you up. You need to get out the house. From the abortion, to seeing Tae with that bitch in the mall, and now this? Girl, you need a drink."

"That sounds comforting Sarah, for real."

After hanging up with Sarah, I reached for the remote on the oak nightstand to power up the plasma so that I could take my mind off of things. I ended up falling asleep watching Judge Hatchett and waking up a few hours later to my Drake, *I'm On One* ringtone. It scared the shit out of me.

"Hello?" I answered with exhaustion heavily in my tone.

"You sleep?" Sarah asked, all loud.

"Yes I was, what's up?"

"Curt wants to beat Eric's ass. You don't have to tell Tae anything, just let Eric get his ass whooped and keep it moving."

I immediately sat up in my bed, wiping my sleepy eyes. "You told Curtis what happened?"

"Yeah! Why not? He's my fiancé now, plus you know he cares about you. He was pissed off when I told him about what happened."

Shit, Sarah thought Curtis was pissed off about what happened to me. Hell, I was more pissed off with *her* for once again telling him my business. That's one thing about Sarah, she told her man everything and it sometimes made me not want to open up to her about a lot of things.

"I don't want him telling anyone about what happened, Sarah damn."

"Girl calm down, my man ain't stupid."

I got up and walked over to the mirror and grabbed my brush off the dresser because I looked a mess. My hair looked like it had not been combed in days and you could see the exhaustion spread evenly across my face. Bags under the eyes of a pretty girl wasn't too appealing.

"What time is it Sarah?" I asked.

"It's almost five; I'll be getting off work soon."

"Alright, I'm gonna get myself together so that I'll be ready when you pick me up. Call me when you're on your way."

"Alright bye.

I slowly untied my bathrobe. I had slept in it as if it was guarding me from being fondled. For some reason, after Eric left I didn't want to take it off. It felt like some sort of protection. I disrobed and tossed it onto my bed. I slipped on a pair of Seven skinny leg jeans and a cute purple fitted top to match the print in the back of my jeans. My outfit was neutral just in case Sarah wanted to go to a restaurant instead of a bar.

Finally satisfied with my appearance, I posed in the mirror, trying to force myself to smile. The pudge in my belly was almost flat but it still looked like I was about a month pregnant.

Suddenly my phone sounded as a text message came through from Tae. It read: *Hey beautiful, I know you don't want to hear from me but I just wanted to tell you that I love you and I hope that you are having a relaxing day.*

I rolled my eyes before pressing delete and proceeded to put the finishing touches on myself. My hair was pulled back into a neat ponytail. I put on my big gold bamboo earrings, applied some eye liner and MAC Lipglass and transformed to finally looking decent again.

It felt like forever waiting for Sarah to pick me up. I sat on my bed, almost letting my weakness get the best of me. I held my cell in my hand, rubbing the buttons with my thumb, contemplating whether to let Tae know that I was stepping out, or proceed with my independent lifestyle that I promised to give myself and leave the house without telling him. I then considered if I should take some meat out of the freezer to unthaw so that I could prepare dinner later.

My strength slowly inched back to the surface once I shut my eyes and pictured Sharece at the mall in her red pumps holding Tae's hand. That's when I decided… fuck him!

He didn't need to know where I was going and I didn't give a damn if he ate dinner or not. I was focused on me, on Janae, for once. I stood tall to look in the mirror and cheer myself along, "You can do this Janae, be strong, he doesn't deserve you."

Then I exhaled.

A little while later, Sarah pulled up in front of my house. She always called me when she was outside because her lazy ass never wanted to get out the car to ring the doorbell.

"Alright, I'm coming." I said before flipping my phone closed. I snatched my keys off the dresser and threw them into my purse, which I picked up from my unmade bed and I left. I didn't give a fuck if the house was cleaned and didn't give a fuck about what Tae thought about the house not being cleaned. I also didn't care about what he thought about my leaving without letting him know or if his dinner would be prepared, I was focused on my new journey.

"You look nice." Sarah said as I reclined in the passenger seat.

"Who?" I said looking around as if she wasn't talking to me.

"You, you look cute, nice and casual," she said eyeing my outfit.

"Well if that's the case, I don't feel the way I look," I said slouching back further.

"Anyways…uh um." Sarah blurted sitting back in her seat using her left hand to play with her right ear.

"Girl if you don't drive this car, let's go." I said.

"Uh umm!!" She blurted even louder tugging on her ear this time.

I didn't know what the fuck she was doing, but I was growing impatient.

"Drive Sarah!" I shouted totally oblivious to the fact that she wanted me to see her ring.

"Bitch you don't realize what I'm doing?" she asked leaning toward me.

I glared at her hand and then I laughed. "Girl I'm so sorry, my slow ass didn't realize what you were doing. Let me see it."

Sarah happily extended her left hand to show me her two carat rock surrounded by two layers of Princess cut stones.

"Aint it the shit?" She asked boastfully.

I held her hand, admiring her engagement ring for a few seconds. I couldn't front, her ring *was* the shit and I was hating on my homegirl and hoping she didn't notice.

"Sarah, all I can say is that Curtis got good taste. It's beautiful."

"I know, my boo do got good taste huh?" she said pulling her arm back and admiring her ring as if she'd never seen it.

"Okay girl, now drive this damn car," I said playfully snapping her out of her zone.

During the ride, I went in depth with Sarah about my plans to leave Tae and how my only roadblock was the fact that I didn't have anywhere to go. Sarah was more than happy to hear that I had finally seen the light.

"Well girl, I am happy for you. I didn't know what it was gonna take for you to leave that dog. That time when you were on the phone with Sharece and she told you that Tae was on his way over to her house and you actually heard his ass on her intercom saying 'it's me boo, let me in'. I thought for sure that was the straw that broke the camel's back. And you still gave his ass another chance after that. But like my mom always says; every woman has her own limit, it takes some women more time to reach their limit to where they decide they'd had enough of a man's shit."

"Yeah girl I have finally reached my limit. Tae will no longer have his way with me." I spoke confidently.

"Yes! Janae, like I said, I'm happy for you."

Sarah pulled into a dark unfamiliar parking lot. She reached in the back seat and pulled a green tank top out of a shopping bag. She unbuttoned her white work blouse and pulled the green tight shirt over her head, taking a little more time to stretch it over her double D's. I curiously pondered what the point of her changing clothes was, until I peered up at a flashing bright sign with a silhouette of a man's body. Then, I noticed flocks of women parading up to the front door of the venue.

"Uh uh Sarah, I know we aint' going in here. We must be going to the restaurant across the street."

"Nope we are going in here boo boo. My mom is meeting us here too, she should be here shortly."

Literally a second later, there was a knock on the window and Ms. Michelle appeared at the passenger side window scaring the shit out of me. I opened the door.

"Ms. Michelle, you almost gave me a heart attack," I clutched my hand over my heart.

"I'm sorry sweetheart, what y'all still doing in this car? Y'all need to hurry up so we can go see some ass."

I still couldn't believe that they had me out at a strip club. That was the last place that I wanted to be.

"Well *y'all* can go in there; I ain't going in no strip club," I said sternly, folding my arms. "Yes the hell you are!" Sarah and Ms. Michelle shouted at the same time.

"Y'all know I don't like places like this, I don't want to see no sweaty balls all in my face, plus I don't have any singles." Ms. Michelle reached into her Baby Phat purse and pulled out a handful of single dollar bills. "I got you covered honey."

Sarah was still primping in the driver's side fold-down mirror. She carefully applied her fake lashes and added some green eye shadow to match her shirt.

Ms. Michelle bent into the car and patted her on the thigh.

"Okay Miss beauty Queen, you look nice. Now let's go." She demanded.

"I know I look good Ma, because I am the bomb like tick tick," Sarah said bouncing her D- cups together. We all shared a giggle before exiting the car.

As we headed up to the club, I noticed there were women in line with bra tops and pum-pum shorts on, dressed as if they worked in the club themselves. It made me feel a bit overdressed. Ms. Michelle was on fire once again that night. She had on a purple corset and a pair of black skinny leg jeans with purple and black pumps. It appeared as if she had lost even more weight since the last time I saw her. She looked damn good and younger than ever.

"Can you remind me why we are here again?" I asked as we were moving up in the line. The other women around us were so pressed to go inside the club, and I was feeling out of place.

"Curtis and his boys went to Diamonds to pick out the women for his bachelor party, so I'm coming here to pick out some men for mine. Now let's go enjoy ourselves while we pick out some cuties."

"I know that's right, let's go see some fly sexy young brothers." Ms. Michelle exuded.

Loud music and thirsty women filled the club. Ms. Michelle's excitement led us to a table right in front of the stage. Not only did I not want to be there in the first place, but I definitely wasn't feeling being right in front of the damn stage. A male waiter approached our table wearing nothing but a small black jockey strap. "Three shots of Patròn please," Ms. Michelle said taking the initiative.

"Patròn!" I shouted scooting to the edge of my seat. "Ms. Michelle, I was thinking of something like a Daiquiri or a Bloody Mary or something."

Ms. Michelle waved her hand at my request so that the waiter wouldn't consider it and demanded that he followed with her initial Patron order.

"Don't mind her. Can we just get the three shots please?"

"Three shots of Patròn it is." The caramel, oily, muscular waiter said walking off.

"Girl don't be up in here acting too cute! Loosen up, you are out with us. You need this more than the both of us. Shake that bullshit off and have some fun."

Ms. Michelle was right; I did need to loosen up. I sighed and sat back in my seat, trying not to look out of place. I searched the room only to see obnoxious women getting lap dances and making it rain on men who looked like they needed to hit the gym before they thought about stripping as an occupation.

"Here are your three shots." The waiter announced as he placed three small shot glasses in front of us. He then put a white napkin in the center of our table and placed three finely cut pieces of lime on it next to a small container of salt. Ms. Michelle put a twenty dollar bill inside of his jockey strap and then smacked his ass.

"Thanks boo," she said watching his tight ass walk off.

Sarah and Ms. Michelle both licked the crease between their thumb and index finger and sprinkled some salt on it.

"Come on Janae, this is how you take a shot of Patròn," Sarah said handing me the salt.

I licked my hand and sprinkled the salt on it. Ms. Michelle was smiling big. "Okay y'all ready?" she said picking up her shot glass.

I scooped mine off the table as well. "I guess so." I said. We counted to three, licked the salt off our hands, threw our shots down and quickly sucked on the lime.

It took a while to remove the sour look off my face because the Patròn went down hard, although it had a mellow aftertaste. My body didn't waste any time absorbing the liquor, especially after shot number two. I was officially *nice*.

I didn't drink too often. And when I did, it was only a glass of wine, so Patron in my system was like liquor to a new drinker. Sarah and Ms. Michelle's tolerance was a bit higher than mine.

They had ordered two more rounds of shots for themselves, but two had already done it for me.

Sarah's face was screwed up all night after crossing out the names of the strippers she had written down as potentials. As she watched them dancing up close, she found flaws in all of them.

Delux was her first choice, but she said that he had too many pimples on his booty. And, the bald head that looked good in his picture was shaped like a sharp egg in person, she said.

Buttercup was her second choice, but she said he danced like a white boy and wasn't going to fuck up her party by dancing off beat.

Handsome Boy was her third choice. He was kind of cute, but appeared a lot older in person than in his pictures. He had a few gray hairs in his low curly fade and it seemed as if he should have retired as a dancer years ago. His muscles were turning soft and he just needed to give it up.

Ms. Michelle, on the other hand, appeared to be in love with him. All of her money went straight to Handsome Boy and she continuously slapped his ass during his entire routine.

"Ma'am, that's enough, you can't touch the dancers." The heavy set bouncer reminded Ms. Michelle. Ms. Michelle kept dancing and pulling on Handsome Boy's thong as if she didn't hear the bouncer.

"Ma'am, consider this your last warning." he announced in a more serious tone.

"It's alright boo, I'm sure you want me to slap your ass too." Ms. Michelle told the bouncer. The big bouncer revealed a slight grin and walked off.

Handsome Boy finished his routine to Ms. Michelle's request to the DJ, Snoop Dog's *Sexual Seduction* by dropping down to a full split. I tapped Sarah on the shoulder cracking up laughing at the visual. "Sarah, that's a little too gay for me, that nigga really just busted into a damn split."

Ms. Michelle sat back in her chair fanning herself with her

hands. "Girl please, he can come over my house and drop that split in my bedroom any day!" she shouted obnoxiously.

Sarah put a line through Handsome Boy's name and put her list back into her purse. "Alright y'all, I'm ready to go."

Sarah was obviously disappointed in her selection. I clutched my purse, ready to head out when the female DJ announced, "We have a treat for y'all ladies. He's ATL's favorite, the ladies love 'em and the men are jealous of 'em. Ladies give it up for Damionnnn Starrr!!!"

The club went wild. You could tell who the regulars were, because they were out of their seats even before he came out. I saw a few pairs of panties fly to the stage. I stood with intentions to walk out the club, but was suddenly knocked back into my chair by the presence of Damion Star.

All three of us were speechless. I couldn't believe that even Sarah was blown away. This man's body was priceless and his face was flawless. He had a very defined facial structure like a perfectly carved ice sculpture. His teeth were bright white and his smile alone could light up a room. His swagger was just as mean. He was like a thugged out sexy ass stripper. He had buttery brown skin, two long Indian braids and a body that looked like it was drawn from a portrait. He had large tattoos covering his chest and back and I couldn't find one thing wrong with this man. He was gorgeous.

"Oh hell yeah, *he* will be dancing at my party." Sarah said smiling and pulling her list back out of her purse to jot down Damion Star's name.

"Girl that is one beautiful man," I agreed.

Something had come over me, or more like the Patròn *took* over me. I snatched a few dollars out of Ms. Michelle's hand and made my way to the foot of the stage. I stood and appreciated this masterpiece of a man as he worked off his snap on pants, revealing his sculpted toned legs. For a moment, it felt like every other woman in the club was muted out. Damion advanced toward me and danced his way closer. He was vibing to one of my favorite songs, *Juicy* by B.I.G.

I tingled with embarrassment as our eyes locked. I felt like a groupie. I quickly snatched the dollars behind my back after realizing that I was stepping out of my realm. This wasn't me. I wasn't the type to approach a man, even if he *was* just a stripper.

I felt someone snatch the dollars from my hands.

"If you ain't gonna give him this money baby, then I will." Ms. Michelle said, waving the money in the air before sticking it in Damion's tight black jockey strap and smacking his ass. "Here you go baby, work it with your sexy ass."

Damion's eyes stayed on me, even while he was grooving with Ms. Michelle. I had never lusted for a man before, but this man was something else. His physical appearance was so perfect, and his aura was like a magnet. I felt myself being pulled in.

"Okay, now I'm going to have to ask you to leave."

The heavy set bouncer had returned, and this time, he brought two skinny bouncers along with him, as if he needed back-up. Over at our table, Sarah was having a little altercation of her own. When Handsome Boy had finished on stage, he joined the crowd to give lap dances and apparently Sarah's ignorant ass told him that he wasn't good enough for her money. The two argued briefly and I ended up having to pull her and Ms. Michelle out of the club, since we were being kicked out anyway.

"Y'all are sooo crazy. I should've known that this night would be an adventure, chilling with two of the craziest chicks in Atlanta." I said.

Ms. Michelle kept fussing about the bouncer. She said that he was mad because he was fat, unattractive and jealous that he wasn't getting attention from anyone. Sarah agreed as she kept carrying on about how Handsome Boy's old, sweaty ass should have tried to dance with someone else.

Through all their fussing, I kept thinking about Damion Star. His presence had graced my mind the entire ride home and all

I could think about was how fly he was. After seeing him, I was actually glad that I went out with Sarah and Ms. Michelle. Of course there would never be a relationship with me and a stripper, but seeing Damion made me realize that Tae wasn't the only man left in the world, and that staying with a man just because I was comfortable and afraid to move on was nothing but a waste of time. There were actually other fish in the sea and I just hadn't caught mine yet.

Chapter 5

Could I be changing? Has our love melted away in his mistakes? Only time will tell, but how much time will it take?

When Sarah dropped me off at home, Tae was actually pulling up at the same time. Judging by the inquisitive look on his face, it was obvious he wanted to know where the hell I had been. The Patròn was still dominating my system so I felt a little bolder than usual.

"What you doing just getting here, Janae?" he asked exiting his car.

"Why are *you* just getting in?" I shot back at him.

"I was working late, what's your excuse?" he asked.

I giggled. "Working late huh? I wonder what construction contract requires that the staff has to work until two in the morning. Save the bullshit okay, Tae. We don't have to answer to each other anymore anyway, because we're through."

Tae waited until we were in the house to respond. He flicked on the lights and scanned my outfit. "Why are you wearing them tight ass jeans? Where the fuck you been? And what's in there for me to eat?" he asked making his way toward the kitchen.

I waved him off and scurried down the long hallway to my room. "I didn't cook shit! Matter of fact, maybe you should call and see if Sharece cooked anything for you. You're free now; you can go out and be with any woman you want. Don't worry about me blowing up your phone or confronting you about it, fly free, I don't even care anymore."

"Stop talking stupid! If I wanted to be free I wouldn't be here. I don't want no fuckin' Sharece, so quit it with this shit!"

He tailed behind me as I walked through the house. I went

into the kitchen for a glass of water and he pointed to the stove feeling like an idiot because I hadn't prepared any food for him.

"A nigga don't get nothing to eat tonight, again?"

"Tae please, go ask Sharece to cook for you because I ain't never lifting a finger for you again, ever." I said rolling my eyes.

I walked away from him and retreated to my bedroom. Again, he followed behind me. I tried to shut the door in his face, but he caught it with his foot.

"Tae, get out of my room, we are through! I have nothing else to say to you. You really lost me this time. I'm serious. I need some time to find a place to move my things out, but I just want you to respect my decision."

He grabbed me by the collar and hemmed me up to the wall. "You can say and think whatever you want, Janae but you're not going anywhere. You're my girl."

I huffed. "Oh I'm your girl? Is that what we have, a relationship? Maybe we are not seeing things through the same set of eyes Tae, but a blind man can see that this shit is broken. You are NEVER HOME TAE! You used to love to be around me, but now it seems like you love staying *away* from me. You were never the type to wear your feelings on your sleeve and tell me you love me every five minutes, so I don't expect that. But the least you could have done was compliment me, notice when I change my hair or when I'm wearing something sexy or when I just want to be cuddled. I don't get any wanted vibes from you. You have me around here feeling like a germ, like you don't want to touch me or compliment me; like I turn you off. I'm only your little sex toy at night when you're feeling horny, other than that, you treat me like I ain't shit."

He released my collar and focused into my eyes, squinting his deep eyebrows. It was a look I hadn't seen him give me in a long time. It was if he felt some sympathy for me.

"I know you don't believe that shit, Janae. That don't even

sound right, I always compliment you and tell you I love you. Stop being dramatic."

"Well if you don't see what I see, then I'm wasting my time trying to explain."

I pushed through Tae, kicked off my pumps and took a seat on the bed. I was too tired and too tipsy for his shit.

"I tell you I love you Janae, you know I do. I always show you how much you mean to me."

I rolled my eyes, waving him off. "Whatever Tae, I wasted my time talking to you. I never got through to you before, I don't know why I thought I would now."

"Fuck it, I don't want to be with you either! You *did* waste your time because I don't want to hear this shit! I told you I don't want to be with Sharece. And she didn't even come to the mall with me the other day, she just happened to be there. So if you want to end our relationship over some stupid shit like seeing me at the mall with some girl and not catching me doing some real shit, then fuck it! It ain't like you seen me fucking someone because I'm faithful to you."

I closed my eyes and nodded at the bullshit he was spitting. "So she *happened* to be in the mall and y'all *happened* to be holding hands? You're so full of shit! And faithful Tae? You're so faithful that you sit around the house calling bitches from our house phone *and* your cell phone? Then I find texts in your phone and all types of shit that you do behind my back but you're faithful huh?" I giggled.

I could only smile through my frustration to keep me from killing his lying ass. He was such a damn performer, he deserved an Oscar. This argument was going nowhere and my decision was still the same.

"Tae can you please get out and shut my door, I would like to go to sleep now."

"I ain't going nowhere. I'm sleeping in here with my woman." He took a seat next to me on the bed.

"Oh I'm your woman again, I thought you just said fuck it?"

He took off his shirt and then tried to pull mine off.

"Stop Tae, I'm not sleeping with you." I resisted.

He stood me up and wrapped his arm around my waist, snatching me close. He peered into my eyes, expecting for me to break like I always had, but I didn't fold. I held my ground. He kept trying to convince me to give in to him, but I resisted. He continued to try and when I didn't budge, he pushed me away.

"Fuck you then Janae. You acting all stupid when I didn't do shit to deserve this. You make a nigga want to cheat, acting like this."

I tucked myself in bed and drowned Tae out. I was so over his verbal abuse. I couldn't wait to leave him.

He stood at the foot of the bed and started acting out of control. He played defensive, yelling and cursing; then he played tough, blaming me for everything; then he would apologize. Then he would play tough again, using words like 'fuck you' and 'I can find a chick with a fatter ass'.

I rolled over and closed my eyes on my pillow while he continued with his Oscar award winning performance. It seemed that my lack of response confused him, so he kept trying to say harsh shit to get a reaction out of me. It wasn't working. It was obvious that he was taken aback at my reluctance to respond, because he was trying so hard to get me mad.

Finally he saw a different Janae, someone who was strong and confident and not giving into him. The shock value even had an impression on me, I was proud of myself; however the liquor did play a huge role in my confidence.

After a few more minutes of Tae's verbal bashing, his voice irritated me.

"Tae I'm tired of this, please just get out!"

"I *am* getting out bitch! I don't want to sleep with your dumb ass tonight anyway."

He proceeded to the door, and as I watched him walk out, I

noticed about five deep red scratches clawed into his back. The scratches were fresh, so apparently he just got them from some bitch.

I quickly threw the covers off of me and sat up.

"Hold on, come here Tae?" I signaled curling my index finger.

He stormed back my way.

"You want me to sleep with you tonight Tae?" I asked sarcastically.

"Yeah, of course I do," he said, as if it wasn't obvious.

"Oh really? Then come here." I stood up and extended my arm for his hand, then I walked his ass over to the mirror with his back facing his reflection.

"Look at this shit!" Tae turned his head at the mirror bending his head to look back.

"So the bitch that just gave you these fresh scratches on your back didn't put it down good enough for you, now you want to fuck me tonight too?"

He quickly spun around to face me. "See here you go with this stupid speculation shit again! I told you I was working late tonight. Some of Eric's equipment had fell on my back when he was working above me on the ladder."

I huffed, his lies were so pitiful and so unbelievable.

"Tae, you're not serious are you?" I folded my arms and stared him up and down pitifully; he was pathetic. "Is that the best lie you can come up with?"

It all began to sink in. This was really our finale. I was actually, really done with Tae. I wanted to cry, but not a single tear formed. I was all cried out over him. Nothing else he could do to me would shock me. And Tae bringing up Eric's name made me feel even more fucked up after what had happened to me earlier in the day.

The scratches on his back and the mall episode reminded me of just how low down he could really be to me. I definitely had to adhere to my plan to leave his sorry ass. Sarah was right. I should've left him that day when I heard him on Sharece's intercom. Hearing my boyfriend on another bitch's intercom saying 'let me in boo' should have sent me straight to the closet to pack my shit and leave.

Instead, that same night he came home and called Sharece in front of me. He cussed her out for setting him up and having me on the phone. He accused *her* of being grimy. Before he called her, he tried lying first. He told me that it wasn't him who I heard on her intercom. After realizing that I wasn't accepting his excuses, he apologized a million times and then called Sharece to blitz on her. He continued to repeatedly apologize and make false promises until I folded. My dumb ass gave in the same night. I gave this asshole the privilege to sleep with me, knowing that he was just at Sharece's house, most likely about to fuck her that night.

I still feel stupid about that situation to this very day. A confusing part of my mind kept telling me that if I showed him that I was down for him and ride with him through his mistakes, that things would fall into place. I sorta felt like I was in a competition with Sharece and I felt like I had won once he was home with me. I knew that it was stupid and that I was only selling my soul to him, but love had me blinded.

A little while after that incident, Tae had stopped dealing with Sharece and he actually did try and prove to me that he wanted to be with me. That's when the rumors that she was supposedly involved in a new relationship started. After all the bullshit we had been through concerning Sharece, I knew for sure that their affair was over.

Thinking back on the turn of events, I now felt like I had it all figured out. I concluded that the reason Tae was being such an asshole to me, not taking me out, not complimenting me and basically dismissing my existence was because Sharece was back in the picture. Tae had Sharece right back in his pocket and either I was in the way or he wanted to have his cake and eat it too.

It was always painful to reminisce about the whole 'Sharece and Tae' affair, so I kicked him back out of my room and didn't indulge in the argument about the scratches on his back. It was a waste of time. He wasn't going to admit it and it didn't matter because my mind was made up, our relationship was a wrap.

The next morning I woke up in Tae's arms. With a face full of disgust, I peeled his arms off of me and wondered how he got through my locked bedroom door again. Luckily, his alarm sounded and it was time for him to get up and get ready to go to work. I was so happy to see him go. I didn't want to be around him any longer than I needed to. Besides that, I wanted to start my day by looking for an apartment and calculating my budget to see if I would be able to afford a spot on my own.

Tae showered, threw on his work clothes and pecked my cheek before rushing out to work. I smeared his kiss off and locked the door behind him. Just the thought of the scratches on his back and who may have put them there made my stomach weak.

I went into the kitchen to calculate my plan. I pulled out a pen and pad from my kitchen junk drawer that I had been meaning to clean out, and squatted down on the leather and chrome kitchen chair to jot down estimates of expenses. I started with first, last and a security deposit on a new spot which would be $1500 to $2000 in total for something luxurious in Atlanta. Then came utilities: cable, lights, and gas in addition to food, car insurance, school loans and other miscellaneous expenses that I would have.

When I finished adding everything up, I was thoroughly stressed out. I rolled my pen across the table, staring at the circled estimated total. There was no way that I would be able to afford it all. I balled up the paper and threw it against the wall.

With Tae paying most of the bills, I never had to keep a tight budget, which is probably another reason why I was so comfortable in my situation with him.

My mom's soft voice of reason rang out in my head, *Janae, sometimes you have to struggle first, it gets greater later.* I smiled at the thought of her. I truly missed her and it was like her sweet spirit encouraged me to face reality. Either I was going to leave now and struggle or stay for a little while and work my ass off to save enough to be stable. I was leaning toward the latter, but was still unsure. This issue became my dilemma for the day.

While laid out on the couch, I flicked on the TV and surfed through the channels, but there was nothing on. Well, nothing to keep my attention because there was too much on my mind. Minutes later, I clicked the TV off and tossed the remote on the couch.

Food became my next objective. I opened up the fridge but nothing seemed to appeal to my appetite. My stomach was growling but there was nothing specific to curb the hunger. I hated the fatigued feeling I got when I would stress out, but this was the life that I chosen for myself.

I kept beating myself up for not leaving Tae sooner, so that I would've already been over this hurdle of regret. On my way to my bedroom, I tripped on one of Tae's work boots and the thought of Eric came into play. That asshole was probably at work smiling in Tae's face and it disgusted me. If I did decide to remain living with Tae temporarily, there would be no way to avoid Eric or Deborah for that matter. I don't even think that I would ever be able to look in Deborah's eyes again without revealing to her what kind of scum she had for a husband.

Being in the house for the rest of the week had me thinking way too much, I was now looking forward to going back to work.

Two weeks had gone by, and I was able to convince Tae to pay my portion of the bills without letting him know that I was saving to leave his ass. He agreed, only because he thought it would put him on my good side. With him paying my portion, I was able to stack an extra thousand dollars in my savings account and use the rest of my paycheck for gas and groceries. Things seemed to be looking up for me and my plan.

Tae was still doing his bullshit; coming in whenever he felt like it and some nights not coming home at all. I tried not to let it bother me since I announced to him each day that we weren't together and I actually convinced myself of the same. One thing was for sure, he knew that his bed was still on the couch and not in the bedroom with me. I avoided him as much as possible, but when his ass was home, he made sure to pay me a compliment, even when I looked horrible. His efforts seemed so forced.

One day I was taking out the trash because his lazy ass never did, he usually just sat and watched me lug four or five heavy trash bags out without asking me if I needed help. But on this particular morning, I threw on some baggy polar bear printed pajama pants, a black and white striped oversized turtle neck and some beat down Reebok classics. After placing the trash out on the sidewalk, I ran back inside. Tae looked me up and down as I shut the front door behind me.

"Look at you, looking all cute." He said as if it impressed me.

I took a look down at my non-matching ensemble and then gave Tae an 'I know you ain't serious' face. All I could do was roll my eyes and walk past him. His bullshit was so fake! Where were the compliments when they were deserved or when I wanted them or when I desired attention from him? Now that I mentioned his shortcomings, he was just throwing compliments in at all the wrong times. His sorry attempt was ignored and I proceeded to ready myself for work.

Tae occupied the bathroom after I was done and he was actually running behind schedule.

"Janae, I'm going to be late for work this morning," he yelled out from the shower.

"Okay," I hollered back at him.

I already had on my cream business suit, purse in hand and was ready to head out. I didn't know what him being late had to do with me.

He yelled out again, "Can you call Eric for me and make something up for me boo? You know how he is about employees being late."

My heart skipped a beat. There was no way that I was calling

Eric. I had avoided him and Deborah for weeks and there was no way that I would call him personally.

"Tae, that's unprofessional, you call him." I reasoned.

"Yo, I'm gonna be like forty-five minutes late Janae. Tell him I'm stuck on the side of the road with a flat tire and that I called you from a pay phone because I left my cell at home."

I heard everything that Tae asked me to say, but pretended not to. I tiptoed to the front door and headed out to my car. As I sat in traffic thinking about it, I felt bad for not helping him out. Eric was pretty hard on his employees for being late, no matter who you were, but Tae had to handle this on his own.

He called me at work shortly after I got settled in and called himself giving me the business.

"That's fucked up Janae, I asked you to do something simple for me and you couldn't even help me out this morning." He huffed. "I don't know what to say about the direction of this relationship. You don't want me to sleep in the bed with you, you haven't gave me no pussy in a few weeks and you look at me like I'm stupid when I compliment you. Man, you're just not being yourself Janae."

"Well you're the one that made me feel like this Tae, remember that."

"What did I do to you except for be faithful to you, love you and pay the bills like a real man?" he asked with confidence.

I gently placed my hand over my forehead and sat my elbow on my messy desk.

"You're not serious right now are you Tae?" I asked.

"What do you mean? Of course I'm serious. You got yourself a good man. That bitch Sarah, Ms. Michelle and all them bitches that you work with would love to have a man like me. You're sitting here pushing me away and acting like a fuckin' little kid. You're always accusing me of shit I didn't do."

"Tae, you're so full of yourself that you probably actually believe everything that you just said. You haven't been faithful to me since day one. I keep fucking up my body with abortions, catching you fucking with Sharece, scratches on your back, sneaking on the phone and shit. Come on Tae, you should understand why I'm acting the way that I am. I'm fed up," I said sternly.

"Fed up with what? I didn't do shit!" he pleaded.

"That's the problem, you're in denial." I stopped at that thought. "You know what? It's not even denial, you're just a liar. You know exactly what you did to me and why I feel this way. You don't even come home half the time, Tae. What faithful man doesn't come home? Face it, we grew apart, we don't need to be together anymore."

"Don't say that Janae." I heard the desperation start to sink in through his tone. He was starting to break down. He tried to convince me that I was just angry and that I didn't mean what I said. "You know I love you girl, we didn't grow apart, you're just mad right now, so I'm gonna let you cool off. Matter of fact, let's talk about everything after work, okay? This nigga Eric called himself sending me home today since I was late, so I'm about to take my helmet and shit and get out of here. That nigga has been acting up lately too, but that's a whole 'nother story. I'll see you when you get home alright?"

"Alright, bye."

The conversation with Tae took a different direction than usual.

Usually when I said something that made him feel like he wasn't in control of the conversation, he would hang up on me. I haven't heard him sound this desperate in years. It seemed like me not giving into his bullshit forced him to realize that I was putting my foot down and shit was real this time. He seemed like he was scared of losing me and couldn't take it. I was proud of how strong I was becoming. The fickle woman that I was in the past was dissolving.

I gave him no other choice but to bow down and try reasoning with me. What bothered me more than anything was Tae's mention of Eric's funny actions. I figured that the situation that happened between Eric and me would come up sooner or later, but I hoped that I would be the one to explain it to Tae.

After ending our conversation, I tried to be cordial at work and conduct business as usual. While filing stacks of admissions applications into the file cabinets in the center of the office, one of my co-workers pointed out that I appeared to be losing weight. The entire office decided to scan my frame with their eyes. I was put on the spot and highly embarrassed, though I managed to keep my composure. The last time I was losing weight rapidly was because of Tae and Sharece's rendezvous and the entire staff knew all about it. They also knew that when I was stressed, I couldn't eat and that Tae and our problems were usually what caused it. I decided to make up a lie so that my business remained under wraps.

"Thanks, I've been going to the gym three times a week." I lied.

"Oh okay, well you look good girl." My co-worker responded with a fake smile knowing that she wanted to pry into my personal life.

Throughout the stress, I got through the work day on a wing and a prayer. Of course, out of all days, it was one of the busiest. When I got home, I was drained. I had taken countless phone calls at work full of questions from prospective students who wanted to start in the Fall. I also had to assist a rush of students with their financial aid. All I wanted to do was kick my feet up and relax.

An aroma of onion, garlic and Lawry's seasoning graciously hit my nose all at once as I stepped inside. Tae was at the stove juggling tasks, stirring white rice, flipping the steak and sifting salt into the boiling corn-on-the-cob.

"Hey boo," he said multi-tasking.

Looking around at the candlelit kitchen table and the scattered rose petals, I greeted him back. "Hey."

I was in total shock! Tae had never done anything like this before.

"Boo, just go take your shower and relax, I'm gonna finish this up," he suggested.

Surprised with the entire set up, including the gift bag beside the table, I decided to adhere to his suggestion. While in my bedroom, I peeled off my clothes in front of the mirror. I felt half anxious and half bitter. I was torn.

Staring at myself, I was convinced that I had to stick to my guns. I softly whispered, "Janae, he is only going to feed you some bullshit because he knows that he's losing you. He's never going to change, so be strong." I took a deep breath, gathered my confidence and headed for the shower.

I was in and out within minutes due to anticipation of how dinner would go. I dried myself off with a thick blue Clark Atlanta towel that I'd gotten from work and put lotion on each body part, before starting on my hair. I made a half part in the front of my hair and brushed each side down, revealing its long straight length. I slipped into something simple yet dainty; a white satin one piece nightie that hit past my knees. I didn't want to tease him by wearing anything any more revealing, because I hadn't let him touch me in weeks and planned to stick with it.

He stood from his seat once I entered the kitchen and he didn't sit back down until I did. Once we were both secure in our chairs, he pointed to my food and decided to boast about his feast.

"I made you white rice with spicy gravy and I marinated the steak in teriyaki sauce and put extra butter on your corn like you like it."

I nodded admiring my dish, "Wow Tae, I'm impressed."

"Thanks," he said accepting the praise with a smile.

We began eating and avoided eye contact whenever one of us looked up. It was uncomfortable for us both. This was the first time that we had sat down together in weeks. He finally revealed what was in the golden gift bag next to the table. He pulled out a bottle of Cristal and popped it open, filling our glasses to the brim.

"Janae look at me." he said.

I peered into his soft eyes which now read extreme desperation. "You're my lady Janae. It hurts me each day when you tell me that we are not together. I miss you boo and I mean that."

Butterflies tickled my stomach, but I dismissed them by picturing Sharece and the deep scratches on his back to maintain my strength. He reached across the table and lifted my hand, holding it with two of his. "Boo, I'm sorry. You were right, I did fuck up and I'm sorry for lying to you."

I glanced away, because his performance was almost convincing. He was actually taking fault for the first time.

"Look at me boo." He pushed his chair closer to mine and placed my hand over his heart. "Janae, I'm nothing without you, I need you."

"Tae, you don't need me, you're just saying this because you know that I'm not taking no more of your shit."

"No Boo listen! I love you with everything inside me. You're my life line. When you told me that I didn't compliment you and that I didn't make you happy, that shit tore a nigga up. I never wanted to make you feel that way and I'm so sorry. I don't know what the fuck I was thinking."

My eyes teared up as I watched his deep brows squint with sadness.

"I should've listened to you when you wanted to start all over and forgive me for everything that I put you through, but I was selfish and I'm sorry. I know I fucked up Janae. I did you wrong and you're the last person in my life that I needed to treat wrong."

I couldn't believe what I was hearing. Tae was actually spitting some real shit. Although he had never taken fault for any of his bullshit in all of our four years together, I couldn't give in to him again. Not this easily.

"Please boo, I'm begging you to forgive me. I want my Janae

back, my sweet loving woman. I don't like this mean person that you've become. I know I'm the reason for changing you, but I made some mistakes and I want you to forgive me. I can change and be that man that you want me to be boo."

My face was now full of tears and I didn't know how to respond. Tae was the cause and cure of my stress and I had missed him so much these last few weeks. His expression was so genuine and his words hit all the right spots. I didn't know what to do or how to handle it.

"I can't Tae, you'll just hurt me again." I said tearfully and now with uncertainty.

"No boo, no I won't." He began kissing my hand. After each word, he placed a few soft pecks up my arm whenever he finished speaking. "No more Sharece, no more staying out, I'm done with that dumb shit. Everything that I want and need in this world is right here in front of me. Please boo, I'm begging you."

I shook my head. "No Tae, I'm not putting up with it anymore. I can't, you're not ready."

"Boo, I'm not saying that I'm ready for marriage right now, but I'm ready to commit. We can take baby steps. Let me prove my love to you boo, please."

I stared into his eyes taking everything in. This man had hurt me more than anyone in this world has ever and probably ever will. But I didn't hate him. I loved him more than life. I took into account how much I had changed recently and I thought, maybe tough love worked on him. Maybe out of all these years, it took for me to really be cold to him for him to see what he had in me this entire time. Maybe he would change.

Weakness began controlling my emotions and my heart fluttered intensely. Suddenly I stopped fighting with myself and I gave in. But giving in never felt so right, until that very moment.

"Okay Tae." I whispered shutting my eyes tight and slowly opening them.

"What you say boo?" He asked only wanting me to repeat what he had already heard.

I sniffed, "I said okay."

He smiled and pulled me close as I cried in his arms.

"Don't cry boo. I'm going to show you, watch. I'm going to make you so happy. You're my baby and you deserve nothing but the best, and I'm going to deliver."

I cried because I was mad at myself for giving in and also because I was angry at how much I loved him. We held each other tight for about five minutes. He rubbed his hand over my hair and kept professing his love for me and how much he was going to change and be the man that I have always wanted.

"Pick up your glass boo." he said after we finished embracing.

We lifted our Cristal filled flutes and Tae made a toast to our new life together and to new beginnings.

It was funny how my appetite immediately returned. It felt like all the stress during the past few weeks had disappeared because I had my man back. I feasted on Tae's dinner like it was the last food on earth and we laughed and had pleasant conversation throughout the rest of our dinner.

When we finished stuffing ourselves, Tae took my hand and led me down to the cool kitchen floor but first he peeled off my satin gown. He ate my pussy for hours like it was dessert, then he led me into our bedroom where we fell asleep in each other's arms.

Chapter 6

Thank you LORD, he's changed! Is it real, or will it be short lived? This is the love that I have always wanted, but how long will it last?

Tae and I were going strong for about a week. He was coming home every night after work, paying me compliments when they were appropriate and was back to being the fun loving man that I met four years ago. His awareness toward my needs demonstrated that he was making attempts to change. He was far from the cold hearted person that used to stress me out. I actually felt like his change was genuine and not something temporary.

I reverted back to my routine of having dinner waiting for him like I used to. The house was kept fresh and clean daily and I ran bath water for us both each night. We would soak in the tub together helping one another wash away our stressful work days and have long conversations about how much fun we had together when we first met.

When we finished in the tub, we would bring our bare bodies into the bedroom where Tae would softly massage baby oil from my neck to my feet. This always led to us making passionate love.

Our love making was better than it had ever been. We were now connecting with each other on a mental *and* physical level, which made for the best sex ever. Each night was better than the last. And after, we'd cuddle in each other's arms and throughout the night he would occasionally squeeze me tight, laying random kisses on my neck and showing his appreciation without having to say a word.

He was surprising me with gifts every other day, making sure I felt appreciated. He wasn't even questioning me about going out with Ms. Michelle as frequently as I was. Because we spent a lot of time together shopping for Sarah's party, we had been running around like chickens with our heads cut off, but it was fun.

We had been extremely busy. Our bachelorette items had arrived, so Ms. Michelle rushed to the mall to pick them up. I had to drop off a deposit at the strip club for Damion Star, then I swung by the South City Kitchen on Crescent Avenue to set up catering services in the midst of hand delivering all the invitations to the invitees. When I got home, I downloaded music for the party on my MacBook. The whole process was exhausting, but doing this for my best friend was worth it.

The day of the bachelorette party quickly crept upon us. I made an early a.m. hair appointment at Marco's Hair Designs and my hairstylist Candy hooked me up with large curls loosely flowing down my back like Beyonce. I rushed to the liquor store to pick up the liquor and then sped home to finish up my look.

My attire made the whole look even more luminous. I wore a sleeveless, low-cut, tight fitting black BCBG mini dress with some hot Manolo Blahnik silver stiletto, peep toe shoes that Tae had got me. They showed off my diamond studded French manicure. I applied light, yet simple make-up, using mineral foundation. I added silver to my eye lids to match my shoes and curled my long lashes top and bottom, finishing with, MAC eyeliner and lip gloss.

"Boo you look stunning." Tae said peering at me as if he wanted to fuck me on the spot.

"Thanks Boo." I replied while putting the finishing touches on myself in front of the full-length mirror.

"Don't let that stripper nigga touch you either. And I hope no other niggas are going to be there." he said playfully, yet semi-serious.

"You're so silly. It's a bachelorette party, there isn't going to be any more males there. And the stripper only stays for an hour."

I was still in disbelief that Tae hadn't had any objections about me going to the party in the first place. On a normal day, he would've told me that Sarah would have to have her fun without me, but he was really changing before my very eyes. So far, I was happy with his transformation.

"Make sure you come straight home so I can fuck you in that dress." He flirted as he continuously scaled his eyes on me taking more time peeking at the way the dress curved to my behind.

I powdered my cheeks lightly with red mineral powder blush and then tossed it on the dresser. I walked up on Tae to flirt back.

"Baby, I'm going to *run* home to this." I said cuffing a handful of his crotch.

"Mmmm, you better hurry up and leave before I keep you here and sweat your hair out." He tucked in his bottom lip.

I giggled, "You're so crazy boo." I pecked his lips twice softly before we locked our tongues. We grasped each other's backs intensely. Tae was rubbing up and down on my ass from the very top down to the cuff and began jiggling it. I stepped back, unlocking my lips from his. "You are a mess baby, let me get out of here because I'm about to jump on you." I said reaching for my lip gloss to re-apply.

"Please jump on me." Tae pled looking down at his manhood that was apparently erect.

"Aw boo, you know I have to go but when I get home it's on." I pecked Tae's lips one more time and I headed for the door.

I hopped in my car and was gloating on our new-found love while driving to Ms. Michelle's house. Me and my boo were happy again and the thought of him gave me chills of happiness. Things were finally how I wanted them to be, we had come a long way and I was proud of myself for sticking beside him and putting in the effort to make it work.

I arrived at Ms. Michelle's house before any of the guests arrived and was able to help her put the finishing touches on everything.

Ms. Michelle was so damn anxious about the party that everything was pretty much taken care of when I got there. She had white table cloths on each table with brown penises imprinted on them. The cake was shaped like an oversized penis with brown frosting to give it the *real* effect and dark chocolate at the shaft covering the two large cakes posed as balls which made it look even more real. The penis hats were on the table beside the cake and she had plenty of room on the two other tables for when the catering arrived.

"I got Ciroc, Bacardi Razz, Hennessey and Remy Martin." I announced to Ms. Michelle while pulling out the liquor bottles from the heavy brown bag.

"That Ciroc and Bacardi shit is for y'all light drinkers, this Remy and Henny is for mama," she proclaimed raising the two bottles of cognac as if she wanted to guzzle them.

I crumpled the brown bag in my hand and looked around. "Looks like you have everything pretty much set, what do you need me to do?"

"Child, just sit down and relax. I put all the decorations up last night. All we have to do is wait for the caterers to arrive." She peeked down at her wrist at an imaginary watch and yelled out, "I know they better get here within the next ten minutes or someone is getting cussed out."

I laughed at Ms. Michelle's dramatics and took a seat on the couch. I couldn't wait to get the night started. I planned on getting a little tipsy while making sure that Sarah had a good time, and then going home to Tae so that he could take full advantage of me. When I was a little drunk it made the sex even better.

Sarah came barging through the door. "Ohhhh shoot, look at it in here. I love it!" She said, looking around at the set up. I stood up to help her unload bags from her hand.

"Doesn't everything look nice?" I asked while unloading the heavy bags near Ms. Michelle's bedroom door.

"Hell yeah, we are going to have some fun tonight." Sarah said doing a slight two step.

I giggled. "Alright Sarah, take all your shit into your mom's room so you can hurry up and get dressed, the guests will start arriving soon."

"Well where the hell is the food?" She asked while glaring at the empty tables.

"Girl, just go get dressed." I insisted, pushing her toward Ms. Michelle's room.

Sarah had brought about five bags full of clothes over. She was so picky with her appearance, every outfit had to show some cleavage and it had to fit her small frame just right. She also always carried a large make-up sack full of MAC and Sephora make-up because she was obsessed with looking her best. To top it off, it took her forever to get dressed and apply the make-up, so I always had to encourage her to get an early start.

The bell rang and I let the caterers in. A few guests arrived at the same time as well. Ms. Michelle and Sarah both stormed out of the bedroom fully dressed, looking glamorous but ruining their looks by acting like two angry crazy women cussing out the caterers.

"What the fuck took y'all so long? I hope y'all don't expect no tip." Ms. Michelle fussed, full of blatant attitude.

Sarah butted in, "fuck the tip, I hope we are getting a discount for your lateness because y'all ruined my party by having the food arrive late. And it better still be hot!"

Before the caterers could defend themselves, I stepped in. I pushed through Ms. Michelle and Sarah and told them to go do something and let me handle the caterers. When the last pan of chicken broccoli and ziti was placed on the last remaining spot on the table, I thanked the caterers and led them out.

Shutting the door behind me, I turned to Ms. Michelle and Sarah and told them that they needed to behave. "Y'all need to stop, we are supposed to have fun tonight, no more drama. I'm about to pour both of y'all a drink so y'all can relax and we can enjoy our night."

I poured Sarah a cup of Sprite mixed with Bacardi Razz and

made Ms. Michelle's crazy ass a cup of Remy straight up. I handed the penis party hats to the five girls that were seated on the couch and told them to help themselves to the food and drinks. When it seemed like everyone was situated, I made my own cup of Razz and Sprite and occasionally opened the door for new arriving guests.

The living room filled up with about twenty-five girls who were mingling, bobbing their heads to the soothing old school Jodeci playing in the background and having a good time. I seated Sarah in her special chair, which was covered in pink and white lace frillies and had it facing the guests so that she could begin opening her gifts. She was more than impressed by the gifts that the guests bought for her, because they were mainly from the store that Ms. Michelle and I recommended they purchase from.

"Oooh, I'm wearing this shit on my honeymoon." Sarah said, holding the purple bustier and string thong set up to herself. I knew her taste, I had a feeling she would love the set.

"Glad you like it." I said with a smile.

She was smiling and thoroughly enjoying herself. It made me feel like all the hard work that Ms. Michelle and I put in had paid off. And of course, Sarah more than appreciated all of the sexual toys. She made it quite apparent that she was excited to use the toys on Curtis. She had us cracking up all night. She continued to open the fancy gift wrappings while guests cooed over each gift. I ran over to respond to a knock at the door. I opened it with the intentions on letting in more guests, but instead, the most handsome, flawless, shirtless man was standing before me. My mouth watered at his presence. We broke eye contact when he lifted his portable radio to press play; it was none other than Damion Star. He danced his way in and placed his radio on one of the tables. I turned off the music we had playing and returned to watch him do his thing.

It seemed as if every single woman in the room was gawking at him. They were pretending to pass out and fanning themselves while appreciating this fine brother that we had the pleasure of seeing take it all off in front of us.

Don't get me wrong, Tae had my heart but there was nothing wrong with appreciating a good looking brother, and Damion was over the TOP good looking. He resembled a more muscular Allen Iverson but with long, coal black, silky hair that he wore in two braids. They hung over both his shoulders, just like he had worn it the night we saw him at the club.

Ms. Michelle dashed in front of him and made it rain on his head. "You can have all my money baby, you can have me too if you want me." She laughed and then began grinding all on Damion's crotch.

"Ms. Michelle let us enjoy him too!" One of the guests hollered out trying to move her out of the way. Ms. Michelle was hogging up the heartthrob; she couldn't get enough of him.

"I'm sorry baby, you'll have your turn. Let me just do this first." Ms. Michelle took both hands and rubbed them over his oily chest down to his washboard abs and hollered as if she just touched platinum.

"Woooooo!!" she squealed.

"Okay, y'all young girls can have him for a little while, but I'm coming right back after another drink," she joked while walking off to the liquor table. Ms. Michelle started coughing as she poured her drink. I followed behind her to give her crazy ass a glass of water and snatched the cognac out of her hand. She was having a little too much fun.

Damion made his rounds, dancing with the guests and giving us our money's worth. When, *Neighbors know my name* by Trey Songz sounded through the speakers, Damion approached the crowd of women and he asked, "Which one of you is the bride?"

I was standing behind Sarah's decorated chair and I pointed down toward her. "She's right here." I answered.

For the first time ever, Sarah's loud ass was speechless. She sat in the chair and pasted her eyes on Damion as he made his way toward her. He stripped his pants off, saving the best show for the bride, but I was enjoying it right along with her. Sarah beamed on him with eyes full of lust as he licked his lips and grooved to the melody. He turned to reveal his muscular church boy booty and Sarah finally broke her trance and put a ten dollar bill in his jock strap. All the ladies on the couch were screaming and hoping that his pants weren't the only thing that came off. He proceeded to give Sarah a lap dance from behind and then turned toward her, grinding on her lap as she sat. For some reason, he was gazing directly in my eyes as I stood behind her bridal chair. After a while, it became a bit uncomfortable because I was intoxicated by his flawlessness. I backed up and walked away, letting Sarah enjoy herself and I poured myself another drink. This time it was pure Razz, without the Sprite.

Damion led Sarah out of her chair and laid her in the middle of the living room floor. He crawled on top of her in a push-up exercise position and put one leg up and grinded his leg and ass in the air. The ladies were going wild and Sarah was screaming just as loud from the floor.

I joined in on the laughter and was pleasantly pleased by Damion's show. I was even more happy that Sarah was enjoying herself.

All the sexual tension in the room had me missing Tae. I excused myself and made my way to Ms. Michelle's room where it was quiet so that I could call him. While it rung, all I kept doing was thinking about Damion's show. I was hot and bothered. The liquor had finally hit me and I wanted to talk a little dirty to my boo.

"Hey baby." I said when he picked up.

"Hey boo, you on your way home?"

"No not yet, the stripper is still here. But Sarah already opened up all of her gifts, so when he finishes up, I'll help Ms. Michelle clean up a little bit, then I'll be home."

"A'ight baby, that nigga didn't touch you did he?"

I giggled. "Of course not baby, the only person I want doing that is you."

"Oh really?" Tae teased.

"Yes, really baby. I hope you're ready for me because I wanna go like four rounds tonight. You think you can handle that?"

"The question is… can *you* handle me?" he asked.

"You know what baby? I ain't gonna answer that, I'll just show you." I said seductively.

"I'll be waiting." He replied.

I pressed end and smiled at the thought of my boo and how wild my night would end.

Ms. Michelle and Damion entered the bedroom as I was walking out.

"You can change in here. Do you something to drink or anything?" Ms. Michelle asked Damion.

"Yes, some water would be fine." He replied.

"Okay sure. Janae can you please bring him some water, I have to use the bathroom." Ms. Michelle said coughing loudly and staggered her drunk butt to the bathroom.

Nervously, I answered. "Sure." I took another peek at his body that was now drenched in sweat and I walked out, wanting to drool.

I grabbed a Styrofoam cup from the kitchen and poured Damion some cold spring water.

Glancing into the living room, I noticed that most of the guests had left and some were gracious enough to clean up after themselves. That only left straightening up the furniture that was moved for the party, which meant that I could hopefully get home to my boo sooner.

Knock, knock, knock. I gently tapped on Ms. Michelle's room door.

"Come in." Damion replied.

I entered slowly and handed Damion his cup of water. Thankfully, he was now fully dressed so it made me less nervous to be around him. His attire added another element to his swag. He wore one of the same black and gray Polo shirts that Tae had, along with some blue True Religion that weren't too baggy. He matched it up with black and Gray Gucci sneakers. He looked even sexier with clothes on.

I tried not to stare at him too hard.

"Thanks sweetheart." He said.

"You're welcome, do you need anything else?" I asked trying to be courteous.

I awaited an answer but he sipped his water and locked his eyes with mine as if he was staring into my soul. I felt butterflies flutter in my stomach and I melted in embarrassment.

The silence was awkward. I looked away because I didn't know what else to say, it was weird. I then turned and made my way to the door.

"Pretty brown, brown." He said as I reached for the knob. I spun in his direction,

"Don't you think that's a little disrespectful?" I asked him.

He advanced toward me, "I didn't say pretty brown *round* like the song, I'm not talking about your booty sweety. I said pretty brown *brown*. I meant that your hazel eyes complement your brown skin tone. You are a very attractive woman."

I felt a little foolish, but I blushed and felt like my cheeks were probably beet red.

"Oh, thanks." I turned and tried to walk out again.

"Wait," he said reaching for my hand, but I pulled it back.

"You asked me if I needed anything else and I do." He said.

"What do you need?" I asked.

"Your phone number." He flirted.

I cracked a smile, "Nice try, but I'm taken."

"You might be taken, but are you happy?" He asked.

"Yes I am, now if you'll excuse me." I was finally able to walk out and had to exhale once the door was shut. It was the first time since I've been with Tae that I've ever felt compromised. I almost wanted to give him my number, but I just wasn't that type of girl; plus he's a stripper. I wouldn't dare ruin what I had at home for him, even if my situation wasn't so perfect.

I pretty much had to do all of the straightening up by myself, since Sarah and Ms. Michelle somehow ended up passing out on the couch. Before they fell asleep, they shared a small pail where they had taken turns vomiting. The duo was pretty much out of commission so I took charge and handled the house.

It wasn't too bad after the furniture was in place. I had to throw away a few plates of food and place the liquor stained table cloths into the trash barrel. I stored the remaining food in the fridge.

By the time I arrived at home, Tae was in the bed knocked out. I undressed and then slowly crept into bed with him. I didn't even bother to wake him; I cuddled beside him and went to sleep in his arms.

So much for my passionate night, but I was satisfied to be right there with Tae.

Chapter 7

How do you know when love is real? How do you know if someone has really changed? What if I'm the one who's changed? I've never felt like this...

I had used Sunday to recuperate from the bachelorette party. Tae and I made a deal that we would sleep in all day. We ordered food, made love, ate some more, made love and then slept. It was the perfect ending to a perfect weekend.

Monday morning was beautiful, it wasn't desert hot outside, it was around 72 degrees and comfortable in Atlanta. Although I had slept all day Sunday, I was still exhausted and wasn't looking forward to going to work. Tae gave me his usual morning call around 10am just to tell me that he loved me and we shared some small talk. Since the office wasn't that busy, I was glad that he had phoned in because I almost nodded off at my desk.

"Boo don't be mad." He said.

"Why Tae what's up?" I asked twitching in my chair.

"I may be late coming home for the rest of the week. This nigga Eric got me working on the Clarendon project. Shit, I told him that he's taking time away from me seeing my boo, but you know how he is about us working on big projects, we gotta be all in. So I guess you can use this as time off. You deserve it. You don't have to have dinner waiting for me when I get home either. Me and the guys will most likely order out each night. So just relax each day until the project is done and when I get home at night, just be waiting in the bed for me with nothing on."

I took in the disappointing news. I was a bit sad, but I didn't give Tae any reservations toward his new refined "work schedule".

I tried to trust him again because we were going strong in our relationship's repair.

I can't front. In the back of my mind, I did wonder if he was about to settle into his old ways and use this time to cheat on me, but I had faith in him and I agreed. I also wondered if Eric had him working on this project purposely to keep him away from me and try to destroy our relationship from a distance.

"Alright baby, don't work too hard." I said.

"Thanks boo. I love you and I'll see you later tonight," he ended.

I placed the phone on the receiver and went about my work day without any distractions.

I took my lunch break at eleven instead of twelve because I had to run to the post office to send out some letters through certified mail. While in line at the post office, my phone rang from an unfamiliar number.

"Hello?" I answered.

"Hi, is this Janae?" A deep voice asked.

"Yes this is, who is this?" I asked.

"So this is pretty brown brown huh?" he replied.

From his words, I knew immediately who it was. "Damion how did you get my number?"

"Oh, you remembered my name? I'm flattered." He said.

"Can you please answer me?" I grew frustrated.

"I begged your friend, the bride's mom for it. I got her number from the club and I called her to ask about you because I couldn't stop thinking about you."

"But I told you that I was taken." I reinforced.

"Yeah that's what you told me. But the bride and her mom told me differently. The bride told me that you were in an unhappy situation."

"Well you know what Damion? Not to be rude and cut you short, but that's actually none of your business and I'm very happy in my relationship so I would appreciate it if you wouldn't call me anymore." I pressed end and hung up on him. I was beyond pissed off.

I wanted to blitz on Sarah. I had to step out of the long post office line and let some old impatient blonde lady take my spot. I stormed out of the building and my anger was on ten. I called Sarah to dig in her ass about how disrespectful I thought she was. My brown complexion turned lollypop and I paced the sidewalk back and forth in front of the post office as the phone rang in my ear.

"Hello?" She answered.

"Why did you tell that stripper Damion my business? He told me that you told him that I wasn't happy in my relationship with Tae, what's up with that Sarah?"

"haaaaaaaaaaaaaaaaaaa!" She laughed louder than a damn ringing bell. I had to pull the phone away from my ear for a second.

"Girl, I sure did tell him that. I told you that you need to go for yours. That nigga is *fine* girl. Tae has been doing his thing, girl go do you."

"Sarah, I thought I told you that Tae and I were happy now."

"For the time being! Y'all always break up to make up and then he pulls the same bullshit. I don't know why you think this time is any different."

"Well it is different Sarah, and if Damion calls and asks about me again please tell him that I'm off the market. And tell Ms. Michelle to tell him the same. And don't tell him any more of my business. I can't believe the two of you!"

"Okay then, grouch." She replied.

"I'm not a grouch, I'm pissed off at you right now. You never cease to surprise me with something crazy or stupid."

"Yeah whatever Janae! Listen, Curtis is beeping in on the other line so I'll talk to you later. You just need to think about giving Damion a chance, you never know, he may be the one."

"Yeah a stripper may be the one for me huh? No thanks, goodbye Sarah."

"Bye girl, I'll call you later."

I lost my train of thought, forgetting about the purpose of my post office trip, I dashed back into the office.

"Do you have the receipts for the certified letters?" My co-worker asked as I took a seat at my desk. I tapped the top of my head, "You know what, I totally forgot. I'll be back in about twenty minutes." I said standing up to repeat the trip.

"Alright Janae, please hurry, there are three students waiting to see you."

I rolled my eyes and rushed back out. My mind was boggled because the call from Damion had taken me by surprise. I couldn't believe he was seeking me out and actually had the nerve to call my phone.

I was so faithful to Tae. I almost felt like I needed to tell him that another man called my phone against my will and that it was Sarah and her mom's idea, but I decided against it. I felt content with the impression that Damion wouldn't call me back after I hung up on him.

After work, I headed to the Waffle House to grab a chicken sandwich since I didn't have to cook for Tae. I was definitely not anticipating the fact that I would probably be asleep when he came home for the rest of the week because of the Clarendon project. I was starting to get used to all of our ample cuddle time together. I had actually gotten used to him coming home every night like he used to. Things were so good between us that they honestly couldn't get any better. We hadn't even had an argument in a while and I hadn't wasted any tears on our problems because they were now non-existent. At the rate we were going, I was convinced that Sharece was a thing of the past and that Tae was all about me.

Missing Tae at home, I showered and retired to bed to watch movies. It was only 7pm but I thought I would just turn in early. I heard a knock at my door about a half hour after I was settled into bed.

Widening my door, I found Ms. Michelle and Sarah standing

on the front door stoop. From the mysterious looks on their faces, I assumed something was up.

"I know this is last minute Janae, but we came to pick you up to get fitted for your bridesmaid dress." Sarah said smacking on a glob of gum.

"Huh?" I asked surprised. It's almost 8 o'clock, where am I getting fitted at this late? And I ain't even dressed." I tugged on my clothes, "look at me, I already took a shower and I'm in my pajamas."

They both barged in.

"Girl so what! Keep them jogging pants on and just put on some flip-flops. You're just getting fitted, it will take no more than twenty minutes." Ms. Michelle insisted coughing and pouring herself a glass of water to clear her throat.

"You know what? I'm officially convinced that the both of you are crazy. It would have been nice if y'all told me this in advance."

I slipped on my flip-flops, combed my hair down and smacked on some lip gloss.

"Y'all lucky I love y'all or we would have had to do this some other time." I said as we headed out to the car.

I used the time in the car to confront Ms. Michelle and Sarah about the Damion situation. They both needed to hear my opinion on how grimy I thought they were for setting me up.

"Okay, now why did y'all give Damion my number and tell him my business?" I blurted out interrupting their conversation about nothing.

Ms. Michelle was driving and she pretended to focus on the road. Then she tucked in both lips to suppress her laughter. Sarah looked out the window to avoid the question as well. The silence ended after a few seconds, and both Sarah and Ms. Michelle snorted out giggles. I cracked a smile and began to laugh with them.

"Mm hmm, we can laugh about it now, but I wanted to kill y'all earlier." I said.

"Girl, if that man wanted me, I wouldn't hesitate. I don't care if I was married to the President, I would take him on the ride of his life."

"You so nasty, Ms. Michelle." I said.

"Why is that nasty? Child, if you don't have a good man at home, there is nothing wrong with getting your groove on. But when you do find yourself a good man, that's when you do everything in your power to make him happy."

"Well I *do* have a good man at home." I professed.

"Urrr" Sarah muttered.

I sat up from the back seat and tapped Sarah's shoulder.

"What does that mean Sarah? What are you grunting for? Yeah, me and Tae had our problems, but he's changed. Trust me, it's different now."

"All I'm saying is that you're my girl. Tae has been shitting on you for years and you've accepted it. You haven't even lived yet. You don't know what another dick feels like. And I'm not even saying that you have to leave Tae, all I'm saying is that you put up with his shit all this time, might as well stay with him and dip in some other chocolate every so often. Because trust and believe, he's going to keep doing it to you. You may think he's faithful and coming home every night, but if a female in the same caliber as Damion Star approached Tae, he would beat that pussy up and not think twice about you. All men cheat, *all* of them! I wouldn't be surprised if my fiancé was out here spanking some chick on the side. But I know that I'm number one and shit, I'm probably gonna be spanking me something on the side too."

Ms. Michelle and Sarah shared a laugh but I didn't think that what she said was funny.

"Well, I don't think all men cheat. I think when a man finds the right woman and knows that she's the one for him, he won't cheat. And if he has cheated on her, he would change his ways once he's in the predicament of losing her."

"Girl you are so naïve." Sarah pitched.

Ms. Michelle pulled into the David's Bridal parking spot. She turned off the engine and proceeded to school us both.

"I'm gonna tell y'all both something. As long as you please your man at home, you don't have to worry about him cheating. Don't get me wrong, he may slip up because men are weak to temptation. But if you keep him pleased in all forms, in the bedroom, in his belly and by being his homey and lover, then that man will fall in love with all those qualities. He will want to make your union permanent and he'd eventually want to marry you. After that, no one in this world would matter to him not even the women he cheats with. You will be his everything. So just keep that in mind ladies. Keeping a man happy is hard work but it's worth it." She preached.

Sarah and I both took in what she said. And on that note, we exited the car and headed inside the bridal store.

A giddy brunette approached me with my dress laid across her forearms.

"Here you go Janae, this is the maid of honor gown that Sarah picked out. It's beautiful, I'm sure it's going to look lovely on you."

Apparently the associate recognized Sarah and Ms. Michelle and knew what our visit was for. Plus, they'd been back and forth to the shop regularly bugging the poor associate and probably giving her a hard time ever since the first day Sarah got engaged.

The dress however was purely Sarah's taste and it was hot. She'd picked out a pink Halter Tea-Length Dress with an attached sash a touch lighter than the original pink color of the dress. It was radiant, yet simple and I loved it.

Sarah snapped her fingers at the brunette associate. "Excuse me, while my friend tries on her dress. Can you go get my wedding dress so that I can try it on and show it to her? Thank you." Sarah demanded in a not so nice tone.

"Sure." The clerk responded holding onto her smile.

Sarah's wedding dress was phenomenal. The top fit like a corset with beaded embroidery stitched over the bust line. The bottom poofed out like a Cinderella dress and included a long curvy tail. It was totally immaculate and I admired it from top to bottom. I glanced in the mirror once I had on my dress, turning from side to side. Something was off about the fit. It was way too loose at the bust line and my butt almost burst through the seams in the back. The associate had to take my measurements to ensure a better fit in time for the wedding.

"Are y'all finished fitting her?" Sarah snapped at the clerk while pointing to me.

The associate took the last measurement, "Yes, she's all set." She said closing her measuring tape.

"Okay good because I have to get out of here before I try on my dress again. I fuckin' love this damn dress." Sarah boasted before handing her dress back to the clerk.

"It *is* pretty." Ms. Michelle said admiring it. She was so happy for Sarah and pleased at how well things were panning out.

After leaving the bridal shop, I was ready to go home and sleep. I noticed that Ms. Michelle was driving in a different direction than my house. "Where are you going Ms. Michelle?" I asked.

"We are stopping at my house for a second. I want to show you *my* dress. I already got fitted for mine and purchased it already."

"Ms. Michelle, it's getting late and I'm tired." I said about to become annoyed.

"Girl we'll only be a second." She insisted.

We arrived at Ms. Michelle's house twenty minutes later. She unlocked her apartment door and Sarah and I followed her inside. "Janae go look in my closet and get my dress, it's the only one covered in plastic.

Naïve to the fact that Ms. Michelle could have gone into her *own* room to grab her *own* dress, I made my way to her room.

A caramel man stood from the bed and said, "hey gorgeous." I put my hand over my chest. I was completely taken off guard. I backed up and stormed out of Ms. Michelle's room. I searched the living room, the kitchen and bathroom only to find that Ms.

Michelle and Sarah had left me. I then realized they had set me up. I retrieved my cell phone from my purse to call them. This time I wasn't going to be easy on either one of them. I couldn't believe they had in the house alone with Damion, trying to force me into dealing with him.

Finally Ms. Michelle picked up the phone dying with laughter.

"Oh y'all think this is funny? Come the fuck back inside this house or I'm going to start breaking all of your antique vases and bash your favorite lamp over your fish tank. This shit is fucked up and I ain't laughing!"

"Calm down girl, we only went next door to the store. We'll be back upstairs in a little while." Sarah screamed through the phone. Apparently, they had me on speaker, "Get your groove on for the time being Janae, tear his ass up."

I shut my eyes and counted to ten because I was about to lose it. I gritted my teeth and managed to speak as calmly as possible.

"Ms. Michelle, get back here and get back here now. And after y'all take me home, lose my number. I'll see you both at the wedding because after tonight, I have two less friends." I threw my phone back into my purse and placed my index finger on my temple to massage my instant headache. I spun around and noticed Damion standing behind me.

He threw up his hands. "Don't blame me for this; they called me to come over here claiming that you wanted to see me. If I would have known that it was the other way around, I wouldn't have come."

I reasoned, "You know what, it's not even your fault. Ms. Michelle and Sarah like to play little games like this." I sighed. "It makes me wonder how I could deal with them both for so long."

He flashed his bright smile, "Man, that Ms. Michelle is something else. I didn't even know that was Sarah's mother at first, because they act like they are homegirls."

I laughed. "That's Ms. Michelle. She's crazy and she's been like that ever since I've known her."

There was a slight uncomfortable pause in our conversation.

"Well, about me calling you, I really didn't mean to disrespect you." He confessed.

I nodded. "That's okay, what's done is done." I said dismissing it.

He walked up closer. "Well let me formally introduce myself, I'm Damion."

He extended his hand out and I put mine out to greet him. "Janae. As if you didn't know my name already." I said shaking his hand.

"Well Janae, it's nice to formally meet you."

"And you as well." I replied.

Silence once again invaded our space like carbon monoxide and we were both looking uncomfortable.

"Well since this didn't go like I thought it would, I'm going to head out. I have to get up for work in the morning anyway."

He headed for his jacket on the leather love seat.

"In the morning?" I asked. I don't know too many strippers that work mornings.

He laughed, slipping on his blazer. "Yes in the morning. I don't strip for a living. Stripping is just for extra money which I use to pay off my school loans. And it don't hurt to use it on maintaining my three properties either. But no I'm not a full-time dancer; I'm a real estate agent and an investor.

I was impressed! What was that saying? Never judge a book by its cover? Well this was one of those cases.

It also put into perspective why he was dressed in a black Italian suit with a crème silk tie. He looked photo shoot ready. Every time I looked at him, my insides melted.

"Oh wow, that's impressive." I said.

"Let me guess, you thought I was an uneducated stripper?" he teased.

"No." I said shaking my head.

"Yes you did. It's okay, women think that all the time and I actually find it amusing. Once they find out how educated I am, some become intimidated."

"Well, I bet a lot of them must think that way, because I'm sure you meet a lot of women at work."

Was I flirting? I had to retract my statement or at least change the subject.

"Ha ha." He laughed. "Actually, I have never in the two years that I've stripped, took any of those women home with me. Women hanging out in strip clubs don't exude class to me." He advanced towards me. "Believe it or not, I remembered you from the night you were there. When I saw you, the attraction was strong. I felt like I *had* to meet you and see what you were about. I didn't think that I would ever see you again. Then I get word about this bachelorette party and there you were. And not to be disrespectful, because I know that you are taken and all, but what were the odds of me seeing you again? Like one in a million right? This may sound corny but I really feel like it was meant for me to see you again. From the first day that I saw you in the club, I knew you weren't like the other women there. Everything about you read that you were raised well."

"Wow." I said. I was impressed by how well he read me.

"I was actually brought up pretty strict and it's funny how some people can read that off of me right away."

"Honestly, I wish I could do more than just read you. I want to get to know you, possibly love you, and treat you to the finer things in life."

"Damion, you don't even know me." I took a step back.

"If you let me get to know you, I promise it'll be worth it." He said.

The sexual energy had me in a trance and I fought to snap out of it. I had Tae at home and a great new-found relationship with him that I had worked hard for. I had to change the subject quick.

"What time is it?" I asked looking at my watch. I have to get home and rest up for work tomorrow too."

"Where do you work?" he asked.

"At Clark Atlanta in the admissions department."

"Beautiful and educated huh?"

I smiled.

"Well can we at least be friends?" He asked.

I replied, "Distant friends, like associates, yes. If we see each other, a casual hi and bye wouldn't hurt. But that's it." I stated.

The front lock slowly unlatched and Ms. Michelle and Sarah crept in.

"Did y'all have fun?" Sarah teased while she and Ms. Michelle stood grinning.

"Take me home!" I said turning my back to Damion and storming past the shady duo.

"I take that as a no," I heard Ms. Michelle saying while I exited.

I was too through with Ms. Michelle and Sarah on the way home. I didn't have shit to say to them. I couldn't believe they would set me up even after I explained time and time again how things were going right at home. They were trying to force me to be like them, and it wasn't right. I took Tae's shit for years and he finally was the man that I wanted him to be, so throwing it away over a booty call with Damion didn't seem to be the right solution.

Surprisingly, Tae was already settled at home when I arrived. This time, he took the initiative to have the bath water waiting for *me* and it was just what I needed.

"I thought that you would get home later tonight Tae?" I asked, tossing my keys on the kitchen counter and then following him to the bathroom.

"Yeah, I was supposed to, but I convinced Eric to let me leave a few hours early. I just couldn't stop thinking about you. I rushed here hoping to surprise you but you weren't home. Where were you?"

My adrenaline was rushing, I felt like he knew that I was alone in Ms. Michelle's house with Damion. I wondered if he saw my heart beating through my shirt. I was at a loss for words. He tapped his fingers in the water to see if it was still hot.

"You okay Janae?" he asked.

"Oh yeah, I'm fine. Um, I was with Ms. Michelle and Janae, they took me to get fitted for my dress."

"This late?" he asked.

I twitched my lips sideways, "That's what I said. They popped up over here unexpectedly, but what else is new with dealing with them two?"

Tae laughed. "That wedding is going to be a ghetto ass mess."

I burst out laughing. "Don't say that baby. Sarah has been planning this wedding since the day Curtis slipped that ring on her finger and if things don't go right at that wedding, then I agree, all hell will probably break loose."

Tae helped me disrobe. Then he peeled off his clothes and joined me in the full bubble bath. I lay between his legs comfortably and almost fell asleep until he took his wet hands out of the tub to massage my shoulders.

"I love you." I told him, my eyes shut, feeling relaxed.

"I love you too boo." he said.

I kinda felt like I had to overdo the 'I love you's' and kisses because I felt guilty for talking to Damion. Secretly, I lusted for him and I felt guilty. I wondered if Tae felt the same way when he was cheating on me the hundreds of times that he had.

After making love that night, I couldn't stop thinking about Damion. I was really impressed with his background. I was curious about him as a person. The guilt was eating me alive, thinking about him while nestled under Tae's arms. I cuddled closer to Tae and dismissed Damion as merely a fantasy and one that I needed to forget quickly.

A whole month passed by and despite a few small arguments, Tae and I were still maintaining a healthy and happy household. It was a refined feeling, yet lonely at times since Tae was still working on the Clarendon project. To our surprise, the project had gotten drawn out for another month so we had to make do with the time we had.

Sarah and Ms. Michelle were calling me off the hook to help with the wedding planning, but I gave them the cold shoulder to teach them a lesson for that Damion bullshit.

It was Tae's birthday and although he had to work and wouldn't be home until later that night, I wanted to surprise him when he came home. I planned to shower him with gifts and a bare bodied me, wearing only high heels.

I headed to the mall after work. I snatched him up a few Polo shirts, cologne and a new diamond earring from Zales.

I noticed a sale going on at Victoria Secret so I strolled in to pick up some items. Victoria Secret was flooded with women and the annual fifty percent off sale didn't make matters better. I picked up a cotton white and blue thong and made my way toward the lingerie section. I told myself that I was only buying underwear and bras, but the skimpy nightwear caught my eye.

While holding up a red see-through teddy, I overheard a conversation between a customer and a sales associate. The voice seemed familiar and the conversation seemed interesting. I tiptoed to peek through the rack of yellow lace bras when I spotted the two women chatting.

"My belly is going to start getting bigger soon so I wanted to know if you had any maternity panties that were comfortable. Also my breasts are already enlarged so bigger bras would be needed too." The customer stated.

"Well, we don't really carry maternity panties or bras, however you have a small frame so going up a few sizes should help you feel supported for a comfortable fit." The squeaky voiced associate replied.

The thin framed girl followed the associate to a large section of bras and I was able to get a good look at her face. It was Sharece, Tae's ex-mistress. She held one hand on her hip, revealing a protruding pooch and seemed to hold excitement in her face about her baby news. I turned my head when she walked by so that she wouldn't see me, but sure enough I saw her, clearly.

My heart stopped as if its battery suddenly died and I just knew that I was about to faint. I tried to catch my breath, but a ball of stress tightened inside of my stomach and formed into vomit almost forcing it to purge from my mouth. From the looks of her pooch she appeared to be 3-4 months pregnant. Crazy thoughts invaded my mind. I figured it was Tae's baby right away. He must've tried to convince her to get an abortion and when she didn't abide by his request he left her and focused on the thought of losing me if I ever found out. I started hating him again instantly. *How dare he deceive me? How dare he be dumb enough to cheat on me and fuck Sharece raw?*

I panicked. I could have anything, a disease, anything! I had to get the fuck out of the mall. I didn't even have the courage to approach Sharece, because I already knew the answer. I knew Tae was the father, but didn't want to hear her tell me. I was embarrassed. I dropped the thongs on the wrong rack and escaped the mall.

I threw Tae's gifts in the car, but I really wanted to burn them. I raced home while bawling all the way there. I tossed all of his bags on the kitchen floor and sat at the kitchen table, face down crying loud and hard.

"Why me!" I shouted out.

Each time I sat up, I daydreamed about Sharece's pooch and how obvious it was that it was Tae's baby. How dare he pretend to change! How dare he hide his upcoming newborn from me! I held my stomach, hating myself for killing my babies. I should have been strong minded like Sharece and demanded that he had no choice in the matter. I hated Tae even harder and my mind drifted away aimlessly as I tried not to pass out.

I needed to talk to someone bad! I was going crazy. I had no choice but to call Sarah because I had no one else to turn to. And if I kept this shit built up inside, I would've gone even crazier than I already had.

"Sarah." I sniffed.

"Janae, you crying?"

"Yes I am." I said.

"What happened, what did Tae do? He cheated on you again huh? See I told you, I told you he wasn't changing." Sarah's persistence to want to know if her expectations of Tae were correct made me opt against telling her. She pissed me off with her assumptions! I was hoping that she would just listen to me instead of throwing out her 'I told you so's.' She basically forced me to lie.

"No, no it's not Tae. I'm just sitting here missing my parents that's all."

It wasn't a complete lie. Every time something bad happened to me, my parents were the first to come to mind. Sometimes, I resented my parents for leaving me in this world alone, but I was also smart enough to understand that I couldn't disrupt what God already planned.

"Aww Janae, you'll be okay. You know how much your mom and dad loved you. They are your Angels now."

"Thanks Sarah. I'm going to go lie down. I'll call you later on if I need to talk okay?"

"Okay." She said. "And Janae?"

"Yes Sarah?"

"I'm sorry about that shit that me and my mom pulled with you and Damion. We were out of line." She paused, "And I'm glad that you and Tae are doing better." She ended.

"Thanks." I said before hanging up.

Tae and I were far from doing better. The situation with Sharece made everything ten times worse. I was in complete and utter shock and couldn't stop crying.

I was in the bedroom when I heard Tae coming through the front door. He went straight to the kitchen first and then trotted through the long hallway toward the bedroom door smiling big with all of his gifts in his hands.

"Boo, thank you! I love everything, especially that earring. That shit is fire."

"Happy Birthday." I said in an obvious nonchalant tone.

When he noticed my puffy eyes, he dropped the bags on the side of the bed and crawled toward me. "Are you okay boo?" He asked pecking my cheek.

"No I'm not." I replied moving my face away from him.

"What's wrong?" He asked.

I thought about it. *Should I ask him about Sharece?* I was nervous and my heart was beating fast. My hands even began to shake a little, the closer he got to me. I already knew it was his, but if he confessed to it, it would only hurt me that much more.

"Baby what's wrong?" Tae asked again. I didn't know how to answer his question because there was definitely something wrong. *He* was what was wrong. I hated him and I wanted him to get the fuck away from me. I needed to be freed from my relationship with Tae for good.

I took in a deep breath. "I was just sitting here thinking real hard about my life. I had two abortions which took the lives of two innocent babies. I so wish that I would have kept my babies, I really wish that I had." I began to cry and Tae grabbed me in his arms and held me tight.

"Boo, I'm so sorry. Don't cry Janae. It's my fault. It was so selfish of me to want you to do that and I'm sorry. Please believe me Janae. The next time you get pregnant, we are going to plan it and I promise you that I would never ever even hint a suggestion of an abortion." He paused, nodded and looked away.

"Damn Janae, this shit been eating me up too. I never suggested for you to get an abortion just to be an asshole. I just didn't think I was ready to be a father. My father was so much of a shitty man and I always compared myself to him which is why I froze up. I thought that if we kept the baby that I'll end up being just like him. I was too selfish to recognize how much I was affecting you in the process. I was only thinking about me. But I'm changing that shit about myself, I'm dead up serious. Every decision that I consider will be in the better interest of *us*."

I held my breath and then cried harder. It all sounded good. But how dare he tell me that he wasn't ready to have a baby knowing that he currently had Sharece pregnant. He held me tight trying to calm me down, but my feelings about him and Sharece wouldn't allow me to stay in his arms.

"Let go of me Tae. I just want to go to sleep."

He reluctantly released me and by the look on his face, I could tell that he wondered if the abortions were the sole issues of my attitude or if it was something else.

"Alright boo, you get some rest. I'm going to go take a shower." He disrobed and then peeked back before heading to the bathroom. "I love you okay? And boo, I'm so, so sorry for everything that I put you through. I'm a changed man, bear with me."

I turned away and crawled under the covers. My entire body began shivering, but I wasn't cold. I was just exhausted with disappointment.

The pregnancy had sealed the deal for me. The fate of our relationship was in my hands. It was up to me to let Tae know that I found out about his unborn child. It was either that or up and leave him without an explanation.

All I wanted to do at that point was sleep. My head was pounding and I wished this was all a bad dream.

The next day, I couldn't focus at work. Every two hours I had to take a walk around the campus to keep myself from crying, but it didn't help.

Students would walk by me outside and I would look the other way so that they wouldn't notice my glossy eyes. I found a secluded spot near one of the monuments and sat down to try to take in some fresh air.

My phone began to ring and although I didn't want to speak to anyone, I picked it up anyway.

"Hello?" I answered.

"Hi Janae, it's Damion. Look, I know you told me not to call you, but I can't stop thinking about you." He explained.

"Damion, this really isn't a good time." I sniffed.

"Oh, I'm sorry. I didn't mean to bother you. Are you okay? It sounds like you were crying?"

I took the phone away from my ear so that I could sniff again without him noticing. Then I took in a deep breath and put it back to my ear. "No, this is just a bad time. I really can't talk right now."

"Well if I hang up, I'll feel bad. Maybe it's something I can help you out with. I don't want to pry, but I'm sure I can assist you. After all, you did say that we could be friends."

His voice presented such a soothing approach that I almost spilled my business to him. Then I thought about it, maybe being friends with him wouldn't be so bad. It would be nice to get a male's point of view on things.

"You can talk to me Janae. I'm just being friendly, that's all." He tried hard to convince me to confide in him.

"Do you really want to know Damion? It's kind of deep." I asked.

"Janae, I have all day for you."

I was vulnerable. I hadn't told Sarah or anyone else about Sharece's pregnancy, and it was eating me up. I proceeded to break down my relationship to Damion. I explained what kind of cool person Tae was when we first met and how much he'd changed over the years into a despondent jerk and had recently bounced back into the Tae that I had fell in love with. I explained how the change came after he finally realized he was losing me. I then let him know about Sharece. I even told him about the baby, I told him EVERYTHING.

It was a relief to get everything out of my system. Damion patiently listened to me vent without a single interruption. I wasn't stupid, I knew there was a chance that he would try to memorize all of Tae's faults and tell me he's the total opposite, but I was prepared in case he wanted to spit game. All I wanted out of our conversation was for him to listen and maybe possibly keep him as a phone buddy.

There was something different about Damion. He didn't have that asshole, immature cocky approach that most men had. Damion was very mature, attentive and articulate. His words were sharp and concise. He was an intellectual, but still hood. His conversation was competent and he was humble with his advice, taking both sides into account.

"Janae, I'm not a hater so I'm not going to tell you that dude isn't sincere. He may in fact have changed and is ready to give you what you always wanted in a relationship. The girl Sharece and the unborn baby may have been the wake up call that he needed to realize what he had at home. It may in fact be a blessing in disguise and he probably appreciates the union he shares with you that much more."

"I mean let's be real. He knows that if he told you about the baby that you would've probably left him right away. So what he might be doing now is trying to devote everything he has into your relationship, so when he does tell you about the baby, you'll want to work through it with him and not leave him."

"Why would I want to work through a relationship with a man that has a kid on the way from another woman? And how is this a blessing in disguise?"

"I don't know, maybe its God's way of telling you that if you can make it through this, then you can handle anything. You said yourself, that before you found out about your man and Sharece messing around again that he was a monster and treated you horribly right?"

"Yes." I replied.

"But once you found out and confronted him, the two of you have since worked things out. And although you haven't confronted him about the baby, you still see change in him, so things may just work out in the end."

I tried wrapping my head around his opinion, but my mind was too much of a mess over the baby.

"I don't know about that Damion, what I do know is that I'm stressed. And in all honesty, it was good to get this all out. I hadn't even told my best friend about this yet. If I would've told Sarah and Ms. Michelle about the baby, they would've given me all the wrong advice and preach to me about how Tae will never change."

"Well sometimes it's not good to listen to your friends, but rather listen to your own heart."

I smiled. "You have all the right things to say."

"I try." He responded.

I sighed. I really appreciated him for listening to me vent. "Thanks Damion, really. I have been crying all day today. This conversation has really helped me. I still don't know what I'm going to do about this situation though."

"Well listen sweetheart, whatever you decide, make sure your heart is a hundred percent in it."

"I will." I said.

"Do you think we can remain friends?" he snuck in.

I looked up in the clear blue sky and took in a deep breath.

Why should I care about what Tae thought? He didn't have any regard toward me when he was fucking Sharece and them other hoes throughout our relationship, so I decided, why not?

Damion was cool and his friendship couldn't hurt.

"Sure Damion, we can be friends." I smiled and ended the phone call.

I rushed back to my desk feeling a little better. Our conversation had relieved some of the tension that I held inside of my heart and I was now able to focus.

I hadn't had another man's advice since confiding in everyone's so-called role model Eric. Speaking of which, I was so comfortable with talking to Damion on the phone that I almost told him how

Eric tried to sexually harass me, but I decided not to. I had way too many issues to iron out and I needed to make power moves, quick.

Chapter 8

Welcome to my new world. This is a new me, and hopefully a better me.

Damion and I talked on the phone just about every day after that first conversation. Our conversations were mainly about me and Tae. I'm sure he was probably tired of hearing me vent about Tae, but he acted as if he understood. I told him how bad my issues at home were affecting me. Speaking to him was like therapy for my soul.

Work was coming to an end on a Friday evening when I got a call from the receptionist telling me that she would help me carry some gifts that had arrived for me back to my desk. Not expecting anything from anyone in particular, I was impressed by the eight dozen bouquets of long stemmed red roses that just about covered the entire front desk. I opened the tiny white card that stuck out from one of the bouquets and it read: *Beautiful flowers for a beautiful lady. Enjoy this gift, my pretty brown brown -DS*. My heart smiled. I took a single rose to my nose and smelled hard. Damion was beginning to grow on me.

"Wow, Tae must looove you." The receptionist who was the same nosy girl that noticed my weight changing about a month ago blurted.

"Yes he does." I said with a smile. It was none of her damn business who sent me the flowers. I was quite surprised that her nosy ass hadn't opened the envelope and read the card herself.

She helped me unload all eight vases of roses on my desk. I retrieved a large blue vase from my job's kitchen area and tried to fit as many roses as I could inside before I left work to lighten the load. I left the full blue vase on my desk and took the rest of the roses out of the office and placed them on my passenger seat in the car.

I would sporadically glance over at the roses and blush, acknowledging that Damion was trying to win me over. Minutes later, I decided to give him a call.

"Thank you." I said, expecting him to already know what my gratitude was for and he did.

"You're welcome Janae, you deserve them. I respect you for still trying to remain level headed throughout everything you're going through. You needed something to keep lifting you up, to assure you that you are beautiful and strong. It was my pleasure."

Light butterflies surfaced in my stomach, I was starting to really dig him. It was as if he was beginning to fill the void that Tae left when he ripped out my heart.

"You're so smooth; tell me why you're still single? You are educated, attractive and you seem like the perfect boyfriend."

"Well I just haven't found the right one. I'm really particular about women. I don't like women with bad reputations, I don't like loud mouth women or women who have no desire to succeed."

"Wow, that's a lot of reservations." I said.

"No, not really. My last girlfriend, well she was my fiancé, she had decided to pursue a career in Korea. She actually expected me to move with her, but I was just completing grad school and I couldn't just pick up to move all the way to Korea. So she left me to live there for good. Just recently, I found out that she is married with a baby on the way."

"Oh wow, I'm sorry to hear that." I sympathized.

"Don't be sorry, everything happens for a reason. It just wasn't meant to be. The only thing that I regret is that I compare all women to her, because she was so pure. She didn't lead a trifling life and was everything that I wanted in a woman, like you. But of course with my luck, I find a woman that fits my standards and you're taken." He ended with sarcasm.

I bit in my bottom lip. I couldn't believe he said that I was perfect. I was blushing heavily. "I'll tell you what Janae, I'll wait for you no matter how long it takes."

"Damion you don't even know me. I think we should remain friends until I decide what to do about Tae. I certainly wouldn't want to ruin our friendship because we have developed quite a chemistry, a friendly chemistry." I pulled into my driveway and turned off my car, "I'm about to head inside my house, so I'll speak to you some other time okay?"

"Alright beautiful, have a blessed night."

"You too." I ended.

I threw a jacket over the roses in the passenger seat and went inside. While heading down the hallway, I heard whispers coming from my bedroom. I crept slowly and quietly.

"Sharece I told you to stop calling me!" Tae said in a high pitched whisper. "I have nothing to say to you. I'm hanging up, don't call me anymore."

I opened the door and startled Tae. "Hey boo." He said rushing to click off his phone, almost dropping it.

"Who were you talking to?" I asked.

"No one." He answered.

"No one Tae?" I asked with an obvious look. I was sure that he knew that I heard part of his conversation.

He shook his head and surrendered. "Okay. Janae, that was Sharece. But you have nothing to worry about, trust me. I told you all that bullshit is over."

I pointed to the bed. "Tae, take that pillow and comforter and sleep on the couch. I heard everything. I can't believe you had the nerve to disrespect me and talk to that bitch in our home *again*!"

"Janae, I promise you it's not what you think!" He pleaded. "But if me sleeping on the couch will make you feel better, then I'll do it. Just know that the call you just heard was nothing, I don't even talk to that girl at all anymore."

I glared at him pitifully and didn't say a word. My expression said it all.

He lifted the brown and crème comforter and took two pillows and dreadfully made his way to the couch.

I shut my eyes in frustration. That asshole still didn't have the balls to tell me about his unborn child.

Child or not, he was not going to disrespect the house we lived in to speak to that bitch. Hearing his conversation made it easier for me to give him the cold shoulder. Our "great relationship" was falling apart more and more each day. I set a timeline for myself. I was going to give it a month and after Sarah's wedding, I would have enough money saved to leave Tae and that's when I would confess to him that I know about his child. I was sure that he wasn't going to mention it, so I had to take matters into my own hands and do something about it.

That night, I couldn't sleep. I stayed up tossing and turning, thinking about Sharece and the baby. It was making me crazy. Tae had killed my hopes for our future. Where was my life headed? Just recently I was happy with Tae, and *boom*! Just like that, I got knocked back off my feet. I didn't even have the courage to tell him why I hadn't been letting him touch me lately. To him, we were still together and I was just hormonal. But to me, our relationship was nothing but pure confusion.

On Saturday morning, I decided to wake up early and go for a jog. Jogging was a stress reliever for me and it gave me reason to get out and take in some fresh air.

I noticed a silver Infiniti creeping slowly behind me on just about every block that I turned to jog on. I kept glancing over my shoulder to see if the person in the car looked familiar, but I couldn't tell who it was. The final street that I turned on, the car sped up ahead of me and parked in an empty space. Out walked a casually dressed Damion.

"What are you doing around here? How did you know that I lived around here?" I asked, hoping that he wasn't stalking me.

He smiled, revealing a perfect set of pearly whites. "Actually I didn't know that you lived around here. I'd just finished showing a house a few blocks back when I spotted you. I kind of thought that it was you, but didn't know for sure, that's why I was creeping behind you for about three blocks."

Still breathing heavy from jogging, I was a wearing a gray sports bra and white stretch pants. I have the type of booty that probably shouldn't be seen in stretch pants without a long t-shirt covering it since it's so large, but I figured no one would be out that early. I felt every bit uncomfortable now that Damion spotted me.

"You're looking gorgeous as ever. In stretch pants or dressed-up you are a force to be reckoned with." He complimented.

I blushed and wiped the bangs that were glued to my forehead from sweating and pushed them to the side.

"Oh please Damion." I said blushing.

"I'm serious, you're effortlessly beautiful." He said.

He took time to check me out. I stood in place feeling even more uncomfortable as he scoped me out. I was hoping that he would hurry up and leave.

"Let me take you out Janae." He said unexpectedly.

"No!" I answered instantly. "You know my situation with Tae. We are still living together and until we are officially apart, I wouldn't dare step out on him."

"Please." He playfully begged. "I'll take you to the River Room Restaurant and Tavern."

"What you know about that place?" I asked. "That place is high end."

He smiled. "I told you that I would only show you to the finer things in life. That's how I live."

I nodded. "I can't Damion, seriously." I looked around, hoping that no one was around who knew me. A few cars had passed us by, but luckily it was no one I knew. "Look, I have to go. I don't want Tae to drive down this street unexpectedly. I already feel bad for being friends with you, we can't cross that line Damion, please understand."

"Well I'm not taking no for an answer. If you don't go out with me, I'll come to your job every day and sit outside of your office."

"No!" I said bucking my eyes and playfully hitting his arm. "You better not do that Damion."

He laughed. "I'm just playing."

I laughed it off with him.

"But on a serious note, I'll pick you up from this spot tomorrow at 4pm so be ready." He said pointing to the spot we were standing.

"No." I hollered as he walked toward his car.

"I told you I wasn't taking no for an answer."

He pulled his car door open and he squatted inside.

He pulled off and I continued jogging; smiling the entire time.

Damion was so charming! Everything about him made me want him. But it wasn't fair to Tae. Shit, a normal person would say that I was stupid for considering Tae's feelings. This man had another woman pregnant and has cheated on me more times than plenty and here I was being soft. I didn't even want to go out to eat with another man.

But it's just my morals. To me, stepping out on someone is more like cheating myself rather than Tae because I just wasn't that type of girl. I couldn't go out with someone else while I still lived with Tae. Therefore, I made up my mind that I was *not* taking Damion up on his offer.

I jogged for about twenty more minutes before I arrived back home. Tae had woken up and was already dressed. He collected everything off the couch and stormed into the bedroom. He threw the comforter and pillows back on the bed and wore an ill attitude on his grill.

"Yo, I'm not sleeping on the couch another night Janae. Why does it feel like now that I'm putting my all into you, I'm getting pushed away?" He asked.

"Tae, I don't want to argue with you right now." I said drying myself off after a hot shower.

"I don't want to argue either. I just want to know what's been going on with you lately. I'm horny as shit, Eric has been riding my ass at work and I just need you to be there for me. I feel like I ain't getting no love from you at all Janae."

"Well I don't know what to tell you Tae. I'm here every day so if you needed to vent you could have done so."

"You been here, but you're not here for me." He said hitting his chest. "When I talk to you, I don't feel like you're listening. I'm starting to feel as if you are the one that lost interest in me."

He looked vulnerable, wearing a face full of pity.

"Tae, do you realize that I heard you talking to Sharece in our home *again*?"

"Nah Janae, even before that happened, you were acting shifty." He squinted his eyes, "something is up with you Janae and I don't know what it is." He nodded and scrunched his brows, then snatched his coat off the dresser.

"I don't have time right now, but we'll talk about this later Janae. I have to head out to work. Eric has been bombarding me with the most work out of everyone and keeping me out late every night. He's starting to piss me off. Anyway, I'll see you later. I love you okay?"

He stood by the bedroom door staring at me waiting for his love in return. "I love you too Tae."

He smiled. "That's my boo."

Staring at Tae through the bedroom window, I watched him toss his hard hat into the car and then get inside. I kind of felt bad for the way I was treating him, but when I thought about how horrible he used to treat me, I only felt bad for myself.

There I sat, about to spend the rest of my Saturday alone. I lay on my bed staring up at the smooth textured ceiling. I was fiddling my fingers, scrunching my toes and contemplating what I wanted to do about Damion. I stood to reason with myself in the mirror as I often had. "Janae, it's just dinner, you need this. Tae has done worse to you."

I snatched my cell off the dresser and called Damion's number. I felt a nervous rush when he answered.

"Hey beautiful."

"Hi Damion, am I interrupting you?" I asked.

"Of course not." He replied.

"Well, I was wondering if you would rather go out today instead of tomorrow." I was staring at myself in the mirror as I spoke, bucking my eyes wide in disbelief over what I had just asked. I bit down on my bottom lip and waited for his reply.

"Hell yeah. Is four o'clock still good?" He asked.

"Four is perfect." I replied.

"Okay, I'll meet you at that spot."

"Alright." I ended.

I clicked my phone off and tossed it on my dresser. I jumped onto my bed like a kid. I couldn't believe myself. *I was actually going on a date.* I didn't even know how to date; I didn't know what to wear or how the conversation would go. I felt like I was doing something wrong and sneaky, but I liked it.

I got up and dashed over to my closet. I didn't want to wear anything that would hug my curves too much and give off the wrong idea. I picked out a champagne colored dress that was tight at the waist, but ballooned at the bottom. It hit mid-thigh and was classy. I scooped up my sexy champagne and silver pumps to match it.

The outfit exuded class, I tried it all on to see if it fit perfectly and it had.

I put on champagne eye shadow and dimmed it down by touching it up with smoky gray on my lids. I applied light mineral make-up and let my hair lay bone straight on each side and added some ivory lip gloss. I squirted a few splashes of my Donna Karen perfume and transferred my belongings from my large Gucci bag into a small silver nifty clutch bag.

4:00 PM arrived. It was starting to get a bit breezy as I stood in the spot waiting for Damion. Impatiently, I kept peeking down the street for the silver Infiniti. A black Escalade pulled up in front of me and I didn't want to look inside in case it was another guy trying to pick me up.

"Janae, come on!"

I squinted for a better look at the driver and then walked toward the large truck once I noticed it was Damion inside.

"I thought you had a silver Inifniti?" I asked.

"I do, but this is my big boy toy."

"Excuse me Mr. Baller." I joked as I hopped inside.

He smiled, kissed me on the cheek and we were on our way.

"Janae, I'm not going to lie. I'm taken aback by the serenity of your beauty. I'm almost fixated on your beauty."

"Damion, you are always complimenting me. You don't have to run game on me, okay? We are going on this date as friends."

"I'm not running game, it's the truth. Did you look in the mirror before you left? You are Halle Berry status, even better. Do you know who you look like?"

"Who?" I asked curiously.

"You look just like Lauren London from the movie ATL. But you have even more added beauty because of those gorgeous hazel eyes and your banging body."

"Shut up Damion, you are so silly."

"Oh no sweetheart, I'm serious. Tae knew what he was doing by not letting you go."

My playful mood switched to serious and I withdrew my smile.

"Damion, can we not talk about Tae tonight?" I gave him a serious look.

"No problem sweetheart, we can make tonight about me and you."

I felt like a Queen entering the restaurant with Damion. He had a neat ponytail that ended with a long silky braid down his back. Shit, it was almost the same length as my hair.

"What is your nationality?" I asked when we were seated.

"I'm Black." He responded.

I smiled, "Yeah right. There is no way you can be just Black with beautiful hair like that. You have to be mixed with something Damion. Your hair is a better texture than mine, and everyone tells me I got that good stuff." I joked.

"Well my mom raised me and I never met my dad. She always told me that he was Black but my aunts had different myths. They would tell me that my father was Puerto Rican or that he was Pakistani or Cape Verdean. So instead of all the confusion, I stick to being Black. It's how I was raised and it's what I am."

"Oh I understand." I replied.

The ambiance of the restaurant was breathtaking. It was decorated in light and warm, yet soothing décor. The sparkling lighting offset the peachy walls and oval ceiling. The round tables were spaced perfectly throughout the open setting full of professionals and people that looked like they were about their business. The waiter had seated us in a perfect spot that was secluded from the other tables.

Damion took the liberty of ordering us both filet mignon in addition to ordering halibut for himself. We downed a few glasses of Merlot and even ordered dessert. During our dinner conversation, he told me about his family who was out of Delaware and how he was regretfully lonely in Atlanta.

He originally moved to Atlanta with his childhood friend for college and a better opportunity. He said that after his friend graduated from college, he left for New York, but Atlanta was where Damion decided to stay and settle. He went on to explain how he was now at a point in his life where he wanted to start his own family and that he only began stripping as a way to pay loans after he graduated.

Once his businesses took off, stripping just became a hobby and was the only entertaining part of his life, since he didn't have many friends in the area. He went on to say that if he found the right woman he would quit stripping instantly.

I also found out that he was pretty well off. The stripping money was paying off a few of his loans but the money that he was getting from his property investments set him up pretty well in the bank. I smiled while listening to him the entire time. He had heard enough about me and Tae, it was time that I got to know him and he didn't hold back.

I did however, tell him about my mom and dad and he was so sympathetic to the fact that I had lost both parents.

We ended dinner on a good note, but not before Damion left a substantially large tip for the waiter.

The dark night sky was beautiful and serene and it made for a great scene to conclude our night.

"Janae, it's only been about a month and I feel like I have known you forever." he said as we sat in the crowded parking lot.

"To be honest Damion, I feel the same way."

He gazed in my eyes from the driver's seat and again I melted right in front of him. He was so perfect. I knew that he had to be too good to be true, so I had to break out of the trance he had on me.

"Okay, you can drive off now." I said turning away.

"I don't want to just yet. I want to look at you." He said.

I sat back in my seat and felt his eyes search me, but I couldn't look at him.

"Damion, I feel uncomfortable. What am I supposed to say while you stare at me?"

"Don't say anything, just let me enjoy you."

My panties were soiled at that point. His words, his looks, his voice were making me weak. I wanted him bad, but I had to take things one step at a time. If I was going to be serious with Damion, I had to at least move out from living with Tae.

He put the key in the ignition and finally pulled away.

The ride back was pretty uneventful. Pleased, I sat staring into the dark streets of Atlanta trying to digest the fact that I had just went out on a date while I was still in a relationship. I wondered if I had done the right thing.

"Here we are." Damion said shifting the clutch into park as we pulled back up to our spot.

"Here we are." I repeated.

"Can I get a hug?" he asked. I reached over and lent him a warm embrace, but I really wanted to jump on his lap. He held me tight, pulling me into his muscular torso. "You smell so good." He said pulling me in even closer. I didn't want him to let me go, but I had to head home and get back to my pitiful reality.

"I really had fun tonight Damion. I'll give you a call tomorrow." He reached over licked his lips and laid a soft kiss on my cheek. I shut my eyes to accept it.

"Bye Damion."

I stepped onto the street and sailed off into the dark streets back home.

Once I got home, I quickly showered before Tae arrived. I wanted to wash the entire date off of me because I was plagued with guilt. I felt like a bowl of dog shit. It was like I had violated Tae more than I ever had. I didn't even want to look at him when he came in. I pretended to be asleep and didn't say anything to him when he crawled into bed with me. As foolish as it sounds, I wanted to apologize to him.

As the night fell, I rested peacefully, dreaming about Damion and how I desperately wanted to see him again.

Chapter 9

Tae was all that I've ever known, could our love finally be outgrown?

Damion met me off campus every day for lunch for two weeks straight. I felt like I knew him more than ever and I was almost growing attached. He made me laugh, he kept all of our lunches spontaneous and had even brought crazy rich people lunches to my job, like escargot, for me to try. I told him that I wasn't into eating snails, but he convinced me to try it. It actually wasn't too bad. We had fun together. Everything wasn't always serious with him. We had picnics at nearby parks and we would just sit by the water and talk. Tae had never taken me on intimate dates where we could bond and connect like I did with Damion.

Damion's real estate job was so flexible that I was able to see him as often as I wanted to.

I was still tip-toeing around the house feeling bad for Tae. I hadn't let him sex me for a long while and our nightly routines disappeared. I cooked dinner when I wanted to and our bath times ceased.

Another beautiful sunny Saturday rolled around. Tae went off to work and I met Damion at our spot around 6pm.

"Where are we going?" I asked, this time being picked up in his silver Infiniti.

"I'm bringing you to one of my favorite restaurants." He said.

I slouched back in the comfortable gray leather seat and let Damion lead the way.

"I missed you Janae, I haven't seen you since Wednesday at lunch."

"I know, I had a lot to do at work on Thursday and Friday and couldn't take a lunch break."

"Let me find out you're starting to get too busy for me." He joked.

I flashed a smile. "I'm making time for you today right?" I joked back.

We arrived at Dailey's restaurant. The atmosphere was informal and congenial. The steak was succulent and the mashed potatoes were delicious. Damion ordered extravagant wine and a decadent dessert as usual. There was never a weak or non-entertaining moment at dinner, we had so much to talk about and Tae wasn't included in our conversation whatsoever.

During the ride home, Damion surprised me and brought him up.

"Janae, I'm really starting to fall for you hard and quick."

"I'm falling for you too." I smiled.

"No, I'm serious. I want you to leave Tae and move in with me." I straightened out my smile. He took me by surprise and I swallowed hard.

"Damion, I can't jump from one relationship to the next. I truly enjoy your friendship, but I can't just up and leave to move in with you. When I decide to leave Tae, I have to be on my own before I make any other major relationship decisions."

While at a red light, I peeked over and noticed a disappointed look on Damion's face. He rested his elbow against the door and played with the light hairs on his chin.

"I want you Janae, I need you. You're the one."

I nodded. "Damion, this is a lot of pressure. I can't give you an answer right now, I'm sorry." I put my hand on my heart.

Damion didn't say anything else. We rode with warm tension in the air until I noticed that the streets began to look unfamiliar. We pulled into a housing community. Surrounding the parking lot was a beautiful brick condominium with a flawless green lawn in front.

"Where are we?" I asked sitting all the way up in my chair looking out the window.

"This is my crib." He said proudly.

I nodded. "No, Damion take me back to our spot, seriously. I'm not ready for whatever you want to happen."

"What do I want to happen?" He asked with a serious face.

"I don't know, but going inside your house is a huge step."

"Janae, calm down. I just want to show you all of me. You know me as Damion Star, the stripper. You *heard* about how I live but you've never *seen* how I live. Come on, let me show you."

I shook off my reluctance and followed him up to his condo.

Inside was an open layout, the wood floors seemed to go on infinitely. He had just the right amount of furniture not to let the open floor plan look too crowded and beautiful art of black celebrities and heroes adorned the walls.

"Your place is really nice Damion." I said glancing around at his glamorous bachelor pad.

"Thanks, I'm glad you like it. You want anything?" He threw his coat on his leather kitchen chair.

"Water please."

His kitchen was small, yet luxurious. The stainless steel appliances complimented the silver outlining on the paintings that hung on the kitchen walls.

"Have a seat!" he yelled from the kitchen.

I made my way to the black and gray two toned leather sofa and tried to shake off my uncomfortable countenance. Being alone in a home with a man who wasn't Tae was frightening.

He handed me a cup of water and then rolled out the drawer from underneath his coffee table. He pulled out a bottle of Dom Pérignon and poured us both a glass.

"Damion, the water you gave me is fine. I didn't ask for champagne."

"Janae, relax. You don't have to drink it if you don't want to."

He powered up his iPod. B.I.G's *Juicy* was the first song on his playlist.

"Oh my goodness Damion, this is the song that was playing

when I first saw you. You were dancing to this for your solo at the club."

"I know." He said grimacing.

He stood in front of me and started swaying his hips, but in a masculine way.

"Let me give you a private dance." He said.

I reached over to the table and traded my water for the glass of Dom and sat back and enjoyed the show. I wouldn't dare pass up a free show from Damion Star. I guzzled down the entire glass and fanned myself when he removed his shirt.

"Okay Damion, that's enough." I said before he was able to take it all off. He stripped all the way down to his boxers and then bent to kiss my face.

"Are you sure you don't want more?" he whispered.

I pushed my legs together because my womanly organs were throbbing and soiling my panties.

"Yes I'm sure." I said receiving another gentle kiss on my neck.

"Are you sure you want me to stop?" He asked again.

I closed my eyes and allowed him to have his way with my neck.

Then I repeated. "Yes. Stop. Please." That's what my mouth told him but my body was telling him differently.

He lay me down on the couch.

"Let me have you Janae." He said.

"I can't, Damion." I whispered, feeling myself becoming slightly intoxicated.

"I need you." He said, stretching my cotton shirt down from my neck and over my shoulder as he kissed my neck and shoulders passionately. I felt his hand hover over my breast and I couldn't push it away because it felt so good.

"Let me show you how good I can make you feel." He peeled my shirt off my stomach and pulled it off over my head. He took my breasts out of my bra and began sucking and licking on them while occasionally looking up into my eyes. I wanted to tell him to stop, but I also wanted him to keep going.

As his mouth found its way to my belly, my insecurity forced my hands to cover the stretch marks on my sides. Once Damion recognized what I was doing, he pulled my hands away and lay approving kisses on my imperfections as if they were as perfect as the rest of my body. I gave a smile of pleasing satisfaction while allowing him to continue on his conquest to my goods. He pulled my skirt down to my knees along with my panties and eventually pulled them completely off. He spread my legs and showed me what his tongue had been longing to do as I melted on his couch in a state of ecstasy.

Damion's tongue pleased me for what seemed like forever, not coming up for a single breath.

"You taste so good." I heard him say every so often. I placed my hand in his soft hair and circled it around as I felt myself drift off into another orgasm. I moaned while winding my hips on his mouth. This man was taking me to an ultimate high.

Tae had never made me cum that many times. He would please me, but after the first orgasm, he was ready to get it on and start fucking. Damion made sure that I got mine over and over again. When Damion finished feasting on me, he stood with a satisfied grin and helped me put back on my clothes. He didn't even expect anything in return. I was shocked.

"Did you like that baby?" He asked.

"Yes I did." I said, meaning every word of it.

"Move in here with me Janae." He proposed the question to me again.

"Damion, why are you doing this to me?" I stood up to finish fixing my clothes and he stood with me, pulling me close. "Janae, be my woman."

I felt tears coming. I didn't know how to answer him, but I was falling for him.

"Can you just give me some time Damion?"

He released his embrace and sat back onto the couch with hurt feelings.

"Damion, if we are going to do this, we have to do it right. I have to leave Tae first." I bargained.

"Then leave him, what are you waiting for Janae? I don't understand how long I'm going to have to wait! You always tell me that you want to be happy, well here I am. I'm your happiness; let me prove it to you."

I was turned on by Damion's aggressiveness. I sat on his lap and kissed his soft lips. I felt the need to make up for the way that he felt. His feelings were hurt beyond belief and he must've held in how he felt for a long time. I felt how genuine he was and how much he wanted to make me happy because his every action spoke volumes. He was the man of my dreams, the man that I had longed for. He had no jealous traits, he was 100% into me and to add to that, he was patient enough to ride along while I dealt with Tae. My only reservation was that we were moving too fast. But somehow it all felt so right.

I was now used to his lunch visits at work and our special Saturday dates. He had become a part of my life, yet Tae was still in it.

As I kissed Damion, I felt his soft tongue slip into my mouth and I allowed mine to join his. We kissed deeply and I felt real feelings pouring out into my kiss as I cuffed the back of his head. Our tongues remained clasped until he began pulling my clothes back off.

"I want you Janae." He said slipping my shirt back over my head and locking his lips back onto mine. He laid me on the couch and pushed up my skirt. He reached for his jeans and pulled out his wallet to retrieve a condom.

"Let me have you." He said.

I wasn't focused. I wanted him, but I wanted Tae too, or did I? I was confused. I couldn't go all the way.

I watched as he slipped on the condom and tears fell from my eyes and slid down the sides of my face.

"I can't do this Damion."

He calmed me.

"Baby, I'll take care of you. It's going to be okay."

"No." I said, pushing my legs closed as he gently opened them again. He lay on top of me and suddenly I felt him about to insert.

"Damion, this isn't right." I said pulling back, inching my body up on the couch.

"Everything about this is right." He said pushing his organ deeply into me. My insides tingled with relief. I had actually let him inside of me and it felt so good and so right. My insides were accepting him by producing pure wetness in return. I didn't even get this wet for Tae. B.I.G was still playing in the background and Damion was stroking slowly and gently. It was that baby making loving. He made sure that every stroke was enjoyable and I moaned with regret, relief and pure satisfaction. I couldn't believe that I went for the gusto and let another man have me. This was it. There was no more Janae and Tae. I really had to leave him now.

This wasn't the type of female that I had set out to be and I didn't know how men could cheat so often. I felt like a hoe, I felt dirty and disrespectful. I was living with one man, yet sneaking around with another. What was I going to do? I had to make a move, now sooner rather than later.

When Damion dropped me off at our spot, I left the car without saying a word to him. It wasn't like he did anything wrong, he did everything right and that was the problem. I didn't know how to control my confusion. I took a little longer to walk home because I wanted to explain things to Sarah. This dilemma was eating me up and even though I was still a little bit mad at her, she was indeed my best friend and I needed her, bad.

"Hey Sarah, what's up?"

"Hey girl, you still mad at me?" She asked right away.

"No, that situation is petty and I'm over it. Speaking of that situation, you're not going to believe what's been going on."

"Fill me in girl, how are you and Tae? Let me know."

"Me and Tae are alright. It's actually me and Damion you should be asking about."

"Whaaaaaaaaaaaat!" She yelled with a long sharp scream that pierced through my ears.

"Sarah don't scream like that, you're making me nervous."

"I'm sorry, I'm sorry. I just can't believe it. I'm so proud of you. What's been going on? Y'all been going out? Does Tae know? Are you growing feelings for him? What? What? What?"

"Slow down girl." I stopped at the curb to let a car drive past me before I crossed the street. Standing on the curb, I shut my eyes as I thought about Damion. "Girl, he is everything that I have ever wanted, in more ways than one."

"Whaaat!!! Okay, Okay finish telling me." Sarah interrupted.

"Well, in the beginning he just listened to me as I complained about Tae. Then our friendship grew into lunch dates and dinner dates and today, girl, he took me to his house."

"Whhaaat! This story is getting good! So what happened? Hurry up and tell me girl! I'm so happy for you. Oh and what about Tae, how have you been able to hide this from him?"

"Tae has been working on a prolonged project at his job and it's allowed me to see Damion more than often. Oh and girl, stripping isn't his full-time gig. He's a big time property investor and let me not forget, college graduate."

"What! Educated, fine and has money? Girl I would have gave up the panties even before I knew all of this, because he had me with his looks. But got damn, he's the perfect package. Speaking of which, did you give up the panties?"

I paused. "That's what I'm calling you for. He just dropped me off and I feel so bad right now because I-I."

"You what? Bitch spit it out."

"I did it. I let him have me." I confessed.

"Haaaa!! You ho! You go girl. Hold on for one second, hold on for one motherfuckin' second." Sarah clicked over and when she returned to the line Ms. Michelle was on her three-way.

"Hey Ms. Michelle." I said, not surprised that Sarah called her.

"Tell my mom what you just told me." Sarah said with excitement.

"No you tell her." I said.

"Shit, you don't have to tell me twice. Mom, Janae did it. She has been seeing Damion and the ho slept with him today."

"Can you be more blunt Sarah?" I asked sarcastically.

"Hell no! I'm proud of you girl, you are finally living. Tae deserves this, that man has put you through some bullshit. Karma is a bitch! Fuck him, that's what that nigga gets."

"I know, but I feel bad." I said.

"You feel bad about what? Girl please, you did the right thing. You're my girl! I'm so proud of you." Sarah continued to shout.

"Janae!" Ms. Michelle called out.

"Yes." I answered.

"You got your feet wet sweetie, but don't get caught up in something you can't control. Either you leave Tae now and be with Damion or leave Damion alone and be with Tae. Whoever you chose, make that man happy so you can spit me out some grandkids. You and Sarah are my babies and I just want y'all happy. I still can't believe you did it, but baby, this ain't you. Choose one of them and slow down before something bad comes out of it." She preached as she began coughing.

"Thanks Ms. Michelle." I said, surprised at how reasonable her response was. "And you really need to get that cold taken care of Ms. Michelle."

"Well I say keep it going." Sarah interrupted. "Tae don't have to know, and he has done the same thing that you're doing with Damion with that bitch Sharece, repeatedly. He was seeing her behind your back for years. If he find out about Damion, lie to him like he be lying to you." she said.

"No Sarah, Ms. Michelle is right. I have to choose one. I can't keep living like this. It isn't fair for either of them." I explained.

I arrived at my front door. "I'm home now y'all, I'll give y'all a call later. Tae is inside."

"Alright girl, congratulations again. My girl done stepped out!" Sarah shouted.

"Sarah, you are making me feel so guilty." I said.

"Go ahead inside Janae. Remember what I told you, choose one." Ms. Michelle encouraged.

"Alright Ms. Michelle, I will, I'll speak to you guys later."

Tae was up waiting for me with dinner ready.

I don't know how men were able to hide their cheating and how they could go about their relationship at home as if nothing happened because I felt sick being around Tae. I felt horrible for what I had just finished doing with Damion. I almost wanted to admit it throughout dinner. I sat eating and daydreaming about what I had just done. I didn't know if I had made a mistake or not. I had a major decision to make.

There was no other way, I had to let go of one of the men in my life. But as it stands, I was having my cake and eating it too. Men do it all the time; I guess I was having my turn. But why did I feel so bad?

Chapter 10

I never set out to share my heart, is it karma or is it a new start?

Tae was growing more irritable by the day because I had refused sex with him for another week. He thought it was stupid of me to use the conversation with him and Sharece as an excuse to hold out on sex since he didn't say anything to her worth holding against him. I had to keep reiterating that speaking to her in our home period was enough for me to hold against him.

My excuse was growing old, and eventually Tae would question the real reason I was holding back from him. He was still working late each night and it afforded me more time to spend at Damion's and I wouldn't feel right sleeping with both of them. Damion and I went at it like rabbits every time we saw each other and I was addicted to him. I couldn't leave his home and then come back and sleep with Tae. So I was riding the phone situation out a little longer.

Things soon changed when Tae came home one night overwhelmed with stress. He stormed in the house pissed off, his brows were bent and he didn't utter a single word. His silence was indeed deadly. He tossed his keys onto the dresser, causing it to chip some of the wood. He kicked his boots off and sat hard on the bed. I was afraid to ask him what was causing his anger. I thought that maybe he'd found out about Damion in some way. I sat calmly beside him; his face was balled up with rage.

"Are you okay Tae? Tell me what's going on." I asked reluctantly.

He was quiet and stared at nothing for a second before he replied. "I'm about to quit that fucking job!" He shouted.

I breathed a sigh of relief. It was calming to know that his issue was about work and not about me and Damion. I figured that I would just listen to him rant until he was calm.

"Yo, tell me why me and this nigga Eric got into it today? This was the first time that we actually argued to the point where I wanted to get physical and knock this nigga out. He even put your name in it." He said pointing at me.

Nerves butchered my insides and my heart thrust hard, it was beating so hard that I couldn't hear myself think.

"What do you mean he put my name in it?" I asked almost stuttering.

"Well the argument started because I started to notice that I was the only one working late, while twenty other niggas got to go home early every night, so I checked him on it. That shit started to become funny to me. I told him that he knew that I had a life outside of work and that I wanted to spend time with you sometimes. Then the nigga said some dumb shit about how I think I know you but I really don't. He said that you are out here like any other chick, sneaking around. I almost knocked that nigga the fuck out. He know you ain't like that, he never kicked no bullshit like that about you before. He always told me to respect you and to know what kind of woman that I have at home. Now he's telling me not to trust any woman, not even you. He was saying it like he knew something."

I turned away from Tae but I felt his eyes still on me. "You would never cheat on me right Janae?" he asked me.

"No." I said turning back to him. I felt horrible for looking in his eyes and lying. But it would kill him if he knew that I was actually really out there cheating.

"I know you wouldn't do no ho shit like that. Sorry for asking you boo. I don't know what got into him though; he was dead serious, as if you were out here doing something."

I was beyond panicked. With Eric saying little shit like that in Tae's ear, it would make him start looking closer at our home situation. I hadn't had sex with him in a long time. But I figured that maybe I should take this opportunity to let him know what Eric had done to me since he was already venting about him. He was mad at Eric for the moment but he really wasn't going to quit his job over their argument because he needed it. But if I told him the situation that happened with me and Eric, he would do something drastic. I hoped that he wouldn't, so I decided to try my luck. Eric wanted to slander my name so it was time that Tae knew the truth about him.

I took both of Tae's hands and held them.

"I have to tell you something, but I don't want you to do anything stupid."

"What? What's wrong?" he asked.

"Just promise me Tae."

"I can't promise you anything Janae because it depends on what it is."

"It's about Eric." I confessed.

He squinted, "about Eric? What about him?" he asked.

I took in a deep breath and exhaled slowly. What I was about to confess to Tae was going to leave a permanent scar inside of him, but it was time that I got the burden off of my chest.

"Tae, about a month or so ago when you were at work, Eric came over unannounced. I figured that he was coming to get something that you needed for work, so I let him in." I paused. "Well when I let him in, he made a pass at me. He grabbed me close to him, tried to kiss me and told me that if we got it on that you wouldn't have to know about it. He said that you have been doing it to me for years and that I should do it to you."

Tae's eyes were enlarging as I spoke and I was sure that he wanted to run out of the house and fuck Eric up.

"What?" he asked.

"I kneed him in the balls and took the phone. I told him that I was calling 911 if he didn't leave and that's when he left."

Tae threw my hands down and quickly stood to his feet.

"Why the fuck are you just now telling me this Janae?" He hollered.

I looked up at him sympathetically. "Because I didn't know how to tell you. I knew that you would do something to cause you to lose your job."

"Fuck that job!" he yelled. "That nigga was trying to fuck my girl!"

I could almost see steam shooting out of Tae's ears. He was hot and looked like he wanted to hurt someone.

He paced the bedroom back and forth. "So he tried to rape you?" He asked stopping in his tracks.

"He definitely came over here with the intentions to have sex, yes Tae." I said.

"I still can't believe you're just now telling me this shit." He continued to pace and nod his head.

"So that's why that nigga been acting funny at work lately. Every time I talk about you he says some negative shit and be trying to keep me at work away from you. That nigga knows you well enough to know you probably wouldn't tell me about this."

He squatted to pick up his boots and began rushing them on.

"Where are you going Tae?" I said sprinting up toward him.

"I gotta get out of here yo, I have to think. I want to go bring it to this nigga, but if I see him right now I would probably kill him. I just gotta get some air."

"Let me come with you Tae." I pleaded.

"Nah stay here, I'll be back." He said seeming out of it.

"No Tae, please, let's finish talking about it."

"What is there to talk about? This nigga been pretending to be like my fucking father. He knew that my real father wasn't shit and how I had to learn how to be a man on my own. I looked up to him as a father figure and he gonna cross the line and fuck with my household? He got his own fucking wife!"

"Niggas at work be telling me that he's jealous of me because I have you, but I never knew why he would be jealous of me. He got his own business and his own wife why the fuck he gotta fuck with me and mine?" He shouted before walking through the hall to the front door.

"Tae, promise me that you won't do anything stupid!" I pled.

He glanced back at me, his eyes looked as if they were about to tear and he shook his head.

"I'll be back."

Once the door shut, I realized that I had just done some critical damage. I blamed myself, wishing that I hadn't let Eric inside that day. Never in a million years would I have thought that he would try to make sexual advances. It seemed as if I had now drilled a hole in many lives; In Tae's life because he would probably never work with Eric again, in Deborah's life because she thought the world of Eric and in my own life because I was gearing up to leave Tae. When I did, he would now be jobless and his relationship with Eric would be forever severed.

I suddenly began feeling sick. I felt that maybe I should've kept it to myself and not messed up Tae's life. How could I be so selfish and ruin the lives of people around me? I needed some calming words, so I called Damion for some sound advice. I hated to bring up Tae to Damion but I needed a sensible person to speak to.

"Hey gorgeous." He greeted me.

"Hey Damion, are you busy? I need to talk to you." I said in a panicky tone.

"I told you to never ask me that, I'm never too busy for you." he said.

"Alright, well I don't mean to trouble you with my problems, but this is something important." I paced back and forth in my bedroom while I spoke.

"Your problems are mine Janae, go on." He assured me.

"Well remember the guy Eric that I was telling you about, Tae's boss?"

"Yeah of course, everyone knows Eric."

"Yeah well, he tried to force himself on me a short while before I met you but I never told Tae about it because I didn't want him to lose his job. All the while it's been eating me up inside because I felt like he needed to know, but I didn't know how to tell him."

"Well I do agree. He does need to know that. His boss shouldn't be disrespecting you Janae."

"See and that's the thing, I held it in up until today. I just told him and he stormed out of the house. I don't want him to do anything crazy. He used to be a wild dude when we were younger. I'm starting to wonder if I did the right thing by telling him."

"Janae, they are two grown men. If Tae don't want to see jail, he isn't going to react irrationally. He may get physical with him, but I don't think anything crazy like guns would be involved. I'm sure Eric is going to deny it because he's married, but you did the right thing. Baby girl, I just can't wait until we are together so I can take you away from all that stress and bullshit."

"Stress is an understatement to how I'm feeling right now, Damion. Thanks for listening. I was really regretting telling him. I kind of feel like all of this is my fault."

"He's married Janae and Tae is his employee, Eric is the only person who is in the wrong in this situation."

My phone beeped and I immediately thought that it was Tae on the other line so I put Damion on hold and clicked over.

"Hello?" I answered.

"You oughta be ashamed of yourself!" A lady stated angrily.

"Deborah?" I asked.

"Yes, it's Deborah. How dare you accuse my husband of making a pass at you! He would never do such a thing."

"Deborah, I'm so sorry. I wish I could have been the one to tell you. I'm sorry that you had to find out like this."

"Don't apologize to me. Apologize to my husband because he's the one you're lying on. As a matter of fact, I hope you got a good lawyer because we will see you in court for defamation of character. I thought you were better than that Janae, you're jealous of my relationship with my husband. Tae is no good for you, so you want to slander my husband's name? Well God don't like ugly so we will see you in court. Tell Tae not to bother coming into work because he doesn't have a job."

She hung up in my ear and I pressed end, even hanging up on Damion. I was at a loss for words. I didn't know how Tae went about confronting Eric and Deborah, and I was afraid to find out. I sunk in my bed, ignoring Damion calling me back. I lay curled up in a ball wondering how Tae presented the situation to Eric and Deborah. I wondered where Tae was, what he was doing and if he hated me for disrupting his life. I grew increasingly concerned until finally I heard his car pulling into the driveway. I quickly erased Damion's calls from my log. When Tae entered our bedroom, he was totally disheveled. His T-shirt was ripped down to his stomach and he had a scratch at the corner of his eye.

"Oh my goodness Tae, what happened?" I asked with frightening concern.

"I fucked that nigga up, that's what happened." He answered with a stone cold face.

He stripped off his clothes and took a quick shower. I was in the bedroom pacing the floor, waiting for Tae to finish.

That's when I realized how much love Tae had for me. He didn't care about his job, he cared about me and how what Eric had done had affected me. He was selfless in this situation and it made me care and appreciate him.

When he got out of the shower, I noticed that his face was still blank and he looked out of it. He crawled next to me in the bed and held me tight.

"I'm so sorry boo, I'm sorry that you had to go through that shit. I don't care about that fucking job, I'll find another one. I just care about you. I let that nigga have it Janae. All I thought about was him trying to violate you and I blacked out. Deborah was sitting there screaming and shit while I fucked Eric up."

"When I first got over there, I confronted him about it. Of course he denied it. Deborah's naïve ass went on about how you're just jealous of their marriage. And when Eric said that he would never try to make a pass at a trifling *ho* like you, I just punched that nigga dead in his face. It was a wrap from there. The old Tae came out on his ass and I beat the shit out of him."

I held Tae tight, the Dove soap seeped into my nostrils as I removed his towel and lay my head on his moist shoulder, deeply appreciating him.

"I'm sorry Tae. I feel like it's my fault." He let go of me and sat up to look me in my eyes. "Janae, this ain't your fault, if it's anyone's fault, it's mine. I never trusted anyone in my life, but I trusted Eric. And the nigga tried to take the only thing I have in this world that is good, and that's you. You're the only one that has never hurt me and I appreciate you so much Janae. I'm so sorry for how I treated you throughout the years. I think that I was afraid to accept genuine love from someone. You are really all that I have Janae, you are such a good person. People like you are one in a million."

I felt myself tearing up as Tae continued.

"When I think about how bad I used to make you feel about yourself, talking about your stretch marks and hurting your feelings, I hate myself for it. I really took you for granted J." He grabbed my face with his hands. "I want you to have my baby Janae. I'm ready, let's start our family boo." He hugged me tight, but I couldn't shake the guilt of sneaking around with Damion.

I had wanted to hear those words from Tae for years. But now, I didn't know if I felt the same way that I did before. The tables seemed to have turned and I didn't know if I was ready for what *he* wanted. Tae was truly changing and here I was cheating on him.

Even if he had Sharece pregnant, maybe we could have still worked it out. It was like Tae needed me. He and his mom were never that close and his father used to cheat on his mom and shut

Tae out. His father never showed Tae affection and he never got to experience what someone genuinely loving him felt like.

Was I being selfish? Had I given up on Tae at a time where things were finally complacent? Should I have ever let Damion into my heart? I was stumped, and the other side of me was falling hard for Damion.

Disturbing my thoughts, Tae lay me flat on the bed and for the first time in a good while, we made love. I felt disgusting. I was now sleeping with two men and was confused about who I wanted to let go.

We cuddled in the dark. I felt relieved that Tae knew the truth about Eric and I could now work on putting it behind me.

"Boo?" Tae asked.

"Huh?" I responded with my eyes shut laying comfortably in his arms.

"Who's Damion?" My eyes opened just as quickly as I shut them. How could he possibly know about Damion?

"Who?" I asked as if I never heard the name. My heart was pumping hard and fast.

"When I was leaving Eric's house he kept yelling something about how you were just lying on him and that the person that I should be asking you about is someone named Damion."

"Tae, he's just making up names to direct the attention away from him." I quickly conjured up.

"I know. That's what I figured." he said pulling me closer.

"Goodnight boo." He said.

"Goodnight."

I was sure that Eric would vehemently deny my accusations, but I didn't know that he knew anything about Damion. I almost forgot how many connections that Eric had around town. He knew a lot of people, but damn, how did he know more about my business than Tae did? I had to do something; I had to end it with Damion before Tae found out.

Chapter 11

I'm torn in between the two, but I really wanna be with "who?"

Tae took on a few temp jobs, but was discouraged about working in an office atmosphere because he didn't feel it was manly enough for him. I had convinced him to stick with it until something better came along.

Working construction with Eric for so long had done him some justice because he was now a part of the union. Somehow, Eric managed to keep his employees working with very few layoffs while other companies struggled. Therefore Tae had to wait patiently for another construction job to open up. In the meantime, he worked the 'lame office jobs' as he called them, to keep the bills paid.

Now that he and I were coming home around the same time, I had to cut down on my time seeing Damion. I missed him so much and was only seeing him about twice a week on my lunch breaks because I had to work through my lunches due to it being busy at the college. Every time he came, he would bring his Escalade so that we could get a quickie in the backseat and then he would beg me to leave Tae and move in with him. He often reminded me about Sharece and the unborn baby that she was carrying and how it should be ample enough reason for me to leave. But it was too hard to leave, because a part of me didn't want to go. Things were going alright at home again with Tae, but my heart was in both places.

Tuesday afternoon, my lunch break was nearing its end and it seemed like Damion and I had been sexing for hours in the Escalade, so I was rushing my suit back on.

"I love you Janae." A shirtless Damion proclaimed out of nowhere.

I pulled my comb out of my purse and soothed down the puffiness of my hair trying not to look at Damion.

"You don't have to say it, but I know you love me too." He said.

I threw the comb back into my purse and stared into Damion's eyes as sensitivity filled my body. I suddenly began to cry profusely. I couldn't take the confusion anymore; this was going on far too long.

He held me tight. "Don't cry baby. It's going to be okay."

I sniffed. "No it's not Damion, I don't know what I'm doing."

"What do you mean Janae?" He asked.

"I'm confused Damion. Please understand. Tae was all that I knew. I never saw myself being with anyone else. Now that I met you, I finally see that there is life outside of Tae, but then again what if I let go and things don't work out with you and me?"

"Things *will* work out Janae. Have some faith in me." He assured me.

"I don't know Damion, it's hard." I wept even harder.

"What's so hard about being happy? How long do you want me to sit back and wonder what you are doing when you are at home with him?" I heard the frustration growing in his tone as he continued. "Do you know what it feels like for me to be home alone at night thinking about you Janae?"

"I think about you at night too Damion." I whined.

"Thinking about me isn't enough. You're going to make me come to your house and tell Tae about us myself."

"No! Damion you can't do that, I have to do this on my own." I pled.

"Well hurry up Janae. I can't just sit back and keep waiting. I'm falling in love with you." He confessed.

I wasn't sure if I was falling in love with him too because I was still in love with Tae. But I knew that I cared for him deeply and I didn't want to lose him.

"Are you still sleeping with Tae too?" he asked.

His question caught me by surprise and I could only answer him with my eyes because I didn't want to lie to him.

He paused and then nodded. "You just told me the answer."

He made his way back into the driver's seat with a face full of disappointment. The hurt was written all over him.

When he dropped me back off in front of the college, I tried to kiss him goodbye but he gave me his cheek.

I thought about him all while I worked that day and I pitied him. Knowing that I was still sleeping with Tae ripped him apart.

I didn't hear from him for the rest of the week. I called him every chance that I got. When Tae went to the store, made a run or even when he took out the trash which he was now starting to do; I was calling Damion.

"Damion, please call me. Stop ignoring my phone calls, I miss you." I stated on his voicemail.

Not speaking to him was killing me. It was literally eating me alive. Although things were great at home with Tae and me, I needed to talk to or see Damion.

Saturday morning, Damion finally called. "Hey Janae, can you meet me at our spot at four?" He asked.

"Yes I can." I replied with a large smile, breathing a sigh of relief.

My heart was completely relieved. Happy butterflies were dancing inside of my belly as if Damion and I were in a brand new relationship. It was so pleasing to hear his voice, but I couldn't profess how much I missed him because Tae was right beside me.

"Who was that?" he asked as he slipped on his jacket.

"Oh that was Sarah. She needs me to help her with some wedding stuff later," I lied. I *was* starting to become a professional liar.

"Oh alright, well hurry home tonight because I have something planned for you." He said laying a wet kiss on my lips.

He rushed out to meet with his boys to watch a game. He hadn't had a men's night out in a while because he was so concerned with spending time with me. As soon as he left, I dashed for my closet to find something hot to wear to meet Damion. I was all smiles in front of my closet searching through my outfits. I decided on a little black dress; it catered to my body like a hand to a glove. I dolled up my hair and make-up and at four o'clock, I made my way to our spot.

Damion pulled up in his Infiniti and wasn't as happy to see me as he normally would be. I on the other hand was kissing all over his face.

"Damion, I missed you so much. Please don't do this to me again."

He shook his head and kept a blank look on his face as he drove toward his crib.

"I had a lot of thinking to do Janae. When you didn't answer my question when I asked if you were still sleeping with Tae, I took that shit hard. I told you that I was falling in love with you and I meant it. I love the fuck out of you and just the thought of that man touching you…" He stopped speaking and shook his head holding a grin of disgust.

All that I could do was sit back and listen to him vent. I knew that there wasn't anything that I could say to console him.

When we arrived at his spot, we quickly settled in and Damion put in Denzel Washington's *American Gangster* DVD. He was still pretty distant. I took it upon myself to show him how much I missed him. I kicked off my heels, hiked up my dress and sat my ass in the middle of his lap. I withered my tongue on his neck and sucked on each side, making my way to his ear. As soon as my lips reached above his lobe, I whispered,

"I love you too."

Pleased with my gesture, he finally smiled. He picked me up as if I were an infant and took me into the bedroom. We had already made love on every piece of furniture in his condo, but his king size sleigh bed was my favorite. After laying me down, he went to the fridge to get some chocolate and he warmed it in the microwave to a temperature just warm enough to put on our bodies. He ate it off my nipples, my flat belly and tongued his way down to his favorite place on my body.

He whispered, "Don't you ever give my love away to him again. This is my pussy."

His words turned me on as he pushed my legs further apart munching and teasing my clit with his tongue. I moaned in exotic pleasure longing for him to enter me. He reached for the protection and gently inserted his gift inside while slowly thrusting his muscular frame on top of me.

"Oooh I love you!" I screamed over and over, meaning every word.

I did love Damion. In such a short amount of time, I felt like I could be with him and begin a new life with him. When I went those few days without speaking to him, I realized how much I adored him and how deep my feelings were. I didn't want to be without him.

"I know you love this baby." Damion groaned as he began thrusting harder.

Looking up at his perfect brown face, I felt like I had entered fantasy world. Any woman in this world would want to be with such a sexy hopeless romantic. He took his time with my body but also knew how to get rough with me.

"I'm about to fuck the shit out of this good pussy." He said thrusting faster and aggressively. Each stroke took me on different levels of highs that were unexplainable. Damion's pipe game was the truth!

"You like that, don't you sexy?" he asked.

"Yes I do Damion baby!" He squeezed his eyes shut and stroked faster and more intense until he released himself. He tossed the magnum into the trash and pulled me close. We were both still breathing heavily as we rested our exhausted bodies on each other with sticky chocolate sealing us together.

"I'm so glad I found you Janae." Damion said holding me tight.

"I'm glad I found you too." I responded.

I rubbed my hand over Damion's bare chest. "I think I'm going to do it Damion."

"You're going to do what baby?" he asked.

"Leave Tae. I'm going to leave him and move in with you."

Damion sat up. His eyes were overjoyed with happiness. "When?" he asked.

"Soon." I replied calmly.

"I want you to have my baby Janae."

"Huh?" I said staring at him in shock. "Damion we can't move too fast, we have to take things one step at a time."

"I feel you but I need you, every piece of you Janae. And to rush things along, as soon as you move in, I'll quit stripping. I wouldn't need to do it anymore because I'll have all the excitement that I need right here with you." He said tickling me.

We headed into his gray stand-up marble shower that was separated from the Jacuzzi style tub in his oversized bathroom and we washed every inch and crease on each other's body. He even got on his knees to deliver one final orgasm before it all ended that night.

Damion and I had a long night full of pure bliss before making our way back to our spot. I regretted the fact that I had to leave him, but was content with the thought of me actually moving on with my life and leaving Tae. I didn't need the stress of him and his new baby with Sharece. I'd rather be with Damion any day.

"I'm going to be waiting for you." He said as he jingled a set of keys in front of me. "As soon as you're ready, these are yours." He teased.

"I won't make you wait too long." I said with my mind made up and tonguing him down with pure passion before getting out the car. I rushed back home because I needed to rinse out a few more sticky pieces of chocolate that was matted in my hair.

To my surprise, Tae was already seated at the kitchen table with a numb look on his face.

"Where were you?" he asked.

"I told you I had to meet Sarah."

"With that skin tight dress on?" He said gazing over at me distastefully.

"Yeah, why?"

"Why wasn't you answering the phone when I called you?" he asked calm, yet stern.

"Because my phone died Tae."

That was the only truth to my story. My phone did actually die.

"Then tell me how was it that you were going to meet Sarah, when she's been calling here for the last few hours looking for you?"

I had to think quick! I had forgot to let Sarah know that I would be with Damion so that she wouldn't get me caught up.

"I don't know Tae, maybe she called after I left her. When she dropped me off, I went to the mall with my friend Karen to pick out Sarah's wedding gift. It's a surprise and I didn't want Sarah's nosy butt to know."

"What's that brown shit in your hair?" he asked pointing to the chocolate matted in my bang.

I had to think quicker on my feet and I decided to reverse things like a man would do.

"What is this Tae? Why are you questioning me as if I'm lying to you? I told you that I was with Sarah and that when I left her I went to the mall and that's the end of it. I can't believe you're still questioning me."

I headed for my bedroom and let out a sigh of relief once the door was shut. I had hoped that he wouldn't follow behind me to do any further interrogating because I wasn't prepared. I had to wipe all signs of Damion off of me. I wasn't as sloppy as Tae was when he was cheating, so if he did decide to check my phone once it was charged, he wouldn't see Damion's number in it at all.

I took off my dress and shoes and slipped into a nighty.

"I wish you would have found a way to call me Janae. I thought I told you that I had something planned for you." Tae said entering the bedroom.

"I'm sorry boo, I totally forgot. What is it?" I asked sitting on the bed.

He reached in his pocket and pulled out a tiny black box. I thought to myself *I know that's not what I think it is.* When he bent down on one knee, I knew that it was. He flipped the box open and took my left hand. His deep brows read seriousness and I could see sweat dampening his forehead as he asked, "Janae, will you be my wife?"

My heart stopped. I had been longing for this moment forever. But now that he wanted to get married, have a baby *and* commit, it was at the wrong time. But how could I say no to him without an explanation? And if I said yes, how could I explain to Damion that I was engaged? Was this the right thing to do? Should I say no, should I say yes? I was confused and it was written all in my bewildered expression.

"Janae?" Tae asked again, "Will you marry me? I want to spend the rest of my life with you."

Tears left my eyes as I stared at the large v-cut diamond. I shook my head and cried out, "I can't Tae."

He rushed to his feet. "What do you mean you can't Janae?" His face was full of confusion. Tae knew that I had always wanted a commitment from him and in the past, marriage scared the life out of him, but it meant the world to me. It puzzled him beyond belief that I would reject his offer.

"Tae, I know about it." I cried.

"You know about what?" he asked impatiently.

"About Sharece and about your baby. I can't marry you when you have a baby on the way."

He sat beside me and took in a large breath before he laughed.

"She ain't pregnant by me, that ain't my baby. You really thought that was my baby?"

I nodded yes.

He turned my head to look directly at his face.

"Boo, when you seen us together in the mall, that was literally the first week that I started kicking it with her again. She had broken up with her boyfriend and begged to see me. Yeah, I admit, I was stupid. I fell for it and started seeing her a few times that week. But something was strange about her. She was throwing up all day and finally told me that she was pregnant by her ex. Shit, I was kind of glad because it gave me more of a reason to realize what I had at home. I realized how much I had hurt you when you saw me and her together and I felt like shit and I deleted that bitch after that."

"Now she keeps calling my phone because her ex doesn't want anything to do with her or the baby, so she's pregnant and alone. I told her that I'm changing my number because she's starting to stalk me."

Tae reached in his Gucci jean pocket and pulled out his phone to dial Sharece's number. He had never willingly called Sharece in front of me to prove his point. I was shocked.

Sharece answered, "So you finally call me huh?" The loud speakerphone echoed.

"Sharece, I'm just calling one final time to tell you to stop calling me. I'm getting married."

"What Tae? Are you serious?" She sniffed and I heard her weeping hard.

"Married? I always wished that one day I would be Mrs. Harris. But I knew you were never going to leave Janae. I wish that I never started seeing my ex because if I hadn't gotten pregnant I really think that things would have worked out with us Tae, and it still can." She said in desperation.

"Be real Sharece, you know that Janae is and will forever be my lady. Me and you were never that serious and no it will never work out."

I heard her sobbing.

"Part of me knew you wouldn't leave her, but I always wished I could change your mind. She could never make you feel like I do Tae." Out of desperation she begged, "Please let's start all over, don't marry her please!" She pled.

Tae huffed. "Whatever Sharece. I just wanted to wish you the best with your future. I hope that you and your child's father will be able to work things out and be happy for the baby's sake."

Sharece released a loud and long cry, she sounded like a miserable puppy in pain.

"Noooo!" she sobbed. "Tae please."

"Goodbye Sharece." Tae clicked the speakerphone off and calmly smiled at me.

"See Janae, that's that. You heard it with your own ears. Sharece is the past. I want you to be my future, forever."

He crawled back on his knee. "Now will you marry me boo? I promise to give you everything, be your everything and fulfill your every desire. You're my world."

My body was beginning to shake and I was unresponsive.

A weight was lifted off my shoulder knowing that the baby wasn't his, but I felt stupid. The baby was one of the main reasons that I started seeing Damion in the first place, what was my excuse now? Staring at Tae on bending knee was mind blowing. I felt like a complete asshole and I wanted to devote my life to apologizing to him.

"Yes Tae, I'll marry you." I cried, sobbing like a baby. He slid the ring on my finger and kissed me long and hard. We hugged each other and wept together in happiness. Tae and I were on the road to being official. But what was I to do about Damion?

Chapter 12

Making the right decisions is one of the most important issues in life. Sometimes you have to make life changing decisions in order to make things right.

Throughout shuffling Tae and Damion, Sarah's wedding was less than two weeks away. I had managed to help her with just about all of the wedding plans beforehand and it had exhausted me more than my own situation. Ordering flowers, picking out the cake, choosing a photographer and the right DJ was a nightmare. Sarah was so picky about everything that we didn't stop until we had the best vendors no matter what the cost was.

Her fiancé Curtis paid for everything and Sarah had stretched his money to the limit. She even picked out a Rolls Royce for her, Curtis and Ms. Michelle to roll up to the wedding in and a Hummer stretch limo for me and the bridesmaids. Ms. Michelle was overwhelmed with joy and expressed how proud she was of Sarah every chance she got.

After Tae proposed that evening and we finished making love, he reminded me to call Sarah. My phone was now fully charged and I called her up later on that night. I just knew she was calling about a wedding issue because that was the content of our daily conversation.

"Where have you been Janae?" A weeping Sarah squealed through the phone.

"I've been here at home, what's wrong?" I asked.

"I've been trying to call you, I'm about to die. Please come to the Emory Crawford Long hospital. I can't breathe right now, hurry Janae, I need you!"

I jumped out of bed.

"Sarah oh my goodness, what's wrong? I'm on my way!"

I didn't wait for her to explain. I slipped on some jeans, a fitted white t-shirt and threw on my brown UGG boots.

"Is everything okay boo, why are you rushing?" Tae asked.

"Sarah is at the hospital talking about she's about to die. I have to go up there, something is wrong."

"You need me to come with you? I told you she's been calling here like crazy for you. I knew something was wrong." Tae asked sitting up and reaching for his shirt.

"Nah baby, I'm just going to go check up on her real quick. I'll call you when I get there. She's probably just being dramatic, if it was something extreme, her mom would have called me or came by to get me by now."

"Alright let me know," he said still expressing concern.

"I will." I replied leaving a sloppy peck on his lips before sprinting out of the house.

I kept calling Ms. Michelle on the way to the hospital, but she wasn't picking up, which concerned me more. What could Sarah be up to?

I parked my car and rushed through the automatic doors. Sarah was at the front desk waiting for me. She jumped out of her fiancé Curtis's arms and ran toward me with her brown face reddened and covered in salty tears.

"Janae, it's my mom!" She cried extra hard stumbling and almost falling backwards. I couldn't understand what she was trying to tell me. Curtis ran behind her and lifted her to her feet. He led us to Ms. Michelle's hospital room.

"Calm down sweetheart, it's going to be okay," Curtis assured Sarah as her screams echoed through the hospital hallways. I was rubbing her back, but I was still clueless as to what was going on. By the way Sarah was acting, I knew it was serious. Curtis widened the wood hospital door and inside laid Ms. Michelle, looking more thin, pale and sickly than ever.

"What's wrong with her?" I asked feeling sick to my stomach seeing Ms. Michelle in that state. I wondered how this particular sickness could hit her so hard, so fast. She was being herself just days ago. Sarah wasn't functioning well enough to let me know what was going on and Curtis kept trying to calm her down. All I could do was stare at Ms. Michelle's sleeping body and wonder why she was hooked up to a life support machine. There weren't any bruises on her body and no other signs of a car accident or anything so I was confused.

Two doctors approached the three of us as we stood near the hospital bed.

"Are you all the family members?" the female doctor asked.

"Yes!" Sarah shouted tearfully. "This is her other daughter." She said pointing to me.

Sarah and I held each other and from the way the doctors approached us, I knew the news wouldn't be good. My eyes teared up immediately. The doctor began delivering the troubling news.

"Well, we told Michelle earlier this month that we were concerned about her rapid weight loss. She had refused all medication ever since she was diagnosed with full-blown AIDS last year." I couldn't hear anything else the doctor explained, all I could do was stare over at the bed.

Ms. Michelle was losing weight, but I didn't know that it was due to being sick. My heart sank as if it were being buried in quicksand. Sarah was getting married soon and if Ms. Michelle wasn't able to attend, it would destroy her. I finally tuned back in when Sarah began to stutter as she asked, "Is, is, is my mom going to make it?"

The female doctor looked at the male doctor and then back at us.

"Unfortunately, by not taking her medication and having full-blown AIDS, she has done a tremendous amount of damage to her immune system and it's too late to correct it. We have done all that we can."

"Noooooooooooo!!!" Sarah screamed breaking loose from my arms. "Mommmm!! Mommmmmy!!" she screamed hysterically.

The doctors exited the room to allow us time to grieve.

I placed both hands to my mouth and cried silently while watching Sarah express her hurt. I couldn't break down because she needed me. Curtis tried to fight his tears but they were falling down his thin cheeks as well. Sarah shook Ms. Michelle's shoulders.

"Wake up mom! I need you, I need you!" she sobbed over her unresponsive mother. Curtis pulled Sarah away and held her tight to restrain her as she tried to fight and break free.

"Baby, please calm down. We will get through this alright? She would want you to be as strong as she would be right now, okay baby? I'm right here." He assured her.

Sarah's loud cries became faint after a while and she looked over at me.

"Did you know?" I asked her in a petite tone.

She shook her head. "No, my mom didn't tell me."

She cried and came to hug me.

"What will we do without her Janae? What will we do without my mommy?" She wept like a young child and I cried along with her.

"We will get through this Sarah, I promise you." I said weeping but trying to remain strong.

We both watched Ms. Michelle's frail body, wondering why she kept this dark secret from us. I had so many questions that no one except Ms. Michelle could answer and the mystery of her secret haunted me as bad as the sight of her vegetable state. We were rubbing her hands and face and taking advantage of our time with her.

Sarah cried while gently stroking her mom's hair.

"Mom, you have to wear that pretty dress that you picked out for my wedding," She sniffed. "Hang in there mommy, you're a fighter, you're gonna make it. I promise." She stared at Ms. Michelle for a second and then peered over at me.

"She's going to make it right Janae?" She asked me.

I stared into my best friend's sensitive eyes. "Yes Sarah, she's going to make it."

That week, we buried Ms. Michelle.

It was heartbreaking and draining for us all. We started out planning a wedding and actually ended up having a funeral first. It was horrible.

Damion showed up at the wake and even attended the funeral. I honestly think that he was more interested in spying on me and Tae rather than paying his respects. He sat by himself watching our every move, scoping to see if we were holding hands or embracing in any way. I felt uncomfortable but was more concerned with Ms. Michelle's homegoing than my own personal life.

I was the one that called Damion days before the funeral to tell him the news of Ms. Michelle's passing, but hadn't spoken to him since. He was calling me off the hook, leaving me messages telling me how he wanted to be there for me and that this was the perfect time for me to move in with him because he would comfort me. But I was receiving enough comfort at home from Tae.

Tae and I hadn't spoken much about our engagement because he was understanding of the time that I had to spend with Sarah.

It had become one of the longest and hardest weeks of my life. I had to put my problems at home on the backburner and help Sarah iron out hers. Right after work, I would rush to her house to help lift her up. She was a wreck and it was up to me to tie up all the loose ends concerning the wedding planning. She often cried and begged me not to leave her at night, so sometimes I stayed with her. Other times, I left while she was sleeping so that I wouldn't keep neglecting my own home.

Ms. Michelle's death dampened the excitement of the wedding. Every night Sarah sobbed intensely, trying to convince me that she needed to cancel it. And every day I would persuade her into following through with it. I told her that it's what Ms. Michelle would have wanted and how much it brought her peace at the end of her life.

Ms. Michelle was always schooling us on how to keep a man and although her ways were probably unethical to most, her daughter had actually followed through with her advice in a strange way. I'm sure Ms. Michelle knew that Sarah and Curtis had something special, Sarah was his rib. Most people didn't have the pleasure in life of meeting their soul mate (you used this as one word on page 37), but Sarah had. I told Sarah that Ms. Michelle would still be a part of the wedding even though she wasn't there physically and it comforted her a bit.

Riiiing!

Days before the wedding, I received a phone call at work from Damion. He normally called my cell, but since I had been avoiding him, he made it a point to Google the phone number.

Riiiing!

"Admissions, this is Janae." I answered half awake.

"So the only way that I can get in touch with you is to hunt you down at work?"

I lowered my tone. "Damion, please don't start with this. You know things have been hard for me after losing Ms. Michelle, plus I have to comfort Sarah. I don't even have time for myself anymore."

"Well you have time for Tae," He said sarcastically.

"Damion, seriously, don't be petty."

"Am I being petty Janae? The last time we were together, you got me all riled up talking about you were moving in with me. Then the next thing I know, I can't even reach you."

"Well I'm not going to sit here and explain myself again. I just told you what's been going on. I don't know why you don't understand that." I assured him.

"No fuck that!" he shouted in a agitated tone.

My eyes enlarged and I took the phone away from my ear and looked at it. He had never raised his voice to me before. This was the first whiff of Damion's attitude that I had received and it was hardcore. It confirmed that I truly had a solid hold on his feelings and he demanded a better explanation.

"I saw that rock on your left hand during the funeral, is there something that you want to tell me?" he asked.

I panicked! He was coming at me hard. I couldn't believe he spotted the ring. There was only one thing to do. I had to face him to see if I really wanted to let him go. I couldn't keep dragging him along. I either had to end it or make it official.

"Meet me up here for lunch Damion, okay? We'll talk about everything then."

I sat the phone on the receiver and stared at it while rubbing my chin in confusion. I had less than an hour to come up with a solution. I massaged my temples to try to collect my thoughts. The truth was that my heart was still in both places.

Tae had ruined many years of my life and suddenly made a transformation into Mr. Perfect. I finally had him at a place where he wanted to commit, even going the extra mile to produce a ring. But who's to say that his change won't be temporary?

And Damion was this perfect man that showed up at the height of my life where I was vulnerable and confused. He proved that he could provide a secure future for us, but what if after a few years, he turns out to be what Tae turned out to be after two years. Should I throw away everything I have with a man that I've known and loved with every stint of my existence, to be with someone who I barely knew but who possessed every perfect attribute? I couldn't settle on a solid answer. I patted the heel of my foot under my desk while thinking hard. I just needed to see Damion one last time before I decided.

Lunch time approached. Damion had never been late for our lunch dates not even once, so I hurried to prepare to meet him. I slipped off my engagement ring and put it in the inside zipper of my purse and popped a piece of gum into my mouth. I escaped outside into his Escalade chomping hard on my gum because my nerves were tapping hard on my emotions.

Damion was well groomed; he looked as handsome as ever dressed in a gray and cream Italian suit.

"You look nice, what's the occasion?" I asked trying to break the ice.

"Work." He answered blankly.

He snatched my left hand searching for the ring and then threw it back into my lap.

"What, you took it off because I was coming?" He asked.

"Damion, I really don't want to argue with you." I said.

"I don't want to argue either Janae. I'm not no damn high school boy. I am a professional businessman and I have feelings. You have to make up your mind and tell me what you want to do. You are not going to continue stringing me along like some fucking puppet."

His aggression was actually turning me on because I loved aggressive men. Plus, I had missed him immensely. But I had to concentrate on the bigger picture here. Damion lifted both of my hands and his sincerity controlled our eye contact. His eyes were sad and defenseless. All I could do was stare at him, almost peering down to his heart. This man was really falling in love with me and wanted to know if I felt the same. I was faced with a decision to keep him and open up the mystery to our future or let him go. Tears graced my cheeks as Damion wiped them with his hands and kissed me like we would never kiss again.

"I love you Janae. Baby please be with me."

It almost sounded as if he were begging. I covered my face with my hands and cried into my palms. I thought about Tae and then I looked at Damion and tried to decipher which one of them I felt I couldn't do without. I had to let one of them go and the time was now.

"The baby isn't Tae's." I admitted.

"What? How would you know that?" Damion asked.

"He called Sharece in front of me and it was confirmed that it's her ex-boyfriend's baby." I told him.

"So what does that mean for us?" he asked with glossy eyes and throwing up his hands.

I hesitated and cried harder and then I nodded.

"I'm sorry Damion, but I'm not ready to move on yet."

Damion sadly gazed at me with a weary look on his face and didn't say anything. He sat all the way back in the driver's seat, staring out at the campus as if he was just defeated.

"I'm sorry." I repeated while letting myself out of the truck. I was actually scared of his reaction and thought that it was best that I left without receiving the backlash. And just like that, I had ended my affair, but inside I felt empty.

I wasn't able to go straight back to my desk because I was too emotional. I had to lock myself in a stall in the ladies room because I felt feverish and had to vomit. My insides were aching and it felt like I was being tortured. I vomited, cried and threw up some more. I tried to cry quietly as traffic came in and out of the bathroom. I soaked half the roll of tissue reminiscing about Damion and hoping that I had made the right decision.

Memories of the passionate nights we spent in his condo, all the extravagant restaurants, thoughtful and meaningful conversations, sex filled lunch breaks and the way he listened and catered to me had me feeling awful for throwing it all away. Again, I questioned if I made the right decision because there was no turning back now. Damion was sick of my shit and honestly I would have been too. I had to take heed to Ms. Michelle's advice and let one of them go before things got out of hand. I remained in the tight pissy bathroom stall for a whole forty-five minutes. My eyes were still slightly red, and my nose was even redder.

When I returned to my desk, I busied myself with backed up work and hoped that the day would fly by.

Driving home after work, I tried to feel at ease with my

decision. I wanted to do everything I could to put some closure to the Damion saga. I flipped open my cell and erased his phone number for good. On the floor of my passenger seat, I still had the aged flowers from the first time he sent me the eight bouquets of roses to my job and I tossed them out of my car window. I let out a few more light tears but was confident that I had made the right decision.

When I got home, I dashed directly into Tae's arms and kissed him like I hadn't seen him in years. It was all the guilt from dealing with Damion.

"Damn boo, you missed a nigga that much?" he asked when I finally let him up for a breath.

"Hell yeah." I said stripping off my work clothes. I forced his body on our bed and kissed all over his neck.

"This is what the fuck I'm talking about." He said letting me have my way with him.

I ripped off his button up and tossed it to the floor.

I stood up in front of him and decided to call the shots.

"Stand up Tae." I demanded

"What?" he asked.

"Stand the fuck up!" I demanded.

"Ooh you talking dirty huh?"

"Take off your pants." I insisted pointing at his crotch.

He unbuttoned the top and unzipped his fly, revealing his Calvin Klein boxers. I stretched them down to his thighs and tugged on his manhood gently before stretching it into my mouth.

"Uhhh." He groaned as I gave him the business.

I felt forever indebted to Tae and it seemed as if I could repay him by blowing his mind in every way. I was prepared to do whatever it took.

I licked and sucked his dick until he sprinkled all over my face. I flashed a seductive smile afterward.

I scurried to the bathroom to get a hot rag to wipe off my face and I laid down next to him.

"What was that about Janae? You never done no shit like that before, I like that. That's better than cooking for a nigga. Do that every day and we'll be married tomorrow."

"Shut up boo, you so crazy." I joked.

"I just wanted to show you how much I appreciate you. You really changed and you made me happy again." I teared up.

"Boo don't cry. I told you, I didn't know what the fuck I had all these years because I was selfish. But don't worry because I will never disrespect you or treat you wrong again."

Chapter 13

I thought this was a new love that I've found, what
do I do when it all comes crashing down?

I decided to leave when Sarah was sound asleep. Curtis opened the front door to help me creep out without waking her.

"Bye Curtis, take care of my friend." I whispered.

"I always do." He said with a smile.

"Hey Janae." He called out. "Thanks for everything, I appreciate it. Sarah definitely needs you right now and you've really been there for her."

"Of course." I said before he shut the front door.

I scurried home, hoping to get some much needed rest. I hadn't gotten a full night's sleep since Ms. Michelle's death and I was tired every day at work trying my best to stay awake. When I got home, Tae was on the couch in the living room with a Henny bottle in his hand, clutching a piece of paper.

"Yo Janae, I need to holler at you for a second!"

From the tone of his voice, I could tell that it wasn't good. His facial expression even pinched every last one of my shaky nerves as I took a seat next to him. I was scared of what he had to say. Plus he wasn't a cognac drinker, he only drank when he was stressed.

"I got a package in the mail today. Eric spoke to management about getting us evicted out of here. He figured since he got us this place that he had the power to get us kicked out, so we got a month to move out."

I placed my hand on my head and sighed deeply, "Aw man Tae, I'm sorry. I can't believe it; this is too much, on top of everything else that's going on. What are we going to do?" I asked.

Tae took a swig from his pint of Hennessey and sat back on the couch looking straight ahead. "I don't know what the fuck you are going to do, but I know what I'm going to do."

"Huh?" I exclaimed. I didn't understand what the attitude toward me was about.

"What do you mean?" I asked.

He handed me the white paper that he held in his hand, it was written in Eric's sloppy handwriting. I read it while Tae reached for a yellow envelope near his foot. The paper read *Look at your innocent bitch now.* I still didn't fully understand until Tae emptied the contents from the yellow envelope into my lap.

Numerous pictures of me and Damion scattered out. The time when I met him at our spot and kissed all over his face after missing him and snapshots of me tonguing him down after being dropped off at our spot. I didn't know what to say, Eric had done it this time! He got what he wanted, he was destroying my life. Tae was now inebriated and probably wanted to murder me.

"So who is dude? Is that the nigga Damion that I asked you about?" He asked. He was still staring straight ahead talking stern and cold, but he hadn't fully raised his voice.

The hurt inside him was obvious.

"Let me explain." I started.

"Shut the fuck up! Answer me. "His tone was now overbearing like a parent to a child.

"Yes." I answered, shitting bricks.

He took another swig of his Hennessey.

"So you been fucking this dude?" He asked with an obvious lump in his throat. This was a question that he wanted answered, but I'm sure he really didn't want to hear me say it. It would rip away at his manhood.

"Tae!" I called out wanting to further explain things.

"Janae, don't fuck with my emotions right now, answer the fucking question!" He was gritting his teeth and his entire face was tensed.

"Tae listen to me okay? I started seeing him when I found out that Sharece was pregnant. I thought that you and I were over because I figured she was carrying your baby. I didn't think things would get deep with Damion."

"Fuck what you're saying right now Janae! Did you fuck this dude or not?" His voice echoed through our living room and my heart was about to break out of my chest.

There was no way around it, Tae wanted an answer. The answer was a single word that would forever seal the fate of our four year relationship. When a man cheated and a woman loved him enough, she would consider giving him a second chance. But once a woman cheated, there were no second chances. Biased as it sounds, it was reality.

In that moment, I realized how much I messed up and how deeply I loved Tae and how he was about to slip out of my life permanently. Giving him this answer would be the end of us.

I began to shake and I stood up, almost losing my footing. I didn't want to be sitting next to him when I told him.

"Yes." I answered, sinking my head into my palms.

Tae bent to place his Hennessey next to his foot and stood up in front of me. I lifted my head to see his face but I couldn't look in his eyes.

He spoke calmly. "We have to be out of here by the end of the month, so make your arrangements on where you are going to be staying. After that, I don't want shit else to do with you."

I thought that he handled the answer better than I expected. Maybe it was the Hennessey that was keeping his anger contained.

SMACK!

That thought was interrupted when a sharp smack came out of nowhere and stung my cheek like a bee. I held my reddened face, crying heavy tears without defending myself. I felt that I deserved that smack and more for what I had done to him. I should've just left instead of dragging his heart into it. Although he hurt me through the years, doing something like this just wasn't in my character.

"You're a ho and I will never fuck with you again!" he said storming toward the bedroom.

My heart sank down to my feet. I felt like a piece of garbage in the middle of the street. I felt nasty, useless and ashamed. No matter how much he cheated, I was better than that, I shouldn't have fought fire with fire.

Before he approached the bedroom, I ran behind him falling to my knees.

Though my mistakes paralleled his, I grew weak because it had sunk in that I had lost him. I made a vulnerable attempt to do the impossible and beg for him back.

He turned and stood over me. I hoped that he would hear me out.

"Tae, listen to me, you are the love of my life. I'm so sorry for what I've done baby. I took four years of verbal and emotional abuse, being neglected, being cheated on and sheltered in the house without having a life."

He interrupted. "Now you see why I used to keep your slut ass caged in."

"Tae, no listen to me. You're talking out of anger right now. You forced me to get abortions, you constantly made me feel bad about myself by picking on my body and you made me feel inferior to you. I know that what I did was wrong, but it's no comparison to what I've endured from you."

A tear snuck out of Tae's eye as he maintained a solid look in mine. I silently said a prayer and hoped that he would at least let my words absorb and understand my position.

"I never meant to hurt you Tae, you have to believe me. I put in work for four years to make us work and you know it!" My face was filled with tears as I clasped my hands together before him while on my knees.

"I'm begging you baby, forgive me like I have forgiven you."

Tae stepped forward and held out his hand.

"Give me my ring back." He demanded.

"Huh?" I shook my head. "No Tae, please, we can work this out." I begged.

Tae stood me up by my arms and took my left hand. He slid the diamond off of my ring finger while I stared into his face. This was it. No matter how much I countered and brought up all of his cheating, I was a female and his pride would never let me back into his heart.

He sniffed and wiped his nose with his forearm. "Go be with that nigga." He said.

He slipped the ring into his pocket, took his Hennessey and keys and left out of the apartment.

I ran behind him and dropped to my knees again in desperation. "Tae I'm sorry baby, forgive me, don't leave Tae. Let's talk about this pleaaase!!!" I begged.

He exited without looking back.

I began to shake. I was in an ambivalent state of mind. As much as I thought that I wanted to be with Damion, home was where my heart was and I no longer had a home. I reasoned with myself, hoping that if I just gave Tae some time to think that he would take me back.

I carried my weak body to my full-length mirror and stared at myself. My eyes were red and puffy, my cheeks were heightened in color and I felt like a disgrace to myself. I ran to the closet and snatched some of Tae's designer shirts off the racks and balled up on top of my bed smelling them and sobbing. I lost him; I lost Tae. The feeling was gut wrenching and I knew that no matter how much I tried and how much I wanted him back, things would never be the same. He would never want anything to do with me.

I rubbed his shirts over my face as if it was Tae's touch and I placed them up to my nose to smell his odor.

"Tae baby pleaseee, I need you, forgive me!!" I cried out

intensely holding the clothes between my knees in a fetal position. It felt as if my ribs were caving into my back.

"Please Taeeee!! Baby!!!!! Don't leave me!" I sobbed all night, yelling Tae's name as if he was there hoping that one day he would forgive me.

"I need you Tae, you're my baby!!" I sobbed forcefully until I fell asleep.

The morning sunrays beamed through my bedroom window and the intense light woke me out of my sleep. I extended my arm beside me searching for Tae's presence but was only met with an empty space. The realness was once again reinforced and the migraine added to the reminder. I peered over at myself in the mirror on the bureau and my eyes looked like I had bags on the top and bottom.

I decided to call in to work as soon as possible because I wouldn't be able to make it through the day with my body feeling like I was dying. I didn't feel hungry, I didn't feel anything but heartbroken. The stress took over the rest of my body. I got up and went over to the window, hoping that Tae would pull up so that we could talk this out and hopefully come up with some sort of resolution. I couldn't take the way that I was feeling. Crying was the only way that I could release how I felt. I paced the house, I even called Tae, but of course he didn't answer. I retreated further into my humiliation.

I left him numerous messages begging him to call me and as pathetic as it sounds I think I even used the words "Tae I'm begging you."

I put my pride aside and was prepared to do anything just to get him to understand me and forgive me. Adding to my tears, were memories of Ms. Michelle and how much I had missed her and it prompted me to call Sarah.

"Hey Janae." Sarah said blankly. She still hadn't returned to her outgoing personality, she was still distant after losing Ms. Michelle.

She was also still on leave from work, so I knew that she would be home and able to talk to me without having to use discretion.

"Hey Sarahhh!!!" I cried her name out. I couldn't speak clearly. Tae was on my mind and it felt like I had lost a body part. It was however, soothing to hear Sarah's voice. After feeling so worthless for what I had done to Tae, I knew that I still had a friend in Sarah and it felt like a breath of fresh air to hear her speak.

"What's wrong Janae, you okay?"

"No I'm not okay Sarah. Tae found out about Damion and he doesn't want anything to do with me anymore. It hurts so bad." I cried.

"Oh my goodness Janae, I'm so sorry. When did this happen?" she asked.

"It happened last night when I left your house. Of all people, it was Eric who delivered the news to him. He sent a letter to him and even included revealing photos to let him know what his 'innocent woman', as he put it, had been doing behind his back. Can you believe that?"

"Yeah right! Damn! Janae, what the fuck! How did Eric know about Damion?"

"Who knows! He probably had someone following me. Ever since I told Tae about what Eric had done to me, I knew that Eric wasn't going to let it go that easy. Shit girl, that's a whole 'nother story. Shit has been so hectic, I wasn't even able to tell you that I finally told Tae about what happened with Eric."

"No Janae, you didn't tell me that. I know Tae must've been going crazy when he heard about that shit. But damn, Eric took it there and sent him pictures and shit?"

"Yes, pictures of us kissing and the whole nine. On top of that, we have until the end of the month to leave. Eric has gotten us evicted and I don't know what I'm going to do." I sobbed in embarrassment. Things had really gotten out of hand.

"Don't cry J. You know you have a home over here."

"No Sarah, I can't do that. I wouldn't dare impose on you and Curtis."

"Janae, as much as I need you right now, I wish that I could move you in here as we speak. Girl, I can't function. When I close my eyes, open my eyes; all that I see is my mom. And Curtis, bless his heart. He tries his best to help me out as much as possible, but he didn't know my mom as long as you've known her. When you're around me, it feels like a part of her is with me."

"Girl, being there for you goes without saying. You're my best friend." I said.

I glanced around at all of my furniture and had to be an adult about the situation. Sarah offered and it didn't make any sense for me not to accept. I had to move out by the end of the month and if I didn't act fast, I would have nowhere to go.

"Sarah, can you talk to Curtis about me moving in with you guys, temporarily of course. And then I'll consider it. I'll just put all of my furniture in storage until I find something."

"Janae please, Curtis loves you like a sister. Whenever you're ready to move, let me know, I'll clear out the spare room for you."

"It may be soon Sarah. I know that Tae doesn't want to be around me. You should have seen him last night, he asked me if I had slept with Damion and I couldn't lie to him."

"Well you know what my mom would have said to that. Once you cheat on your man and he finds out, you might as well walk away without any scratches and surrender, because the battle is already lost."

"And that's the hardest part for me Sarah; I know that the battle is lost. Men don't take back a cheating woman. And girl all that shit that I put up with Tae, now look at me. I broke it off with Damion so now I have neither one of them, but I'm going to deal with this like a woman. It hurts like someone is torturing me, but Sarah I'm going to pick myself up and own up to my mistakes."

"That's what I want to hear. From now on, we will be here for each other."

Sarah's conversation was so much more adult. If Ms. Michelle were still alive, Sarah would be preaching to me about how Tae got what he deserved and that I shouldn't fret over his feelings. Instead, she listened and let me vent without throwing out her own interpretations of my situation and we actually had a viable conversation.

"Janae, there is one more thing that is very important to me that I would like for you to help me with after the wedding."

"Of course Sarah, anything you need."

"I want you to help me clean out my mom's apartment. I'll send some of her things to my family in Alabama, but there are a lot of her belongings that I'd like to keep. I just can't do it right now, the wedding is days away and I have to save all the strength that I have to get through it."

"I agree, after the wedding will be the best time to do it. I will help you out with no problem. It's going to be hard for the both of us, but we'll be there for each other."

"Thanks Janae."

"No problem, girl."

I sat the cordless next to me on the couch. Hearing the pain in Sarah's voice made my situation feel so minute. She had just lost her mom and me of all people, knew exactly how much pain she was in. Her loss was still fresh and she was still grieving. My ass was crying over a man, more importantly for mistakes that I had made. I was the one who put myself in the position that I was in.

I proceeded into my bedroom and took down my old Kenneth Cole suitcases from the top of my closet and began removing my folded clothes from each drawer and packed them tight. I stuffed my car with all of my belongings from my side of the closet that Tae and I shared. I hoped that I would have everything removed before Tae got home.

I decided to leave everything in God's hands. If Tae and I were meant to be, then he would return to me. For now, I was going to begin the withdrawal process.

Chapter 14

From happiness to pain, what happens next will forever change things…

It was two days before the wedding and I had been swarming myself with activities to keep my mind off of Tae. Most activities pertained to Sarah's wedding and it was undoubtedly keeping me busy.

On this particular day, she and I had an appointment to get our faces done by the wedding's make-up artist to measure her skills. I was actually quite impressed. It was rumored that she was one of ATL's exclusive make-up artists, so I couldn't wait to see what she could do. She had an impressive resume that included making up some of Atlanta's biggest R&B and hip-hop stars like Keisha Cole and Da Brat. I couldn't wait for my turn.

She added dramatic fan-like lashes to our lids and found foundation to match our skin tone's exact colors. She dabbed light shimmery brown blush to lighten my cheeks and added pale pink blush to highlight Sarah's cheekbones. She smudged nude glossy lipstick on our lips and finished with lilac eye shadow. The results were phenomenal. We resembled professional models.

Standing up to look in the studio mirror, I examined the entire make-up job and was highly impressed. I turned my head side to side and could find not one flaw.

"Sarah, she is the truth!" I shouted.

The thin make-up artist smiled largely, folding her arms and resting her body against the wall with one leg up, hoping that Sarah would agree.

"Yeah she is the truth." Sarah said just as amazed with the results. "I absolutely love it." She said in a more heightened tone of satisfaction.

"I want you to do my make-up just like this for the wedding." she told her.

"No problem." The make-up artist agreed with a beaming smile.

"Janae, we can't just go back to my house looking this good. Let's go out for a drink or something. We haven't gone out in forever. You've lived with me for the last couple of days and all we've been doing is sitting in the house feeling sorry for ourselves. Let's go get a drink and hopefully catch a few laughs."

I gave it some thought while putting on my sleeveless gray top coat over my sweater dress. I hadn't spoken to Tae since I've moved in with Sarah and was probably the last person on his mind. And Sarah was right, all we did at her house was soak in each other's misery, with sorry attempts to lift each other up. We weren't fooling anyone, we were miserable.

"Okay." I agreed. "Let's go out."

We gave our goodbyes to the make-up artist and headed to Uno's Pizzeria. It was nice and low key and not particularly crowded. We didn't need to overdo it at an extravagant restaurant anyway. We just needed a spot where we could let our hair down and chat. We took a seat in two high stools at the bar and ordered two pomegranate martinis. We were receiving praises and compliments left and right on our make-up by patrons at the bar as well as customers passing us by.

I noticed that Sarah had zoned out for a moment but I didn't want to bother her with questions.

She finally began to speak. "I almost don't want to live anymore." She said after taking a sip from her martini glass."

"Look at me Sarah." I turned her head to mine. "Don't ever let me hear you say that again. You are one of the strongest people that I know and I always tell you how much I admire your strength. Your mom wanted nothing but great things for you. You have to make her proud." Tears began to slip from her eyes and she didn't bother to wipe them.

"You are stronger than me Janae. You lost your mom *and* your dad and you are still living your life. Your mom was one of the nicest people that I have ever known and although your father was a little distant, losing both parents in any capacity hurts. I still don't know how you did it, because I don't think that I can. To add insult to injury was how my mom died. I almost hate her for keeping her health issues from me. Then I feel stupid for not knowing. All the coughing she used to do when she didn't even have a cold, all the weight she was losing. How didn't I notice what was going on. I regret so much Janae and I feel stupid. It all hurts too bad and I just can't handle it."

"Yes you can. Use me as a living testimony. Yes I lost both parents and it was the hardest thing that I had to conquer in my life, especially losing them back-to-back. But I prayed for strength every day and I'll continue to stay in the battle. Maybe Ms. Michelle had her reasons for not telling us about her health. Maybe she didn't want to burden us because she knew how worried we would be. We will probably never have those answers and it will only stress you to keep thinking about it. You just have to think of all of the memories and meaningful conversations you had with your mom and keep them alive in your heart. It takes time, but it gets greater later, trust me."

"I can't do it." Sarah announced with her face down sobbing and shaking her head.

"Yes you can, and you will." I assured her.

I couldn't take seeing my friend in such pain, I had to intervene.

"Uh uh girl. You dragged me out here so we are going to have some fun. Now lift up your glass." I held my glass out in the air waiting for hers to meet it half way. She smiled through her tears and lifted her glass and clanked it lightly against mine.

"To our future and to that good man that you are about to marry." She wiped her tears and drank to the toast. Once Sarah's tears disappeared, we had a few laughs and a few more rounds of martinis while reminiscing on how much Ms. Michelle made an impact on our lives. Her liveliness would never die.

Curtis greeted us at the door when we arrived back at Sarah's house.

"Where y'all been?" he asked holding the door open for us. "And I hope neither one of you was the designated driver. Y'all look tore up." He said.

Sarah and I looked at each other and giggled.

"We needed to get out Curtis, and we actually ended up having a good time." I told him.

Sarah stumbled over to Curtis and kissed his lips. "I love you Curtis." She said.

"I love you too, Ms. Drunk Lady." He replied.

We laughed and Curtis escorted his fiancé into their bedroom. I smiled at their admirable connection before making my way to the spare room where I had been staying and I shut the door behind me.

That's when everything hit me again and I was unable to hide from the truth. I was alone. Dealing with Damion gave me the realization that there were other men in this world besides Tae, but my heart wouldn't be ready to fish for someone new for a long time. I had to recover from the wounds that still bound me to yearn for Tae.

Damion was on my mind too, but Tae front-lined my thoughts especially. I decided against turning on the TV. No movie or reality show would be more intriguing or despicable than my own life story. I took off my pumps and lay back with my hands behind my head, staring at the ceiling. I didn't want to talk to anyone, I didn't want to listen to music or be bothered. I just needed to think. Of all times, my cell phone began to ring and I almost didn't answer it. I shuffled through my purse and flipped my phone open.

"Hello."

I heard a breath but no one replied.

"Hello?" I asked again.

"It's me." A deep voice replied.

"Tae?" I sat straight up on the bed. His voice sounded so

soothing to hear and my insides were roaring. I didn't want to overdo it, so I just listened to him.

"Yeah it's me. Where are you?" he asked.

"I'm over Sarah's house. I'm going to stay here until I find a place." I replied.

"Oh, I thought you had moved in with that nigga."

"No. Tae I told you that was over. You're who I want to be with. I just thought that you had Sharece pregnant and I couldn't take it. That's why I did what I did."

I heard him begin to get choked up. "I miss you like shit Janae." Then I heard heavy breaths as if he was crying.

"I miss you too boo." I began to tear up as well.

"Nah, don't do that." He stopped me. "Don't talk sweet and do all that bullshit. I miss you so much, but I'm mad as fuck at what you did. You can never undo that shit." He sniffed and then continued. "I know that I fucked up and did my dirt, but I told you over and over how sorry I was. But this just isn't you man." He sighed. "You gave another nigga my pussy J. What the fuck!"

I had to defend myself.

"Tae, I know that I could never undo the past, but don't you think it's selfish of you to excuse your actions and enforce how mine could never be undone?"

"No I don't. I had higher expectations for you. I proposed to you, I wanted you to be my wife man. I gave up all that dumb shit I was doing and all that. And if there is one thing that I've learned from all of this is to NEVER trust a woman." He paused again.

"Man, I just wanted to hear your voice Janae. I'm glad you're a'ight but I gotta go."

"Wait Tae, that's it? You just called to hear my voice? You don't want to talk about anything?"

"Nah man, ain't nothing to talk about. It's a wrap."

Tears slid over my make-up and I was back to the same state that I was in the day that I confessed.

"Well are you still coming to the wedding?" I whispered while crying silently.

"Nah man, I don't think so. I don't want to see you Janae. I'm all fucked up, you don't understand Janae. But yo, tell Sarah I said good luck and shit. I'll see y'all whenever."

"Tae, I need you."

He sighed. "You don't need me Janae. You didn't need me when you was over there fucking that dude. So, have a good life. See you when I see you."

He hung up the phone and I sat feeling like someone had just knocked the wind out of me. I regretted picking up the phone. I was doing semi-well before I talked to him. I should have continued on the road to getting over him, but instead I only tortured myself by picking up.

I tossed my phone back into my purse and stretched on the full-size bed, sinking my head into the pillow and cried myself to sleep.

I was a wreck all the way up until the wedding day. No calls from Tae or anyone for that matter. I kept my phone turned off to preserve my energy for the wedding.

I tried to show some excitement for Sarah, but her low energy washed off on me and we were both in low spirits.

The wedding day was very nerve wracking, but we were ready to get it over with. Curtis spent the night at a hotel with his relatives so that he wouldn't see Sarah the day of the wedding. We had to keep it traditional in the aspect of the groom not seeing the bride on the big day.

The make-up artist and bridesmaids arrived early in the morning to get prepped. When it was all said and done, everyone looked amazing. The pink bridesmaid dresses offset the white and powder pink flowers that Sarah held and her wedding dress was to die for.

Sarah had lost a lot of weight in the past couple of weeks, but her hour glass figure formed a perfectly beautiful shape in her wedding dress. It looked great when she showed me the dress in the store, but seeing it worn up close and personal was no comparison.

The corset shaped top formed perfectly around her very curvy bust and the slim fitting bottom led out to a long white tail which I had to hold while walking her to her Rolls Royce.

The church décor was astounding. There were large powder pink and white bows at the start of every pew and large standing bouquets of the same colors in the vestibule. Some of the guests even decided to wear either pink or white to contribute to the theme.

The church was filled with about a hundred or so guests, most of whom had tears in their eyes, still grieving the loss of Ms. Michelle. Everyone knew how special this day was for Sarah, Curtis and most of all Ms. Michelle and they were all happy that Sarah still went through with it.

The wedding music sounded in the church and the guests stood to welcome the wedding party. We bridesmaids made our way down the aisle first. We scattered pink and white rose petals from our small white baskets onto the white carpet as we strolled by.

Cameras were clicking and videotapes were rolling. I managed to keep a smile plastered over my face the entire time. Finally, the wedding party was all in place at the pulpit and Sarah and Curtis stood at the start of the white carpet ready to make their grand entrance. The signature *Here Comes the Bride* wedding music began and Sarah and Curtis walked arm and arm down the carpet.

In Sarah's free hand, she held an 8x10 portrait of Ms. Michelle against her torso. She had planned this beforehand. It was her way of making sure that her mom was experiencing her dream wedding along with her. When Sarah and Curtis made their way down the aisle, they stood face-to-face gazing into each other's eyes while the Preacher read the Word. He read a beautiful scripture and then informed them that it was time to read their personal vows. Sarah and Curtis both read sensitive words that came deep from their hearts. It was hard to hold back tears but I somehow managed to, although Curtis' mom was sobbing loudly from the front row.

"May no man break this union that God has brought together, you may kiss the bride." The Preacher announced as Sarah and Curtis locked lips.

The entire congregation stood to clap and support their union. I clapped and smiled, musing about how months of all of our hard work had ended with a 45 minute church session that turned out beautifully. My best friend was now married and about to start a new life with a great man.

It was at the reception that Sarah announced her pregnancy. She had just found out the night before the wedding and held the news to herself until now. God took a life and gave a new one I thought to myself while channeling precious memories of Ms. Michelle. I was completely and utterly excited for Sarah. I knew that the baby wouldn't fill the void in Sarah's heart, but I had high hopes that it would certainly patch it with new happiness.

I could almost feel Ms. Michelle's warmth through Sarah and Curtis's enlarged smiles about their baby news. At the same time, an inkling in the back of my mind was forcing me back into my own reality because I definitely had to move out of Sarah's house now. She and Curtis needed this time together. They were now newlyweds and it would be selfish of me not to let them share the growth of their new bundle together. They didn't need a spectator in the mix.

I didn't want them to keep worrying about petty things like if I had enough to eat for the day or if my bedroom was warm enough or my bed comfortable enough. Besides, I was a grown ass woman and had to tackle my own problems.

I idled at the circular pink and white flower decorated table full of champagne glasses and sank down two complete flutes of champagne as if it would take away my problems. I saw Sarah's friends and family giggling and slow dancing on the shiny hardwood mid-section of the room and it felt like the music slowed down.

I felt a bit faint and struggled to maintain my composure. I reached behind me and sat my glass down on the table. I shut my eyes for a moment and put my hand on my head trying to dismiss all cloudy and distorted thoughts about my recent mistakes. I leaned back against the table almost sitting on it so that I wouldn't fall over. Either this feeling was the result of drinking champagne and not eating in days or stress consuming my body to an extraordinary weakness.

Suddenly I was able to escape my trance as I was approached by a seemingly familiar face.

"Damion?" I asked as if I were seeing things. "I didn't know you were coming." I blurted, now completely startled that it was in fact *him*.

His presence struck a sensitive chord in my heart and I almost cried at the sight of him. He smiled and made his way beside me.

As usual, he was dressed in a suit that looked like it was meant for P. Diddy. Flawless, perfectly cut, neat invisible seams and a brilliant pearl colored vest inside his blue suit jacket. He had on blue Gator shoes, his line-up was neatly aligned around his mouth and chin and his silky lengthy jet black hair was pushed back in a neat ponytail. He looked suave and his style was astonishingly tasteful.

"I wasn't going to show up at first. I wasn't sure if I would've been met with the sight of you and Tae hand-in-hand. But something told me to still come through." He said.

His brown eyes searched the empty area beside me and then he glanced around at the dance floor before scoping out the entire room. I knew exactly who he was searching for. "Is he here? Is dude here?" he asked after not spotting Tae.

"No." I said sinking my head down.

He lifted my left hand, "No ring either?"

It's over Damion." I said blankly. "Tae and I are over."

Damion let my words sink in for a second. He stood without saying anything and then turned and grabbed himself a glass of champagne. After that, the questions began to flow.

"How long has it been since it's been over? Why didn't you call and tell me that it was over? Did I really not mean that much to you? I've been patiently waiting for you to leave that dude and when you do, you didn't have the decency of calling me?"

He chugged down the champagne and sloppily placed the glass on the table, then angrily walked away.

I realized how much his feelings were still caught up. I felt like an asshole. I stood there for a moment and then decided to chase after him. He exited the reception hall into a tight hallway leading to the elevators. We were no longer able to hear the music and we seemed to be the only two people in the hallway.

"Damion wait. You asked me a bunch of questions, don't you want me to answer them?"

He pressed the down elevator button and told me that I had one minute to talk and that my explanation really wouldn't matter anyway.

I tried to talk fast to explain myself.

"Well, I think I owe it to you to explain. Shortly after I broke things off with you, Tae found out about us. Apparently, his boss Eric had someone photograph us together and he sent the photos to Tae. I came clean and told Tae that we had in fact been together and he didn't want anything else to do with me. I was too embarrassed to contact you, especially after the way that I broke things off. I didn't think that you ever wanted to hear from me again."

"Well you would have found all of that out if you would've called me. I'll admit; I was upset at the way you ended it, but that wouldn't have stopped me from working things out with you." He paused in frustration, his forehead wrinkled and his face scrunched up, "Damn Janae, this was some real selfish shit. You got me feeling like a real clown, I feel played and I don't appreciate it at all."

I placed my hand over my heart expressing sincerity, "I didn't mean to make you feel that way. I was just stuck between a rock and a hard place. I still am."

The elevator arrived and the steel doors parted open, Damion stepped inside and turned back to face me.

"Well that's not my problem Janae, that's yours." The doors closed, and I stood in front of them feeling numb and cold. Damion was right, this was *my* problem. I got myself into this love triangle knowing that I was playing Russian Roulette by juggling two men and I hurt them both. But, most of all, I hurt myself.

I took in a deep breath and sucked back my tears before I walked back into the reception area. I tried to keep a steady face, but Sarah noticed right away that I was out of it. She looked inebriated herself and the tail on her wedding dress was badly stained with dust from wiping on the dance floor all night. It didn't matter though because she appeared happy and that's all that mattered to me.

"Girl you are pregnant, I hope you weren't drinking." I told her.

"Girl calm down, I had two glasses of red wine. I called the hospital yesterday when I found out that I was pregnant to see if it was okay if I drink red wine on my wedding day. The doctor said that it was fine. I couldn't get married and not at least have one or two drinks at the wedding." she laughed.

She took both of my hands and led me to the dance floor as the song *Ladies Night* resounded through the loud speakers.

"Come on now J, you are not going to be upset at my wedding. Put a smile on your face and let's get down." She clapped her hands and winded her body to the beat and I finally hinted at a smile while grooving along with her.

Although the alcohol played an immediate role in Sarah's happiness, I was very happy that she went through with the wedding and was having a great time. When the song ended, Sarah took my hand and led me toward Curtis and two handsome professional looking gentlemen over by the cake table.

"Janae, these are Curtis' two brothers, Mike and Isaiah."

"Nice to meet you." I smiled greeting them both.

"They came down from Chicago. Mike is the oldest, he's a *doctor*."

She put a heavy emphasis on doctor. "Isaiah is the youngest, he's in grad school and they are both single." she winked.

I was now hipped to what Sarah was trying to pull. She was trying to get me to mingle with one of Curtis' brothers, but I just wasn't up to it. She pulled Curtis by the hand and moseyed back onto the dance floor to allow me to get to know his brothers. Instead, I informed them that it was a pleasure meeting them and went my own way.

The reception was wrapped up about an hour later and everyone, even in their drunken state, rushed out to their cars. The white stretch Hummer limo was out front waiting for me and the bridesmaids. I hugged Curtis and Sarah and wished them a safe journey on their honeymoon to sunny Jamaica before I went inside the limo.

"I love you Janae. Thank you for everything, I really enjoyed myself, the wedding was perfect." Sarah said.

"I did too Sarah, you look beautiful and everything turned out amazing."

She smiled and hugged me tight, "I'm going to free my mind on this trip Janae. When I get back don't forget that I need your help with clearing out my mom's apartment. I'm still not looking forward to it at all girl," her face saddened.

"Don't even think about that right now Sarah, just enjoy your honeymoon with your husband and take full advantage of your relaxing adventure."

"I plan to." she agreed.

Curtis waved me a brief goodbye and they jumped into their Rolls Royce and drove off with the "Just Married" sign on the back of the car waving in the wind. I could sense that they were a bit relieved that I was residing at their place in assurance that their home wouldn't be tampered with for the two weeks they'd be away.

I blew a kiss to the car and headed inside of the limo.

Most of the bridesmaids were passed out on the spread leather seats. They had danced their shoes off and drank more than they could handle. Curls were now frizzy and straight hair was now crinkled due to sweat. My make-up and French twist up-do on the other hand was still intact, but my face was as stale as coal without a hint of happiness. I gazed out at the dark Atlanta streets with thoughts of Damion, which had quickly replaced memories of Tae. I felt like I had lost my chance at a good relationship by trying to make it work with Tae, but most of all, I felt the pain of being alone.

When I arrived at Sarah's place, I peeled my dress off immediately and walked around comfortably in my panties and bra. Stress was still suppressing my appetite, but not my urge for something sweet. I discovered a pint of vanilla ice cream deep in the freezer and popped in one of my favorite movies, *The Color Purple*. My night was ending up to be pretty relaxing and the sadness was subsiding a bit. I took my cellphone out of my purse and discovered that I had two missed calls.

The number looked familiar, but since I had erased Damion's name and number out of my phone, the digits took a while to register.

I pondered calling him back, I didn't know if he wanted to finish venting or if he wanted to talk on a casual level.

After executing the pint of ice cream, I sat the empty carton on the nightstand and decided to give him a call. What was the worst that could come out of calling him?

"Hello?" I greeted him nervously.

"Hey, I didn't think you were going to call me back." He responded.

"Well, I did have to give it some thought. I really don't want to argue with you or be chastised over my mistakes."

"Let the past be the past. What's done is done. Seeing you tonight brought back so many feelings that I thought were behind me. You were as flawless as an airbrushed picture."

I smiled. "I see things haven't changed. You still like to throw the compliments my way."

"Well it's true. You are a very fine specimen. I've always told you that." He paused. "I'm sorry about the way that I acted today. Seeing you tonight and then finding out that you weren't with ol' boy and haven't reached out to me really got under my skin. But as I sat and thought about it, I had to respect your opinion."

I was now at ease.

"I'm glad you understand. This whole journey has been very bumpy for me. I'm staying at Sarah's right now, because Eric got Tae and I evicted. I'm just saving up to get my own place. I think after I move out, my life will start to pick back up."

"Well I see that you have things figured out. That nigga Eric really did you dirty in more ways than one."

"Tell me about it. I try not to think of him, because I get angry. I'm just going to let God have his way with him. And I hope that his wife someday finds out the truth about her husband."

"Oh she will, I'll put money on that."

I smiled.

"Wow, you're still a good listener, I miss that about you." I told him.

"There's a lot of things I miss about you." he said in a sexy monotone.

I had to cross my legs because his voice was getting to me. I was tingling in an area that hadn't been touched in a while. Just the thought of his sexy body and gentle touch was enticing.

"Whatever Damion." I brushed him off.

"I do. I'll tell you what. How about you jump in your car and swing through here so that I can show you what I mean."

"Come on now Damion, we just seen each other for the first time in who knows how long. I can't just jump back into your heart and I can't just push you back into mine."

"Why not?" he asked. His forwardness was so attractive. It was luring me in, but I had to keep my cool.

"Because it's too early. Besides, who knows what women you have been seeing in the meantime."

"None." he replied.

"I find that hard to believe Damion."

"Janae, please just get in your car and come through. We don't have to do anything; I just need to see you."

I spotted my pink jogging suit in the closet, peeked at myself in the mirror to make sure that my make-up was still up to par, and then decided that I was going to go.

"Alright Damion. But we aren't doing anything and I'm only staying for a little while."

"Okay." He agreed.

As soon as I hit the door, Damion pulled me in and kissed me like he was making up for every day we missed. He was ripping through my velour jogging suit and hadn't even greeted me with a hello. I had sunk down a glass of wine in the car before I came up to his crib, so the alcohol courage helped me face him and it was now playing a major role in me not resisting his touches.

I released myself to him letting him have his way with me. In the sober part of my mind, I was thinking that this was never the type of woman that I was. But I had already done damage, I was a cheater and I was now single. I kind of felt like I deserved this, I deserved to be pleased after being hurt for so long.

My body was now bare and Damion laid me on his sleigh bed and made a feast out of my body parts. He started from my titties, he caressed them with his mouth, giving each one an equal amount of love. He twisted his tongue down my stomach, stopping at my belly button to massage it with his mouth. Then he made his way below to my kitty cat and my body thanked him naturally. I let out moans of gratitude and came within minutes. It had been a while and he was doing everything perfectly. Every touch, every motion was on point.

"Tell me you want me." He said reaching for protection.

"I want you." I moaned.

"Tell me again." he said.

"I want you Damion." I said with seductive eyes.

He topped the condom over the head of his penis and rolled it down. He slid it inside me with ease. My body's wetness accepted him and it made his body quiver in satisfaction. It felt like the best love making ever. Better than Tae's, and better than any other session Damion and I had. We went at it for what seemed like hours and after, we lay in our body fluids out of breath and full of smiles.

"I missed the fuck outta your lil ass." He confessed.

I smiled, "I missed you too."

"Wanna go again?" he asked.

"Please Damion, you can't handle the truth." I joked laying my face on his bare muscular chest.

We stayed up all night catching up. We talked about what we wanted out of our futures and where we saw our careers in five years. He was still the same attentive listener that he had always been and our conversation flowed smoothly.

I couldn't help but notice that his closet seemed emptier than before and the condo didn't feel as homely as it once was.

"Where are all of your clothes?" I asked peering over at the half empty closet.

"What do you mean? They are at the cleaners." he replied.

"Oh, just wondering." I said dismissing it.

"Well, just wonder how you're gonna handle this dick." He rolled me over and we went at it again.

Throughout the two weeks that Sarah was away, Damion and I connected as if we had never left each other. We may have been moving a little too fast, but after giving it a little thought, I decided to move in with him.

When Sarah and Curtis arrived from their trip I was pretty much packed up. Sarah supported my decision, although she expressed that it was a bit risky and too soon. But she went with the flow. I didn't care what anyone thought, I was falling for Damion again and Tae hadn't even crossed my mind since we reconnected.

Damion was placing my last piece of luggage into the trunk of his Escalade. I hugged Sarah and Curtis and thanked them for the stay and we were off. Sarah and Curtis waved us off from their porch stoop.

"I hope I'm doing the right thing Damion." I said in deep thought as we rode away.

"Baby of course you are, do you know how long I've been waiting for this?" he assured me.

"I know but I kinda feel like we should take it slower."

"For what? Don't go switching up on me again. This time let's do it right and be all about each other."

I loosened up. "You're right, I'm happy. And I really think that you and I were meant to be. Forgive me for being apprehensive, I just told myself that any next move that I made would be on solid footing."

"Well baby, I'm going to take care of you and you'll never have to worry about being unhappy again. I'm sure we'll get into petty arguments over small issues like normal couples do, but I would never do anything to break your heart."

I adored the fact that Damion had answers for all of my concerns. It seemed that he had the right things to say to everything. But it felt like everything about this man couldn't be this perfect. How could I be so lucky?

I sat staring at Damion and then pulled the lever to let the passenger seat back and I just enjoyed the moment while my man drove us to what was now *our* home.

We arrived at the condo and I stopped Damion before he got out of the truck.

"Do you promise Damion?" I asked. "Promise you'll never hurt me. I just want to be happy."

He peered over at me confidently, "I promise."

That was the last reassurance that I needed to feel good about my decision. I had moved on from Tae and this time things were going to be good.

Once Damion and I finished unloading my belongings into the condo, I left to meet Sarah at Ms. Michelle's house. This had been something that Sarah and I had dreaded to do for some time now. When I arrived, Sarah was still in her car and she was crying dramatically. I lightly knocked on her window to get her attention.

"Are you okay Sarah?"

She rolled down the window. "No. I've been sitting here for like ten minutes. I don't know if I can do it, I can't get out of my car Janae."

"Come on Sarah, you can do it. I'm right here with you, okay? Would you like for me to call Curtis?" I started to retrieve my cell from my pocket.

"No. You don't have to call him. This is something that I think that you and I should do since she considered you her daughter as well. Plus, I cried every day on our honeymoon and I don't want to seem like a cry baby to my husband."

"Girl trust me, your husband understands. You lost your mom and if there is one thing I can say about Curtis, it's that he has patience. He had the patience to deal with your crazy ass this long, trust me he can handle you now."

She smiled, "Alright, I'm coming out."

She rolled the window up, shut off the car and met me at the door. We held hands and entered Ms. Michelle's apartment together. It was the only way either one of us had the strength to make it in.

Unfortunately, Sarah's strength ended abruptly. She began sobbing right away.

"Janae, why can't she just come out of her bedroom and greet us? Why did she have to leave me Janae, why?"

I held my tears back, Sarah sobbed hard and I sat her down on the couch and held her.

She looked around, "It feels cold in here now Janae, it feels like the house knows that she's not here anymore."

I had no words. I didn't want to say the wrong thing to make Sarah even more sentimental so I just held her. And after some time, she gathered herself.

"Okay Janae, I think I'm ready."

"You sure?" I asked her.

"Yeah, we have to get this out the way because I want to make this my last time coming here. I can't do this anymore. Let's start here in the living room." She stood up.

"My Aunt in Arizona wants this living room set, she said she'll come down to get it shipped. You can help me put all the pictures in boxes and I'll send them to my grandmother in Alabama. I've also arranged for my mom's bedroom set to be sent to my grandmother. All that I want is her personal possessions like her pearls and jewelry that she cherished. It will mean a lot to me to pass them down to my children."

"Well let's get started." I said.

We discovered five large boxes in Ms. Michelle's hallway closet and we packed all the pictures that once hung from the olive colored walls into the box. We had the living room's pictures and antiques packed up within an hour and it was all done in silence.

The whole situation was eating Sarah up inside and there was nothing that I could say that would comfort her. Tears were quietly graduating down her cheeks as she smiled at some of the memories from the pictures we packed.

We then made it into the kitchen after clearing out the hallway closet. Sarah packed up some of her mom's pots and pans for herself and the rest we either threw out or put in a box to send to other family members.

After completing the kitchen, Sarah faced her mom's bedroom door. Entering Ms. Michelle's room was a feat that we once again had to conquer together. I took Sarah by the hand clearing her out of the trance she had gone into, staring at Ms. Michelle's oak bedroom door.

I reached for the knob. When I opened the door, a cool breeze whisked over us and it seemed as if it was Ms. Michelle assuring us that it was okay and that we needed to be strong. I led Sarah inside and all she could do was stand by the door and look around. She didn't want to disrupt or touch any of her mom's belongings, because it was the way Ms. Michelle had left it. The bed was unmade, the small garbage pail was full and she had paperwork lying across the dresser.

"Janae, can you excuse me for a minute?" Sarah asked.

Her face was stone cold and serious, so I stepped out of the room to give her time to grieve or whatever she needed to do to feel better.

Minutes later she called me into the bedroom sobbing.

"Janae, come here, quick! Look what I found, read this."

On top of Ms. Michelle's crème colored bureau was a letter addressed to Sarah. It was put in position as if Ms. Michelle left it for Sarah to find. It read:

Dear Sarah, my little girl, my angel; my everything:

If you're reading this then you probably found out the truth about me. You now know why I was living my life to its capacity for the past few years because I knew that I didn't have many years left. I was diagnosed with HIV about five years ago and have been living with full-blown AIDS for the past year and a half. I never told you about it for one specific reason. You're strong like me but when it comes to something severe such as this…

I knew that you wouldn't be able to handle it. I kept it from you to shield you from being tortured for my mistake. I hope you don't hate me for keeping this from you, but I couldn't make you suffer along with me. I still don't know who infected me but I've come to a point in my life where I forgive that person. Life is short and it shouldn't be lived with regret. When I found out that you were getting married, it was like God had granted me my final wish.

I knew that I didn't have much time left because I refused to take the large dose of meds the doctor prescribed. God blessed you with someone perfect to look out for you in my absence. I've adored Curtis for the two years that I've known him and he's going to make a great husband and father someday. Yes I said some day because the two of you will make beautiful grandkids.

Make sure you tell my grandkids all about grandma Michelle and how much I love them even before they were even born. Tell Janae that I love her and to never forget me and that I also expect some grandkids from her as well. Please use me as an example. Always respect yourself, don't make the same careless decisions that I made just for lust. Make decisions using your heart and your intellect. And always remember to keep God first. Once again my dear Sarah, mommy is sorry. Don't cry for me, smile with me and always know that I'm with you.

Until the day we meet again, see you soon.

Mom

Sarah and I cried together after reading the letter and at the same time it gave us some ease. It was like Ms. Michelle was speaking to us through the paper and it finally gave us some closure.

"She was right." Sarah sniffed wiping her tears.

"What do you mean?" I asked.

"If she would have told me that she was infected, I probably would have killed myself. She was my mother, my sister and my best friend all in one. I would have died the day she told me," she said shaking her head.

"See, she shielded you from that Sarah. Every mom knows her child."

Sarah smiled through her tears. "Yes, she truly knew me. I'm so glad that I found this letter; it brings a bit of peace to my heart. And I don't know if you noticed lately Janae, but I've changed. I've become a better person and I'm going to be the best wife for Curtis and great mom to my new baby."

"Aw Sarah, you got me crying again." I wiped my tears and smiled. "But girl, of course I noticed your change. You're still crazy but you've slowed down a bit and I'm proud of your transformation. Treat him right, like Ms. Michelle would say, please your man."

Sarah and I giggled and hugged and finally continued to pack up the rest of the house.

For months Damion and I lived like we were newlyweds. After work, our nights were full of great conversation and sexual escapades, we couldn't resist each other. We were each other's dessert, dinner and breakfast.

My appetite resumed to normal, my weight was healthy and I went into work each day with a pep in my step and a new-found bubbly attitude. I was however a bit saddened by some rumors that were spread around the office about Tae seeing a new woman. It bothered me for a moment, but seeing as though I was completely happy with Damion, I let it go.

That's how I knew that I was really falling in love. Things couldn't have been going better for us… until I started seeing some of Tae's traits in Damion.

Chapter 15

A new life with an old love, could it be real or was it lies I've been told?

The first night my suspicion began was when he didn't come home. He wasn't sneaky like Tae to just stay out without explanation. He did call with what appeared to be a valid reason, but I was still unsure of what to make of it.

I was sitting up in the bed in the dark with my arms wrapped around my knees when he called. It was the first time that I had to stay in the condo alone.

"Janae baby, I'm on the road. I have to show a property in North Carolina in the morning so I'm driving out tonight."

"Why would you be telling me this now Damion? It's two in the morning; you could have mentioned this earlier."

"I know baby, but situations like these are spontaneous. If I sell this property I could make a lot of money for us."

"I understand, but I just wish you could have told me this earlier. I've been up all night waiting up for you." I said pissed but trying to sound more concerned.

"Aw my baby wants daddy there to spank that ass huh?"

"Something like that." I teased.

"Well I'll be back tomorrow and I promise I'll make it up to you."

After our call ended, I was still a bit uneasy. I've learned from dealing with Tae that any spontaneous actions that a man springs upon you last minute usually had some type of bullshit behind it.

For the next few months, the North Carolina excuse was used at least three times a week and I didn't understand it. He always told me that the showings didn't go very well and that all of the houses that he showed in North Carolina still have not sold. I tried to convince him that it was not only a waste of gas money but not worth the time when there were plenty of properties in Atlanta waiting to be sold. He told me that traveling was a part of the real estate business and that I needed to adjust because it was his way of living. Something about it still just didn't sit well with me.

I stopped wanting to have sex with him because I felt like I hardly saw him and my trust was fading slowly, but surely. His clothes that were in the so-called cleaners, never returned to the closet. I just couldn't put my finger on what was going on with Damion.

If cheating was the issue, I don't know what could have been his reasoning. Our sex life was great and he enjoyed paying all the bills so I would pay for the groceries. He pretty much spoiled me and I spoiled him in other ways. I bought him expensive suits and expensive shoes and tried to keep him pleased.

But with his recent absences from home, I was starting to stress out again.

I tried to go to work with a clear head on a bright Monday morning. I had avoided traffic and got a great parking spot in the college lot, so my day was already heading down a smooth path. My phone rang just before I left my car to head inside the office.

"Hello?" I answered.

"Hey boo, I missed you so much."

"Tae?" I asked.

"What, you don't know my voice anymore?" he replied.

"Well it's been a while. I wasn't expecting to hear from you."

"What I can't call my girl anymore?"

"Your girl?" I asked.

"Let's keep it real Janae, that pussy will always be mine."

I took the phone away from my ear and looked at it. "You're not serious right now Tae are you? Don't you have a woman now?"

"She ain't you! No one can fill your shoes."

"Well Tae now that I'm over you, I believe that everything happens for a reason. Maybe it was good for me to have done what I've done because I would probably still have been stuck dealing with another four years of being cheated on. Look what you are doing right now, you have a woman and you're calling me and telling me that my pussy is yours? Is this what you used to do to me behind my back? What? Did you and your girlfriend have a fight so you think you can call me to stunt off or something?"

"Stop being so sensitive! I'm calling you because I missed you and I want to get up with you. I reserved a hotel for us. Let me hit it one last time."

"You know what, you really disgust me Tae! I can't believe you are calling me to assist you in cheating on your girl. Sorry but I would never do that to her."

"What? Look who's talking, you was out here sleeping with some lame ass nigga and you fucked our relationship up. Don't try to blame the shit on me and act like your shit don't stink."

"Well guess what Tae? I *am* blaming it on you because if you'd acted right in the first place we would still be together. But your weak ass had to keep cheating on me, lying to me and breaking my heart. Now that I'm over you, I look back and want to kick myself in the ass for staying so long. So on that note, good luck with your relationship, I wish that sister all the best because she is going to need it. You were never going to change Tae and it's sad, but guess what? I don't have to deal with it anymore EVER again. I gotta go."

I hung up with my dignity laying solid across my smile. Now that the heartbreak was over, I realized that Tae and I weren't meant to be and I wasted years trying. I was always afraid to move on and now that I have, it felt like my greatest accomplishment. The change that he made when we were together was obviously temporary, seeing as though he could cheat on his new girl so easily. A dog was going to be a dog and I was glad that he was now in the past.

Now I just had to work on things with Damion. I needed to see if he had some sort of hidden agenda.

I had called Damion all morning and afternoon and he hadn't picked up any of my calls. I took my frustration out on students who came into the office asking questions that could easily be answered by reading the college brochures. I tossed a few brochures into the hands of students who stood looking dumbfounded by my reaction.

I realized that I had to collect myself and not scare anymore students out of the office. I had to conduct business properly and professionally. But Damion was pissing me off! This episode was reminding me of all the times that I used to call Tae when he wasn't answering his phone due to being with a female, and I got myself worked up.

Normally, even if Damion went to North Carolina, he would call me at least three times in the morning just to talk about nothing. Things now seemed more and more unusual and I wasn't feeling it. He finally called me at 4:00 PM which was almost quitting time and I liked to had cussed him out.

I snatched the phone off the receiver once I saw his number flash across the screen.

"Where have you been and why weren't you answering your phone?" I barked.

"Damn baby, what's wrong with you?" He asked.

"No, what's wrong with you? Why are you just now calling me at four o'clock? I'm sure you seen numerous missed calls from me on your cell and you're just calling me now?"

"Okay, first you need to calm down. I'm sorry. I was handling business. I had to close on two houses this morning so I've been in the court house helping to finalize the paper work."

"Why didn't you tell me about this last night? I didn't know anything about you closing on any homes today. You usually always keep me updated on what you are doing."

"I know baby, I'm sorry. I didn't think that it would be a big deal." He said calmly.

Still sensing attitude in my tone, he took a deep breath and tried to make good out of the situation. "Okay look, how about you to go to the mall after work and pick out something hot to wear because I'm going to take you out tonight, so that we can celebrate me getting these two deals done."

I took in a deep breath myself, and then came down off of mad mode.

"Okay. I guess I was just overreacting. But, Damion?" I started.

"Yes baby?"

"Can you please not pull anything like this again? I'm not saying that I have to be all down your back knowing where you are every two minutes, but just don't shut me out and not answer my calls. I don't want to bring my trust issues into our relationship, but it's still something that I'm dealing with."

"Baby, you have nothing to worry about and again I'm sorry. Just make sure what you pick out today can be easily taken off after dinner."

I smiled, "alright, I'm getting off soon. See you at home."

After work, I made my way to the Lenox Mall and found a pink form fitting freak 'em dress. I also picked out some pretty silver accessories that looked like they would match well with a pair of shoes that I already had at home that I thought would complement the dress. I planned to look fabulous for the night, dismiss my leery trust issues with Damion, and appreciate the fact that I had a good man before I scared him away.

After leaving the mall, I pulled into the condo parking lot next to Damion's truck full of excitement. I couldn't wait to get into my new dress and mesmerize Damion with my curves. As I made my way up the stairs, I spotted a light skinned girl shaped similar to me standing in front of my door with a toddler latched at her hip. I started toward her to see if she had the wrong door.

"Hi, who are you looking for?" I asked nearing the door and grabbing my keys out of my purse.

She smiled and said, "You got to be kidding me, I knew it."

"You knew what?" I asked.

"I knew he had another girl here."

"He who? Are you sure you have the right house?" I asked again.

She smirked and pushed out her hip that secured the baby. "Doesn't he look familiar?"

The gorgeous silky haired, brown eyed little boy appeared to be one or two years old and was the spitting image of Damion.

I dropped my bags along with my keys on the ground and liked to have had a heart attack.

"Oh no boo, don't be shocked. I been through this plenty of times." she said.

My heart beat uncontrollably as I bent to pick up my belongings.

"I don't want no drama. It ain't you I'm mad at, it's him." She said, hovering over me.

"Damion? You're talking about Damion?" I asked while I stood up, just to be clear.

"Yes Damion, my fiancé. My lying, cheating ass fiancé and father of my two kids."

"Wait, fiancé? And did you say *two* kids?" I asked.

"Yes we also have a five year old and we've been engaged for two years."

My breath was now shortened even more and I had to put my hand over my chest to calm myself down. I felt like a fool.

"He owns a few other houses and every so often, I pop up and catch him having a female living in it. He puts the charm on her, lies to her and make her feel like she's his one and only, but it's all game. I've been through it far too long. I'm sure he lies to you every so often and tells you that he's on trips to show houses in other states. Well that's bullshit. He's either home with me or with one of the other girls. Each time I catch him, he tells me that the girl living in the apartments are tenants of his which I'm sure he's going to say about you."

"I mean, I'm sure you were probably wondering why his clothes aren't here. I know you had to sense something. He has a family, we live together."

I didn't have anything to say to her, I just wanted to get to the bottom of this. She was a very pretty girl, but I could see the stress all in her face. She was hurt and I've been in her predicament before, so I knew her pain. However, I had my own pain to confront as well as to confront Damion.

"Daddy!" the little boy shouted at my apartment door.

The girl looked at me and shook her head. "He ain't answering the door. He's had me standing out here for a good while because he knows that if I come in there and see your stuff in there, then he's caught. We've been arguing at home all morning because I knew that he was out here cheating."

I huffed, feeling foolish and shook my head, "I guess that's why he wasn't answering the phone this morning, because he was with you."

"Oh trust me, his phone was ringing like crazy and I kept telling him to answer it, but he wouldn't." she said.

I had heard enough, I took my key and opened the door. I was more than ready to confront Damion.

When we got inside, Damion was sitting in the kitchen with his hands folded at his chest looking at us.

"So you have a family Damion?" I asked.

"What?" he asked.

He then looked at his fiancé. "What did you tell her Ariana?"

"I told her the truth. I'm tired of you doing this to me and the kids, I'm sick of it!" She placed the baby on the floor and he ran to the couch. Tears formed at her eyes and she began yelling at Damion.

"Come home, get your stuff and get out! I'm not dealing with you anymore. You and her can be happy because I'm done!"

"Ariana, what are you talking about? This is Janae, she's a tenant. She's been looking for an apartment, so I let her stay here."

I gazed at him with a look of pure evil. At that moment, it had sunk in that I was his mistress. He made a complete asshole out of me.

"Your tenant? Nigga, you're supposed to be living here with me."

"Don't listen to her Ariana, she's lying!"

"I'm lying? So why are you in here right now Damion, why have you been staying here with me?

"You called me to fix your sink." He lied.

"What!" I screamed in shock.

This was the first time that I was able to see Damion's true colors. He was blatantly lying and making it seem like I meant nothing to him.

"So everything was a lie huh? You're engaged and you have kids? You hadn't even mentioned having KIDS!" I shouted.

Ariana scrunched up her forehead looking at me and then at Damion, "You didn't even tell her about our kids?" she asked pissed off.

"She's lying Ariana, of course she knew I had kids. Why does it matter anyway, she's just my tenant."

At that point, I threw my hands up. I wasn't going to sit around and watch him lie and make it seem like I was just some random girl.

"You know what Damion, I am out of here. I don't need this drama or this stress. I can't believe you lied to me and that I never knew who you really were. You always tell me not to worry about anything and you were the one who was pretending the entire time. You were the cause of my last break up and then you lead me on, only to break my heart?"

He looked at me with an empty and blank face. Sweat was collected at his forehead and I could tell that he was ashamed, but he was trying to save his family.

I pointed towards him. "You better not ever in your life call me or come near me, or I will kill you." I said firmly.

I gave him the look of death before I headed into the bedroom and began packing my belongings. I was too mad to cry. I pulled my clothes off the hangers and was throwing them into suitcases while Damion and Ariana remained in the kitchen arguing. I never thought that I would be anyone's mistress and there I was, living with someone else's man. I knew that Damion had to be too good to be true, he was just *too* perfect. He was everything that I wanted Tae to be, yet he wasn't even my man.

I overheard Ariana hollering that Damion needed help and that she had hoped that after quitting his job at the strip club, his sex addiction would've decreased. She screamed about all the porno's that she found hidden in their closet at home and that if he didn't get any help with his addiction that she would leave and never look back.

Damion was trying to shout over her and assure her that I meant nothing and that he didn't have a problem. He told her that she was all that he needed and more and that he was sorry that he hurt her.

Thankfully none of the furniture in the apartment was mine and if I had left anything behind, they could just toss it out. I had all of my clothes in a suitcase and a single duffle bag and I lugged it through the living room to the front door.

Damion had his son in his arms and Ariana had her head buried in his chest crying. He peered over at me and mouthed the words "I'm sorry" without saying it aloud.

"Good luck to you and your family." I said.

I opened the door and was on my way out. I thought that I handled myself well. I really wanted to claw his eyes out for lying to me and misleading me. But after dealing with a liar, cheater and deceiver, I shouldn't have expected anything less.

"Wait!"

Ariana came running behind me and stopped me when I was at my car.

"Honey you don't have to worry about me ever calling or trying to be with him again. I'm not mistress material, I thought him and I were exclusive." I explained.

"That's okay; you don't seem like the type. I just wanted to ask you something really important before I consider giving him another chance."

She helped me place my bags in the trunk of my car and I don't think that I was prepared for what she wanted to ask me.

"Has Damion ever told you about his cousin that moved to Atlanta with him?"

"Yeah, the one that came up here with him for school, his old roommate? What about him?" I asked.

She looked a bit leery and she inhaled. "Well it's rumored that he wasn't his cousin or just his roommate. People have told me that they were more than roommates."

"What do you mean?" I asked.

"Well, I've caught him cheating on me with different girls, and I've been stupid enough to stay, mainly for the kids. But if he's on the down low, then that's something that I need to know. Kids or no kids, I would leave him right away."

Once again my heart fluttered, I thought of Ms. Michelle and how she died from the virus. If he had all types of women and possibly sleeping with men too, who knows what I could have caught from him.

"Honestly, this is news to me." I told her. I was shocked out of my mind. "I really hope that it's untrue for the sake of you and your kids. But just ask yourself this. All the money that he makes from real estate, why in the world was he working at a male strip club for?" I asked.

I left her with that thought. I got in my car and drove away. This time, my destination was the clinic and I didn't care how long the wait was. Damion and I always used condoms, but you never know.

As I sat in the waiting room, I couldn't wrap my mind around the fact that Damion had a family the entire time, even when I was with Tae. He was the one encouraging me to leave Tae so adamantly each day and he had a family of his own all along. *And* he was possibly gay! This was just too much for me. I did believe that God did everything for a reason, and that he placed Damion's girlfriend Ariana in my presence today to get me out of my situation before my heart was any deeper into it. Who knows how long Damion would have kept up this pretend life with me.

After waiting for twenty minutes, I was called in to get my blood drawn and a pap smear. I told the doctor to check me for *everything* and even told her how I would be practicing abstinence from here on out. I had almost given up on men after dealing with two complete dogs. I was convinced that neither Tae nor Damion would ever change and the thought of wasting my life with another man who would potentially take advantage of me was not in my plans.

After leaving the clinic, I decided against going to Sarah's house. I didn't want to explain to her what happened, I was too embarrassed. I ended up checking in at the Comfort Inn which ended up turning into two week stay. I needed the time to myself to reflect on my mistakes and to determine my next move.

The Monday of week two, I received two pleasant phone calls. One was from the clinic. My results were all negative for any and all STDs. The second call was from a luxury apartment complex that I had applied for. They called to tell me that my application was approved. I was excited and rushed over to the apartment complex and collected my keys. They informed me that by Thursday, I would be able to move in.

I was excited about my new place and I wanted to call Sarah to let her know about it. Just as I was about to call her, a text came through my phone from Damion's number. Right away my smile turned into a frown. What nerve he had to be calling himself texting me! I opened the text and it read: *you'll always be my pretty brown brown.* I almost vomited in my mouth. He now had me convinced me that he was insane. After ruining my life I couldn't believe that he enabled himself to send such bullshit.

As I was erasing his text, my phone began ringing from a private number. I figured that it was Damion and I was too livid to even hear him so much as breathe through the phone so I kept hitting the ignore button. I was on the verge of shutting my phone off because it kept ringing and it was aggravating me to the point where I wanted to throw it out of the car window.

After about the twentieth ring, I finally picked up to find out who wanted to get a hold of me so badly. I pulled in the hotel lot and put the car in park, so if I needed to scream on the person on the other end, I could do so in my car.

"Hello?" I said with undeniable attitude.

"Janae?"

"Deborah?" I asked in a calmer tone.

"Yes it's me. I have to talk to you about something very important."

Her tone was cordial, she no longer sounded like she wanted to kill me for accusing her husband Eric of what he had really in fact done to me.

I took the key out of the ignition and sat them in my lap.

"Well first I want to apologize for the way that I spoke to you the last time that I called." She paused and it seemed as if she was starting to cry. I heard whimpering.

"Deborah, what's going on? Is everything okay?" I asked.

"No." She cried. "Things will probably never be okay for a long time."

She sighed and I listened as she continued in a rather shaky tone.

"Well when word got out about what you accused my husband of doing to you, other young women came forward accusing him of the same thing."

I shook my head while Deborah went on. I wasn't too surprised to hear what she was telling me. After he tried to sexually assault me, lie about the situation and then try to destroy my life with Tae, I knew that the respectable persona that he showed the world was just a front. It was obvious that he tried to break up what I had with Tae so that I wouldn't tell Tae or anyone else about his flaws and further expose him.

After hearing how hard Deborah cried while telling me her next words, I couldn't help but to sympathize with her.

"Janae, he has done it to several other of his worker's girlfriends and wives and a few women at church. And to add insult to injury, he has been molesting our young daughters for years and I had no idea." She was crying extremely hard and at times it sounded as if she couldn't breathe.

"I'm so sorry Deborah, I really am."

I sympathized with her, almost in tears.

Eric had caused her and her family a significant amount of pain and I've never heard Deborah sound so powerless.

"You don't have to be sorry honey. I was actually calling to apologize to you. There are a lot of law suits that are being put in place against Eric and I had him arrested immediately after our girls told me what he had been doing to them. I filed for divorce and the construction company is being rendered to me and I have already found a seller. The sum that I will receive from selling the company is going to be substantial. I wouldn't feel right if I just walked away without saying thank you to you for exposing him. I've always thought that I was one of the lucky ones when all along I was living a lie.

"If it weren't for you, I wouldn't have known what he was doing to our precious little girls because they were too scared to say anything. And for that, I would like to offer you fifty thousand dollars. It's the least I could do."

My heart stopped, this was completely unexpected.

"Fifty thousand dollars?" I asked sitting up in my chair.

"Yes." she responded.

"I-I don't know what to say." I replied.

"You don't have to say anything, I owe you way more than that." She sighed. "Again, I want to say thank you Janae. Thank you, thank you, thank you. Now I can move on with my life and put this behind me. My daughters have started counseling and we have a long road ahead of us. Just keep us in your prayers and text me an address where I can send you your check. I want to send it as soon as possible because my daughters and I are leaving Atlanta. I'm planning to start a new life somewhere else and wash myself clean of all memories of Eric."

"Deborah, I will definitely keep you and the girls in my prayers. I wish you all the best and I'm so sorry that you all had to go through this. You take care of yourself okay? I will text you the information shortly. Give the girls my love."

"Thank you Janae, God bless you."

I texted Deborah my work address right after our phone call ended and as promised, she sent the check ASAP and it cleared right away.

Two months later, I was settled into my new apartment and happened to be watching the news. A story of a deeply depressed woman who was heavily medicated with anti-depressant pills was headed out to drive her and her two daughters cross-country, but allegedly fell asleep behind the wheel and crashed into a service truck, killing herself and two daughters on impact. I was in disbelief when they showed a family picture of Deborah and her two daughters across the screen. I cried right away.

The accident had killed all three of them but the truck driver had survived. He was on the television giving his statement about how he kept beeping and shouting at the driver to stop, but her head was on the wheel as if she nodded off. They collided head first. It was hard to dismiss the hate that I had in my heart for Eric because he had destroyed so many lives and in a sense killed his own family. How could a man be so selfish and destroy the lovely life that he had, for his own personal pleasure? I just couldn't understand it. Deborah and her daughters' deaths really had a huge effect on me and I took it hard. I vomited for a week straight every time I thought about the situation. I couldn't shake the last conversation that I had with Deborah. I told her that I would pray for her and the girls and now they were gone.

Eric now had to sit in jail with the burden of not only losing Deborah's companionship forever, but that of his two daughters' death as well.

When I found out that Eric only had to serve eight years in prison and pay nominal amounts in fines, I was pissed! I felt like justice wasn't served and the only way he got off so easily was because the court only admitted testimonies of the women that he assaulted in court. His daughers weren't alive to testify against him which became an advantage for him.

That monster would be released in ten years and it just didn't seem fair. Unfortunately, there wasn't anything that I could do about it. As much as I wished him harm, God had already repaid him by causing him to lose everything in the end.

Chapter 16

This is a new chapter in my life. I'm lonely and single but things finally seem right.

For months I lived alone. At times it got lonely, but I felt free. I had no one to cook or clean for, and no one to worry about cheating on me. I was stress free. I involved myself in extra hobbies to make myself happy. I joined a gym and even befriended a few girls that I met there. Things were going quite well. It felt like my health was intact, I was at a healthy weight again and my confidence was at an all-time high. I even changed my phone number so that neither Damion nor Tae had access to me. I used the money that Deborah gave me and I put a down payment on a condo.

When I moved in, I furnished the fuck out of my condo, oriental style. I even had my friends from the gym meet me at the furniture store to pack their cars with Asian paintings, oriental clocks and exotic plants. My life was fantastic. Even work was slowing down and all I did was shop on the Internet all day long.

Sarah was beginning to seem pretty upbeat each day as well. Her pregnancy came and went as did her pregnancy weight. She was back to her normal size in less than two weeks after the baby was born. She gave birth to a beautiful baby girl. She named her Nariah Michelle Walker. The baby wore Sarah's button nose and Curtis's pouty lips but her eyes were the spitting image of Ms. Michelle's. Sarah and Curtis were so in love with their new baby; the aura of their joy was contagious. They were so happy.

Seeing them both overwhelmed with happiness sparked the loneliness that I tried to fight. I sat on Sarah's couch and watched them as they admired their daughter.

Sarah placed the baby in Curtis's arms.

"Here baby, can you change her, I think she just pooped."

Curtis cradled the baby in his arms and kept kissing her plump cheeks all the way up until he made it into the baby's room to place her on the changing table.

I guess my loneliness was obvious because Sarah had a devilish grin on her face when she sat next to me.

"Girl, I know you said that you're not ready to date yet, but there is someone that I want to hook you up with."

"Sarah, don't even go there, I don't have time for a man in my life right now. I've told you this plenty of times."

"I know, I know. But this isn't just any man."

"What do you mean this isn't just any man?" I asked.

"Remember Curtis' brothers that I introduced you to at my reception?"

"Yeah, the clean cut business brothers." I said with my fingers formed in quotations.

Sarah looked back to see if Curtis was returning from the baby's room and then replied, "yeah them. The older one is moving here this weekend and he asked about you. So I told him that you'll be glad to meet him for lunch this Saturday."

"What!" I said standing up off the couch.

"Shhhh, I didn't even tell Curtis. They really aren't that close anyway. I took the liberty of setting this up for you myself. Just go out on one date, if you ain't feeling him, then you don't have to see him anymore. But girl he is fine, I think he's the one for you." Sarah said proudly.

"I can't believe you done set me up on a blind date. Let me find out the old Sarah is resurfacing."

"No honey this is still the new me, I just want to see my friend happy. So just do this just this one time, I promise you won't regret it." She assured me.

I stared at Sarah while pondering on her suggestion. I thought about how fine Curtis' brother looked the day of the reception and I was sold.

"Alright I'll go." I said.

Sarah flashed a pleased smile.

"Yes." She said.

"I just hope he don't have baby mama drama, kids in every state or crazy ex-girlfriends." I said.

"Girl he is Curtis' brother, his family bred some good men so you won't have anything to worry about."

"I hope not." I ended.

My nervousness was coupled with excitement about my Saturday date. I daydreamed how the date would go and hoped that he would finally be someone with some substance, someone sane and would permanently sweep me off my feet.

When Saturday rolled around, I was a nervous wreck. I tried on at least five dresses before settling on a cashmere, fitted elegant Dolce and Gabanna dress. My make-up was light and dainty and I wore pearl accessories.

Sarah told him to meet me in the Waffle House parking lot because I wasn't down with showing him where I lived just yet. I took in about four deep breaths while sitting in the semi-empty lot waiting for my date. Out of nowhere, a gentleman wearing a black suit and silk gray tie opened my door and gestured for me to step out.

"Hello." I greeted him while he helped me out of my car.

"Hello yourself, you look absolutely beautiful." He complimented before placing a soft peck on my hand.

His lips felt like heaven on my hand. It was the most action that I had gotten from a man in months.

He led me to his S-series Benz and opened the door for me, then shut it when I was seated. The crème leather seats smelled brand new and judging from the plastic on the TV system and headrests, I knew the car was recently purchased. When he was seated inside, he keyed an address to the restaurant in the Navigation system and we were off.

The spot he ended up taking me to was even more elegant than any of the places that Damion had taken me and I was quite impressed.

Our date was going better than any daydream I could have ever imagined. We even danced to jazz music, something that was totally out of my element. I was an R&B girl, but dancing with him felt comfortable. I found myself laying my head against his chest on the dance floor, feeling like I was right at home. It almost felt like I was dancing with my future husband. He smelled good, looked good and he was smart as hell.

After the band ended the last song, he led me back to our candlelit table.

"So Ms. Janae, tell me more about yourself, I want to hear everything."

I took a sip of Chardonnay and began telling him all about me. I was confident, had great things going for myself, a new condo, money in the bank and a great career. I was boasting. I didn't want to scare him with my hopes and dreams of settling down and having kids as soon as I found the right man, so I just kept our conversation basic but provided enough info for him to find out who I was.

"Enough about me, tell me about yourself." I ended.

"Well I accepted a position here at Atlanta Medical Center as a surgeon. I'm excited to be here in Atlanta, I get to be close to my brother Curtis and his new family and I'm hoping to settle in as quickly as possible."

"Well if there is anything that you need, just let me know. I'm an ATL veteran, I've been here my whole life." I informed him.

"I can tell by your accent." He laughed.

I blushed. "You think I have an accent?"

"Yeah, but it's cute, I like it a lot." He said with a smile. He had the whitest, straightest teeth that I had ever seen on a man.

The date continued to go perfectly. The only downside was that I was unable to read him. I mean, I could tell that he was into me because he kept reiterating how beautiful and intelligent I was, but he hadn't hinted around for another date. I didn't want to suggest it because I didn't want to seem thirsty, so the ride back from the restaurant was fairly silent.

"I would really like to see you again Janac."

My heart melted. The right words had finally come out.

"I would like that." I replied with a smile.

"Listen, my new place is just around the corner from here and Sarah was telling me about that oriental feel that you put on your new place. I mean, all of my things are in boxes but maybe you can tell me if my place has potential."

I was hesitant at first, but I let my guard down and agreed.

His house was just like I would imagine a surgeon's house to look. It was huge! It was modern but had an old school charm to it. It was a six bedroom mansion and I wondered just how he would furnish the unused rooms.

"Wow, this place is gorgeous." I said looking around as he took off my coat and hung it on the ball of the staircase.

"What do you think, does it have potential?" he asked walking closely behind me.

"Does it have potential?" I repeated, "Look at this fireplace, it's all marble, the possibilities are endless. If this were my house, I would drape it in all soft colors. I would hang valances on all of the high windows and paint the walls a light green and then…"

I turned around and the next thing I knew, his tongue was deep down my throat.

I found myself not holding back, because I was yearning for it until I realized that we had just met and I pulled away.

"We don't even know each other, let's not do this, the time isn't right." I said.

"Janae, I felt the chemistry all night, we both want this. Let's just let tonight be our night." He walked up on me again and kissed me until the thoughts of me regretting it melted away in his touches.

He led me down to the warm hardwood floors and served my kitty a treat that it hadn't felt in a long time. He pulled my dress over my head and feasted on my breasts. My body was caving in to him and I was wetter than a river bank. I watched as he rolled the condom on his dick. It was erect and ready to be inserted. He pulled his shirt over his head revealing a body that only steroids could create.

"You are so beautiful." He said before entering me.

As he stroked and laid his body against mine, I moaned and cried at the same time. I wanted him to respect me. I didn't know what he was going to think of me now that I had given it up to him on the first night.

This woman that I was turning into was scary. First I cheated on Tae, now I was out having a one night stand. I hoped that the muscular body that was on top of me wouldn't see me as only a booty call. I wanted to be Sarah's sister-in-law. I wanted to be with him long term. I could see myself having his kids and raising them in the beautiful mansion that we were christening.

His body thrust harder and stronger and I could see his face tense up. "Aw this is some good pussy." He moaned, then he came.

He laid his body on top of me and I pushed him up, grabbed my dress and ran into the bathroom. I looked in the mirror and cried silently, but managed to pull myself together so that he wouldn't think that I was crazy. I fixed my hair to fight the frizz and I exited the bathroom.

"Are you okay?" he asked waiting for me right outside of the bathroom.

"I'm fine." I sniffed, trying to produce a smile.

He slowly approached me. "Okay, I hope you don't feel uncomfortable because of what just happened." He said.

I hesitated whether or not to tell him the truth but then I

forced myself to. "Honestly I *am* a little uncomfortable because I've never done anything like this before."

"Aw sweetheart, don't feel like that because I would really like to see you again." He said.

His approval helped the one night stand settle with me, or settle a little better, because I still didn't feel too good about it.

On the ride back to the Waffle House, I let him do all the talking. He talked about where he wanted to bring me on our next date and repeated how much he was digging our chemistry. And although I hadn't said much on the ride back, I was looking forward to seeing him again.

"Well here we are." He said pulling beside my car.

"I will give you a call next weekend, I'm going to use this entire week to settle into my house and get things in order at the hospital." He said.

"I can understand that." I told him.

"Well just know that I'm looking forward to seeing you again. I really like you Janae."

"I like you too." I said meeting him halfway to peck his lips. He put his left hand on the steering wheel and his right hand on the clutch. As I peered over at his left hand I saw a shiny object on his ring finger, I couldn't believe I didn't notice it the whole night. I even had to squint my eyes for a better look.

"You aren't married are you?" I asked.

He looked at me as if I was supposed to know. "Yeah, you already know that."

"What? How the fuck was I supposed to know that? Sarah didn't tell me you were married! Do you really think that I would have given myself to you after the first date or even went out on a date with you in the first place if I knew that you were married?"

"Janae, I thought we had an understanding here."

"An understanding about what, for me to be your mistress? What kind of girl do you think I am?"

"Janae, what do you think I have a six bedroom house for? I have a wife and four children."

I smacked him across his face with the force of a punch. "Don't even say another word to me. That smack was for your wife and for all the women around the world that has ever been cheated on. It's men like you that make women want to stay single. I hope your dick falls off and your wife leaves you when she finds out what kind of a sick man you are."

He held his face in shock. No words exited his lips. He was a witness to a woman scorned. I took the frustration that was built in me from Tae and Damion out on him and I slammed his door hard hoping to shatter the glass.

I called Sarah right away when I got in my car.

"How the fuck are you gonna hook me up with a married man Sarah?"

"What? Married? He isn't married."

"Try again, he is married with kids. With four kids!" I shouted.

"Hold on a second Janae." I heard Sarah call out for Curtis. "Curtis is your brother married?" She whispered.

"Yeah why?" he whispered back.

Sarah put the phone back up to her ear. "Oh my goodness, I'm so sorry Janae."

I shook my head and squeezed out a tear.

"Sorry isn't good enough Sarah."

I heard Curtis talking to Sarah in the background, "What are you saying sorry to Janae for? I hope you didn't try to hook her up with my brother! Is that what you and him were around here sneaking and talking about? My brother is no good, he has a good woman at home but has been sneaking around on his wife for years. I hope you didn't try to set her up with him, he's the biggest player I know."

"Please forgive me Janae." Sarah pled. "I really didn't know; I feel so bad."

I hung up the phone and threw it on the passenger seat.

Tears cascaded down my cheeks as I tried to maintain a steady pace home. I was frustrated, hurt and I resented men. I hated myself for allowing another man to have my goods for nothing. I felt pathetic and used and I swore off all men from that point on. I didn't want to entertain the thought of a good man because I felt like a good man didn't exist. Looking back on the women in my life, I couldn't think of many that had luck with men, except for Sarah.

Ms. Michelle was the mistress to so many men throughout her life that it ended up handing her a death sentence. Deborah was the faithful wife to a man who didn't deserve her love and it ultimately destroyed her life and her children's lives. Not to mention my mom who stayed with my father only to keep our family together and she was miserable until the day she died. And look at me. Lonely, and full of hate for men. Do I think all men cheat? Well looking back at the spiral of events that took place in my life, I would answer with a definite yes. Do I think all women should too? I guess every situation is different so I'll leave that up to them to decide.

A month had passed and I hadn't called Sarah nor did I pick up when she tried to call me. I was still mad at her for setting me up with Curtis' married brother. I knew that it was just a matter of time before she showed up at my front door because I had avoided her heavily.

I became depressed and only left my apartment for work. I stopped going to the gym and even avoided the new friends that I'd made there. I spent my days crying, vomiting and feeling nauseous and I thought that it was due to depression. When I missed my period, I also blamed it on depression until it didn't come the next month either. On top of that, I couldn't stifle being sick every morning and my body was going through noticeable changes which prompted me to take a pregnancy test.

I sat on my toilet staring at the two pink lines with tears rolling down my face. I always wanted a baby, but not like this. I was pregnant by a married man and it just didn't sit right with me. I remembered seeing Curtis's brother put on the condom but I guess it must've broke.

I tossed the test into the trash and sat in the bathroom in silence. I didn't know what to do or who to call. All I knew was that abortion was not option for me.

I scheduled an appointment to confirm the pregnancy and I *was* in fact pregnant. I was still in disbelief sitting uncomfortably on the hospital bed. I held my belly wondering if I should accept the news as a blessing or addition to my stress. The young doctor went on to explain how important prenatal care was to the baby and then handed me my first prescription for prenatal pills and told me congratulations. Just then I traded smiles with the doctor and it was the first time I had smiled in a long time.

I began filling my prescriptions monthly and attending all of my appointments alone. I wasn't going to let the father of my child know about the baby because I didn't want to disrupt his family. I felt that I shouldn't burden his wife with my situation and so I took matters into my own hands.

When I found out that I was having a boy, I painted his room blue and decorated it with powder blue and white boy accessories like teddy bears and blue and white stuffed cars. The mahogany crib and dresser offset the blue walls and the room was ready for the baby's presence.

I felt bad hiding my pregnancy from Sarah. She continued to pop up at my house. She would bang on the door for hours screaming out how she knew that I was inside because my car was parked out front. But I never opened the door.

The only people that knew of my pregnancy were my co-workers because that's the only place that I spent time at besides home. I worked all the way up until my ninth month. I used my time at home to get to know myself. I read the Bible and often talked to my baby. I would rub my belly and tell the baby stories about my mom and dad and even told him about Ms. Michelle. I had a lot to say because I hadn't been talking to any of my friends.

I had acquired lot's more stretch marks on my stomach and hips, but wore them as motherhood badges of honor. I was proud of all of the changes that pregnancy bestowed upon me. Everyone at work would compliment me and say that I was all belly and hadn't gained weight elsewhere.

My boss dismissed me on my due date and told me not to come back into work until after my maternity leave was up. I informed her that although I was overdue, coming to work didn't bother me but she still dismissed me for my leave.

One week passed and I was tired of just sitting at home. I decided to use the rest of my pregnancy to become active in my community. Ms. Michelle inspired me to raise HIV awareness, so I decided to network with other non-profit organizations to help spread the word about the deadly virus. The two weeks I was overdue was used to meet with different HIV groups that were making large strides in the community.

I used a portion of the money that Deborah gave me to start up the Ms. Michelle foundation. I was very proud of how things were coming along. I was just setting up for my first fundraiser when I began going into labor right outside the vendor that I'd used to host the event. I was rushed to the hospital in an ambulance and an hour later, I gave birth to my son Andre Perry.

I cried tears of joy when the doctor placed my warm eight pounder up to my chest. I kissed him and held him tight. Immediately, he meant the world to me. He was perfect in every aspect of the word. He had my eyes and nose and his skin was peanut butter brown. I was fixated on him and grew attached right away.

The doctor took him away to clean him up and I was so exhausted after giving birth that I fell fast asleep.

Later in the afternoon, I slowly opened my eyes and noticed

that I had visitors. Sarah and Curtis were standing at my bedside with a large balloon that read congratulations and attached was an adorable blue teddy bear.

I cried right away and so did Sarah.

"I missed you so much Janae." Sarah cried kneeling over the bed to hug me.

"I missed you too." I cried hugging her tight.

She stood straight and wiped her tears.

"After you were ignoring my calls and avoiding me when I would come by your house, I went up to your job and your co-workers told me that you were pregnant. I was so happy for you and I couldn't understand why you didn't tell me." Sarah said still wiping her never-ending tears.

I wiped my own and shifted up on the hard hospital bed. "I was too embarrassed." I cried.

Curtis butt in, "Don't be embarrassed Janae." He placed his hand over his chest, "I sincerely want to apologize to you on my brother's behalf. Sarah told me everything. You didn't deserve what my brother has done to you and whether you decide to tell him about the baby or not, I'll leave that completely up to you.

"Thanks Curtis." I said.

The nurse pushed the high clear cart that held my baby boy inside and Curtis and Sarah moved to the other side of the bed to make room for the baby. Sarah peered over him and smiled. "He's so gorgeous." she said admiring my son.

"Hey lil guy." Curtis said.

"Would you like to try breastfeeding?" The bright eyed nurse asked me.

"Sure" I told her.

"Alright, I'll excuse myself." Curtis said as he made his way out of the room..

My breasts were full of milk and the baby latched on as if he knew how healthy the milk was for him. Sarah admired him and held his hand as he fed himself.

"Our babies are going to grow up together Janae. They aren't that far apart in age. And once you recover, you and I are going to put the babies in their strollers and stroll down to the cemetery to see my mom. She would be so happy for you right now; we all knew how much you wanted a baby."

"That'll be nice. Sarah." I agreed.

Sarah stayed with me the whole afternoon while Curtis went home to look after their daughter. We caught up on what we'd missed in each other's lives in the past months. I had told her about the Ms. Michelle foundation and she cried.

When I was released from the hospital, I spent most of the time in the house bonding with the baby and my free time on the Internet networking with organizations in other states for my foundation. Things were coming together very well.

I brought the baby to his doctor's appointments and got myself checked out as well. It seemed as if my life was back in order and the new addition to my household made me complete.

Six months had gone by and I couldn't be more proud of how much my foundation had blossomed. I had custom designed *Let's find a Cure* T-shirts and buttons made and they were selling off my website like hot cakes. The profits were beginning to become quite lucrative and it was well worth it for the cause.

It was a bright, beautiful Tuesday afternoon and Sarah had come over to help me with some follow-up work for an upcoming fundraiser. My phone had been ringing non-stop with sponsors. I had been so busy during the months leading up to the fundraiser that I hadn't even gotten back in touch with my doctor who had been leaving messages daily. Sarah and I both were dedicated to this new movement.

"Sarah, can you answer the phone?" I asked taking a break from working. I headed toward my son's room to see if he'd awakened for a feed.

"Janae!" Sarah called out.

I peeked in the room and saw that the baby was still sound asleep in his crib and then I made my way back into the living room.

"Huh?"

"Telephone." Sarah said pushing the cordless phone toward me. "They said that it was important."

"Hello." I answered.

"Hello, Janae?"

"Yes this is she." I answered.

"This is Dr. Klein. I had been leaving you messages for some time now. I'm calling to inform you about the results of your pap."

I plopped down on the couch.

"Is something wrong?" I asked.

Sarah stood in front of me with a face full of concern. My face couldn't fight the worry.

"Janae, your pap test showed abnormal cell changes and we would like to do other tests to look for precancerous or cancer cells on your cervix." I put my free hand on top of my head. I was beginning to panic at this point. I stood and walked away from Sarah and I began pacing the hall. "Well-well when should I come in?" I stuttered.

"Right away." Dr. Klein informed me.

I hung up the phone and took in a deep breath and exhaled. I slowly walked back toward the couch and sat down. I stared at the wall trying to digest the news hoping that the tests were mis-read.

"What, what is it, what did she say?" Sarah asked curiously.

"They may have found cancer on my cervix." I told her.

Sarah covered her mouth with both hands and began to cry.

"What?" She asked.

"They want me to come into the hospital right now." I said as I sat in shock.

"Janae, go up there, go see what they want. I'll watch the baby. You have enough milk pumped in the fridge to last me the rest of the night. Go! Hurry up, call me a soon as you get there." She rushed.

"Okay." I said.

I took my time retrieving my coat from the closet. Something about this didn't feel right to me. I made my way to my baby's room to kiss him before I left. He was awake in his crib cooing and smiling at me. I began to cry as I kissed on his innocent face. I said a prayer hoping that whatever was going on with my body was temporary or hopefully nothing was wrong with me at all.

I took my time driving to the hospital. I honestly didn't know what news I would hear so I didn't see the point of rushing to possibly hear my fate. When I arrived, Dr. Klein led me into the small cold hospital room. I traded my clothes for an all-white hospital gown and allowed the doctors to conduct their tests. I was nervous, and all that I could think about was my mom. I remembered when she received the same type of phone call from the doctor when she was diagnosed with cancer and it kept replaying in my mind. I squeezed my eyes shut and kept praying for a miracle.

The doctors performed tests after tests and unfortunately, I didn't make it home that day. I spent several days in the hospital waiting on the results and when they were confirmed, I was told that I was diagnosed with advanced cervical cancer.

"I wish this was something we could've caught earlier Janae." The doctor began to explain. "Women diagnosed postpartum, in other words, after giving birth, have worse survival rates than those diagnosed during pregnancy. Particularly if they delivered vaginally which I can see from your records was the case for you, correct?" she asked.

"Yes." I said in a whisper. I just couldn't believe what I was hearing. I was in shock and all I could think about was my baby. I had to be strong and make it through this; I had to fight this for Andre's sake.

The doctor then told me how the disease was so advanced

that I had to be treated with chemotherapy and radiotherapy because a cure was not possible. She then explained that the aim of radiotherapy was for local disease control or symptomatic relief. I braced myself for everything that was about to happen to me. I had no choice but to allow them to treat me so that I could continue with this fight.

Everything began to happen so fast. It seemed as if the moment I was treated, my hair began to shed and my body began to weaken. I wasn't even in pain before treatment but now, I felt how I looked. I had lost weight, I had patches of stringy hair left on my scalp and I didn't feel like myself anymore.

When Sarah learned how critical my disease was, she quit her job and spent almost every day and night at the hospital with me. She was like my guardian angel. She held the baby for me when I grew too weak to hold him and she would place his face up to mine so that I could kiss him and whisper in his ear.

My disease was incurable and the doctors wasted no time informing me that I was knocking on death's doors. Although I was in pain the majority of the time, I was able to get things set up so that my son would be alright in the event of my death. I had Sarah continue to keep the Ms. Michelle foundation going and gave her my bank account numbers so that she could make sure my son had whatever he needed.

I then arranged for Sarah to inform Curtis to talk with his brother and his wife about the option of adopting my baby. I'd hoped that they would agree.

Soon after she met with them and explained my condition. Curtis, his brother and his petite wife paid me a visit to speak with me about adopting Andre. Sarah handed the baby to Curtis' brother and I managed toproduce a smile while he and his wife both admired him.

His wife walked up to me and took my hand. She was beautiful and seemed very down to earth and motherly.

"I admire you, you're very brave," she said.

"Thank you." I whispered, feeling weak.

"We will provide the perfect life for little Andre, I promise." She informed me. I actually saw tears forming in her oval shaped eyes.

Curtis had assured me beforehand that she was one of the greatest moms he knew and it made me feel even more at ease after meeting her.

My eyes were half closed and I kept smiling at her while she held the baby. I was too weak to talk but I felt good about meeting her. She was different than what I had expected and I was glad that I had a chance to see what type of parents would raise my child. She appeared very nurturing and I hoped that her husband would change his ways after seeing what I was going through and be committed to his family.

Life was too short to spend time cheating and sleeping around. Life was about being happy, laughing, loving each other and appreciating family. I hoped that in my short life, that I've touched everyone around me and that my son would grow up being proud of his mom for giving back and most of all for loving hard. Although I never found true happiness in a relationship, I found it in my son and most of all, I had finally found it within myself.

Suddenly the pain stopped and my heart began to weaken. My vision was fading as I watched Curtis' brother and his wife cradling the baby in front of me. It was as if this meeting was meant to happen at this very moment.

"Goodbye Andre." I said in my mind, but my lips wouldn't move. I felt myself slipping away. My eyes were opening and closing and then I heard the machine flat line.

"Somebody get the doctor!" Sarah shouted out in tears. She was hysterical, screaming and crying loudly. All of a sudden, the sounds in the room started fading out and everything was moving in slow motion.

"Janae! Janae!" Sarah cried lifting my hand to her face. Her cries were becoming more and more faint.

I wanted to reach out and tell her that I was okay, but I couldn't move. She continued to shout and scream for someone to do something, tears were streaming down her face, but I felt absolutely fine. I wanted to tell her that I was no longer in pain, but my mouth wouldn't open. I wanted to express to her how wonderful I felt. I've never felt so at home, so loved, so at peace. My body seemed to be pulling me in a direction that I couldn't fight but it was so comforting.

Suddenly I couldn't re-open my eyes and when I did, I was no longer in the hospital. I was greeted by a bright light as a set of doors opened.

"Mom, Dad!" I yelled in tears as they both stood at the doors wearing smiles. In back of them stood Ms. Michelle. She was wearing a white robe and the most peaceful smile that I've ever seen.

She greeted me and said, "Welcome home Janae. Welcome home."

I hugged her and realized that I didn't lose the fight. In fact, I had won. It was just my time to go. I was finally at peace, I *was* finally home.

I will always be with you Andre. Mommy loves you…Good bye….

Acknowledgements

As always I have to thank my Heavenly Father GOD for blessing me with the opportunity to display my talent to the world. Without him, none of this would be possible and I am truly thankful. To my two beautiful children Shyna and DeVandre, I love you both more than life. I hope that I'm making you both proud because you both continue to make me a proud mom. To my mother, Della, thanks for having my back and being there for me as my foundation was being laid. Words can't thank you enough for your love and support. To my brother's Andre and Darryl, my army, my team, I love you both so much! Andre, although you are not here, I will continue to make you proud and live for the both of us. I'll see you when I get there! Big bro, D, I'm so happy that you are home! We are going to take over the world and do it big for Dre's sake! On dogs! Lol…

To all of my friends and family, thank you all for having my back. It's too many of you to name but you all know who you are, I love y'all and I'm thankful to have you all in my life.

I would like to thank my new team: Tracey Cooper, Lisa Mabry, Bernard Bell and the AMAZING Scott Royster for recognizing my vision and helping me turn my dreams into reality. We are making magic happen together and I couldn't ask for a greater team. Thank you all for your hard work and believing in a lil Hood Chick like me, lol.

Scott, thank you for helping with the transitioning of StreetDreamz Publications and LSDV Productions. All the behind-the-scenes negotiations and long meetings were all worth it! I always said that this was bigger than books for me and you saw my vision as if we had the same pair of eyes. I don't know how to express how thankful I am to have you on my team. All

I gotta say is, I hope the world is ready for what's about to take place!

A VERY *SPECIAL* THANK YOU goes out to ALL of my readers!!! Without your support, I wouldn't be where I am today!! All credit goes to all of you and I mean that from the bottom of my heart. I appreciate the fan mail, the emails, the fb and twitter comments and most of all for you spreading the word. To say that I'm thankful for you all is an understatement.

Visit my website at www.lashondadevaughn.com for my Facebook, Twitter, Pinterest, BlackPlanet page and to follow my blog!

Don't forget to "Like" my Facebook Fan page: Author LaShonda DeVaughn

Upcoming LSDV Productions Titles

The Naked Eye, By Kaie Golson

Married But Available, By Tracee Boyd

American Thug, By Darryl DeVaughn

I'd Rather Be Single 2, By LaShonda DeVaughn

CPSIA information can be obtained at www.ICGtesting.com
Printed in the USA
BVOW040748010612

291565BV00001B/3/P